NIGHTFALL TWO

In 1941, at the beginning of his writing career, Isaac Asimov published a story, 'Nightfall', which almost immediately became an SF classic.

But 'Nightfall's' resounding success has irritated its author ever since.

As he reasonably says, thirty years of solid star-studded professionalism (think of the world-famous *Foundation* trilogy, of *I, Robot*, *The Caves of Steel*, etc, etc,) must surely have produced stories as fine as and possibly far superior to that early tale. Yet there are still people around – and people whose opinions Asimov respects – to tell him that 'Nightfall' is the finest thing he ever wrote. Finally, in 1969, in an effort to exorcise 'Nightfall's' ghost once and for all, he made his own selection of twenty stories from the scores he has written and presented them in chronological order in *Nightfall and other stories*. It was an instant bestseller.

For technical reasons this first paperback edition of *Nightfall and other stories* is published as two companion volumes. This volume, *Nightfall Two*, ranges across the Asimov worlds from 'In a Good Cause – ' (1951) to 'Segregationist' (1967).* Each volume is a self-contained collection. Together they compose an unparalleled selection of the best of Asimov chosen by Asimov himself.

Nightfall One, already published, ranges from 'Nightfall' itself (1941) to 'C–Chute' (1951).

Also by Isaac Asimov in Panther Books

Isaac Asimov

Nightfall Two

Science fiction stories

Panther

Granada Publishing Limited
Published in 1971 by Panther Books Ltd
Frogmore, St Albans, Herts AL2 2NF
Reprinted 1972, 1973

Nightfall Two includes the last fifteen stories
published by Rapp & Whiting Ltd in *Nightfall
and other Stories*, 1970
Copyright © Isaac Asimov 1969
Made and printed in Great Britain by
C. Nicholls & Company Ltd
The Philips Park Press, Manchester
Set in Linotype Plantin

Contents

to John W. Campbell Jr.
for making 'Nightfall' possible,
and for thirty years of friendship
and
to the memory of Anthony Boucher
and Groff Conklin

There is a perennial question among readers as to whether the views contained in a story reflect the views of the author. The answer is, 'Not necessarily –' And yet one ought to add another short phrase '– but usually.'

When I write a story in which opposing characters have opposing viewpoints, I do my best, in so far as it lies within my capabilities, to let each character express his own viewpoint honestly.

There are few people who, like Richard III in Shakespeare's play, are willing to say: 'since I cannot prove a lover to entertain these fair and well-spoken days, I am determined to prove a villain.'

No matter how villainous Tom may appear to Dick, Tom undoubtedly has arguments, quite sincerely felt, to prove to himself that he is not villainous at all. It is therefore quite ridiculous to have a villain act ostentatiously like a villain (unless you have the genius of Shakespeare and can carry off anything – and I'm afraid I haven't).

Still, no matter how I try to be fair, and how I try to present each person's views honestly, I cannot make myself be as convincing in presenting views that don't appeal to me, as in presenting those that do. Besides, the general working out of my story usually proceeds as I want it to; the victory, in one way or another, tends to lie with those characters whom I particularly like. Even if the ending is tragic, the point of the story (I hate to use the word 'moral') is usually one that satisfies me.

In short, if you ignore the fine details of any of my stories and consider it as a whole, I think you will find that the feeling it leaves with you is the feeling that I myself feel. It isn't a matter of conscious propaganda; it's just that I am a human being who feels something and who cannot help having that feeling show in the story.

But there are exceptions –

In 1951, Mr. Raymond J. Healy, an anthologist of note, was planning a collection of original science fiction stories, and asked me to write one. He made only one specification. He wanted an upbeat story – something which, in my own more unsophisticated way, I called a 'happy ending' story.

So I wrote a happy ending, but since I always try to beat the rules out of sheer bravado, I tried to write an unexpected happy

*ending, one in which the reader doesn't find out till the very end
what the happy ending really is.*

*It was only after I had successfully (I think) managed this
particular* tour de force *and had had the story published, that I
realized that my interest in technique had for once blinded me
to content. Somehow this particular story, 'In a Good Cause –,'
doesn't quite reflect my own feelings.*

*Groff Conklin, the late perceptive science fiction critic, once
said that he liked this story, even though he disagreed with its
philosophy, and to my embarrassment, I find that that is exactly
how I myself feel.*

First appearance – New Tales of Space and Time, 1951.
Copyright, 1951, by Henry Holt and Company, Inc.

'IN A GOOD CAUSE'

In the Great Court, which stands as a patch of untouched peace
among the fifty busy square miles devoted to the towering buildings that are the pulse beat of the United Worlds of the Galaxy,
stands a statue.

It stands where it can look at the stars at night. There are
other statues ringing the court, but this one stands in the center
and alone.

It is not a very good statue. The face is too noble and lacks
the lines of living. The brow is a shade too high, the nose a shade
too symmetrical, the clothing a shade too carefully disposed.
The whole bearing is by far too saintly to be true. One can suppose that the man in real life might have frowned at times, or
hiccuped, but the statue seemed to insist that such imperfec-
tions were impossible.

All this, of course, is understandable overcompensation. The
man had no statues raised to him while alive, and succeeding
generations, with the advantage of hindsight, felt guilty.

The name on the pedestal reads 'Richard Sayama Altmayer'. Underneath it is a short phrase and, vertically arranged, three dates. The phrase is: *'In a good cause, there are no failures.'* The three dates are June 17, 2755; September 5, 2788; December 21, 2800; – the years being counted in the usual manner of the period, that is, from the date of the first atomic explosion in 1945 of the ancient era.

None of those dates represents either his birth or death. They mark neither a date of marriage or of the accomplishment of some great deed or, indeed, of anything that the inhabitants of the United Worlds can remember with pleasure and pride. Rather, they are the final expression of the feeling of guilt.

Quite simply and plainly, they are the three dates upon which Richard Sayama Altmayer was sent to prison for his opinions.

1 – *June 17, 2755*

At the age of twenty-two, certainly, Dick Altmayer was fully capable of feeling fury. His hair was as yet dark brown and he had not grown the mustache which, in later years, would be so characteristic of him. His nose was, of course, thin and high-bridged, but the contours of his face were youthful. It would be only later that the growing gauntness of his cheeks would convert that nose into the prominent landmark that it now is in the minds of trillions of school children.

Geoffrey Stock was standing in the doorway, viewing the results of his friend's fury. His round face and cold, steady eyes were there, but he had yet to put on the first of the military uniforms in which he was to spend the rest of his life.

He said, 'Great Galaxy!'

Altmayer looked up. 'Hello, Jeff.'

'What's been happening, Dick? I thought your principles, pal, forbid destruction of any kind. Here's a book-viewer that looks somewhat destroyed.' He picked up the pieces.

Altmayer said, 'I was holding the viewer when my wave-receiver came through with an official message. You know which one, too.'

'I know. It happened to me, too. Where is it?'

'On the floor. I tore it off the spool as soon as it belched out at me. Wait, let's dump it down the atom chute.'

'Hey, hold on. You can't –'

'Why not?'

'Because you won't accomplish anything. You'll have to report.'

'And just why?'

'Don't be an ass, Dick.'

'This is a matter of principle, by Space.'

'Oh, nuts! You can't fight the whole planet.'

'I don't intend to fight the whole planet; just the few who get us into wars.'

Stock shrugged. 'That means the whole planet. That guff of yours of leaders tricking poor innocent people into fighting is just so much space-dust. Do you think that if a vote were taken the people wouldn't be overwhelmingly in favor of fighting this fight?'

'That means nothing, Jeff. The government has control of —'

'The organs of propaganda. Yes, I know. I've listened to you often enough. Buy why not report, anyway?'

Altmayer turned away.

Stock said, 'In the first place, you might not pass the physical examination.'

'I'd pass. I've been in Space.'

'That doesn't mean anything. If the doctors let you hop a liner, that only means you don't have a heart murmur or an aneurysm. For military duty aboard ship in Space you need much more than just that. How do you know you qualify?'

'That's a side issue, Jeff, and an insulting one. It's not that I'm afraid to fight.'

'Do you think you can stop the war this way?'

'I wish I could,' Altmayer's voice almost shook as he spoke. 'It's this idea I have that all mankind should be a single unit. There shouldn't be wars or space-fleets armed only for destruction. The Galaxy stands ready to be opened to the united efforts of the human race. Instead, we have been factioned for nearly two thousand years, and we throw away all the Galaxy.'

Stock laughed, 'We're doing all right. There are more than eighty independent planetary systems.'

'And are we the only intelligences in the Galaxy?'

'Oh, the Diaboli, your particular devils,' and Stock put his fists to his temples and extended the two forefingers, waggling them.

'And yours, too, and everybody's. They have a single government extending over more planets than all those occupied by our precious eighty independents.'

'Sure, and their nearest planet is only fifteen hundred light years away from Earth and they can't live on oxygen planets anyway.'

Stock got out of his friendly mood. He said, curtly, 'Look, I dropped by here to say that I was reporting for examination next week. Are you coming with me?'

'No.'

'You're really determined.'

'I'm really determined.'

'You know you'll accomplish nothing. There'll be no great flame ignited on Earth. It will be no case of millions of young men being excited by your example into a no-war strike. You will simply be put in jail.'

'Well, then, jail it is.'

And jail it was. On June 17, 2755, of the atomic era, after a short trial in which Richard Sayama Altmayer refused to present any defense, he was sentenced to jail for the term of three years or for the duration of the war, whichever should be longer. He served a little over four years and two months, at which time the war ended in a definite though not shattering Santannian defeat. Earth gained complete control of certain disputed asteroids, various commercial advantages, and a limitation of the Santannian navy.

The combined human losses of the war were something over two thousand ships with, of course, most of their crews, and in addition, several millions of lives due to the bombardment of planetary surfaces from space. The fleets of the two contending powers had been sufficiently strong to restrict this bombardment to the outposts of their respective systems, so that the planets of Earth and Santanni, themselves, were little affected.

The war conclusively established Earth as the strongest single human military power.

Geoffrey Stock fought throughout the war, seeing action more than once and remaining whole in life and limb despite that. At the end of the war he had the rank of major. He took part in the first diplomatic mission sent out by Earth to the world of the Diaboli, and that was the first step in his expanding role in Earth's military and political life.

2 – *September 5, 2788*

They were the first Diaboli ever to have appeared on the surface of Earth itself. The projection posters and the newscasts of the Federalist party made that abundantly clear to any who were unaware of that. Over and over, they repeated the chronology of events.

It was toward the beginning of the century that human explorers first came across the Diaboli. They were intelligent and had discovered interstellar travel independently somewhat earlier than had the humans. Already the galactic volume of their dominions was greater than that which was human-occupied.

Regular diplomatic relationships between the Diaboli and the major human powers had begun twenty years earlier, immediately after the war between Santanni and Earth. At that time, outposts of Diaboli power were already within twenty light years of the outermost human centers. Their missions went everywhere, drawing trade treaties, obtaining concessions on unoccupied asteroids.

And now they were on Earth itself. They were treated as equals and perhaps as more than equals by the rulers of the greatest center of human population in the Galaxy. The most damning statistic of all was the most loudly proclaimed by the Federalists. It was this: Although the number of living Diaboli was somewhat less than the total number of living humans, humanity had opened up not more than five new worlds to colonization in fifty years, while the Diaboli had begun the occupation of nearly five hundred.

'A hundred to one against us,' cried the Federalists, 'because they are one political organization and we are a hundred.' But relatively few on Earth, and fewer in the Galaxy as a whole, paid attention to the Federalists and their demands for Galactic Union.

The crowds that lined the streets along which nearly daily the five Diaboli of the mission traveled from their specially conditioned suite in the best hotel of the city to the Secretariat of Defense were, by and large, not hostile. Most were merely curious, and more than a little revolted.

The Diaboli were not pleasant creatures to look at. They were larger and considerably more massive than Earthmen. They had four stubby legs set close together below and two flexibly-fingered arms above. Their skin was wrinkled and naked and they wore no clothing. Their broad, scaly faces wore no expressions capable of being read by Earthmen, and from flattened regions just above each large-pupilled eye there sprang short horns. It was these last that gave the creatures their names. At first they had been called devils, and later the politer Latin equivalent.

Each wore a pair of cylinders on its back from which flexible tubes extended to the nostrils; there they clamped on tightly. These were packed with soda-lime which absorbed the, to them, poisonous carbon dioxide from the air they breathed. Their own metabolism revolved about the reduction of sulfur and sometimes those foremost among the humans in the crowd caught a foul whiff of the hydrogen sulfide exhaled by the Diaboli.

The leader of the Federalists was in the crowd. He stood far back where he attracted no attention from the police who had roped off the avenues and who now maintained a watchful order on the little hoppers that could be maneuvered quickly through the thickest crowd. The Federalist leader was gaunt-faced, with a thin and prominently bridged nose and straight, graying hair.

He turned away, 'I cannot bear to look at them.'

His companion was more philosophic. He said, 'No uglier in spirit, at least, than some of our handsome officials. These creatures are at least true to their own.'

'You are sadly right. Are we entirely ready?'

'Entirely. There won't be one of them alive to return to his world.'

'Good! I will remain here to give the signal.'

The Diaboli were talking as well. This fact could not be evident to any human, no matter how close. To be sure, they could communicate by making ordinary sounds to one another but that was not their method of choice. The skin between their horns could, by the actions of muscles which differed in their construction from any known to humans, vibrate rapidly. The tiny waves which were transmitted in this manner to the air were too rapid to be heard by the human ear and too delicate to be detected by any but the most sensitive of human instrumentation. At that time, in fact, humans remained unaware of this form of communication.

A vibration said, 'Did you know that this is the planet of origin of the Two-legs?'

'No.' There was a chorus of such no's, and then one particular vibration said, 'Do you get that from the Two-leg communications you have been studying, queer one?'

'Because I study the communications? More of our people should do so instead of insisting so firmly on the complete worthlessness of Two-leg culture. For one thing, we are in a much better position to deal with the Two-legs if we know something about them. Their history is interesting in a horrible way. I am glad I brought myself to view their spools.'

'And yet,' came another vibration, 'from our previous contacts with Two-legs, one would be certain that they did not know their planet of origin. Certainly there is no veneration of this planet, Earth, or any memorial rites connected with it. Are you sure the information is correct?'

'Entirely so. The lack of ritual, and the fact that this planet is by no means a shrine, is perfectly understandable in the light of Two-leg history. The Two-legs on the other worlds would scarcely concede the honor. It would somehow lower the independent dignity of their own worlds.'

'I don't quite understand.'

'Neither do I, exactly, but after several days of reading I think I catch a glimmer. It would seem that, originally, when interstellar travel was first discovered by the Two-legs, they lived under a single political unit.'

'Naturally.'

'Not for these Two-legs. This was an unusual stage in their history and did not last. After the colonies on the various worlds grew and came to reasonable maturity, their first interest was to break away from the mother world. The first in the series of interstellar wars among these Two-legs began then.'

'Horrible. Like cannibals.'

'Yes, isn't it? My digestion has been upset for days. My cud is sour. In any case, the various colonies gained independence, so that now we have the situation of which we are well aware. All of the Two-leg kingdoms, republics, aristocracies, etc., are simply tiny clots of worlds, each consisting of a dominant world and a few subsidiaries which, in turn, are forever seeking their independence or being shifted from one dominant to another. This Earth is the strongest among them and yet less than a dozen worlds owe it allegiance.'

'Incredible that these creatures should be so blind to their own interests. Do they not have a tradition of the single government that existed when they consisted of but one world?'

'As I said that was unusual for them. The single government had existed only a few decades. Prior to that, this very planet itself was split into a number of subplanetary political units.'

'Never heard anything like it.' For a while, the supersonics of the various creatures interfered with one another.

'It's a fact. It is simply the nature of the beast.'

And with that, they were at the Secretariat of Defense.

The five Diaboli stood side by side along the table. They stood because their anatomy did not admit of anything that could correspond to 'sitting'. On the other side of the table, five Earthmen stood as well. It would have been more convenient for the humans to sit but, understandably, there was no desire to make the handicap of smaller size any more pronounced than it already was. The table was a rather wide one; the widest, in fact, that could be conveniently obtained. This was out of respect for the human nose, for from the Diaboli, slightly so as they breathed, much more so when they spoke, there came the gentle and continuous drift of hydrogen sulfide. This was a difficulty rather unprecedented in diplomatic negotations.

Ordinarily the meetings did not last for more than half an hour, and at the end of this interval the Diaboli ended their conversations without ceremony and turned to leave. This time, however, the leave-taking was interrupted. A man entered, and the five human negotiators made way for him. He was tall, taller than any of the other Earthmen, and he wore a uniform with the ease of long usage. His face was round and his eyes cold and steady. His black hair was rather thin but as yet untouched by gray. There was an irregular blotch of scar tissue running from the point of his jaw downward past the line of his high, leather-brown collar. It might have been the result of a hand energy-ray, wielded by some forgotten human enemy in one of the five wars in which the man had been an active participant.

'Sirs,' said the Earthman who had been chief negotiator hitherto, 'may I introduce the Secretary of Defense?'

The Diaboli were somewhat shocked and, although their expressions were in repose and inscrutable, the sound plates on their foreheads vibrated actively. Their strict sense of hierarchy was disturbed. The Secretary was only a Two-leg, but by Two-leg standards, he outranked them. They could not properly conduct official business with him.

The Secretary was aware of their feelings but had no choice in the matter. For at least ten minutes, their leaving must be delayed and no ordinary interruption could serve to hold back the Diaboli.

'Sirs,' he said, 'I must ask your indulgence to remain longer this time.'

The central Diabolus replied in the nearest approach to English any Diabolus could manage. Actually, a Diabolus might be said to have two mouths. One was hinged at the outermost extremity of the jawbone and was used in eating. In this capacity, the motion of the mouth was rarely seen by human beings, since the Diaboli much preferred to eat in the company of their own kind exclusively. A narrower mouth opening, however, perhaps two inches in width, could be used in speaking. It pursed itself open, revealing the gummy gap where a Diabolus' missing incisors ought to have been. It remained open during speech, the necessary consonantal blockings being performed by the palate and back of the tongue. The result was hoarse and fuzzy, but understandable.

The Diabolus said, 'You will pardon us, already we suffer.' And by his forehead, he twittered unheard, 'They mean to suffocate us in their vile atmosphere. We must ask for larger poison-absorbing cylinders.'

The Secretary of Defense said, 'I am in sympathy with your feelings, and yet this may be my only opportunity to speak with you. Perhaps you would do us the honor to eat with us.'

The Earthman next the Secretary could not forbear a quick and passing frown. He scribbled rapidly on a piece of paper and passed it to the Secretary, who glanced momentarily at it.

It read, 'No. They eat sulfuretted hay. Stinks unbearably.' The Secretary crumpled the note and let it drop.

The Diabolus said, 'The honor is ours. Were we physically able to endure your strange atmosphere for so long a time, we would accept most gratefully.'

And via forehead, he said with agitation, 'They cannot expect us to eat with them and watch them consume the corpses of dead animals. My cud would never be sweet again.'

'We respect your reasons,' said the Secretary. 'Let us then

transact our business now. In the negotiations that have so far proceeded, we have been unable to obtain from your government, in the persons of you, their representatives, any clear indication as to what the boundaries of your sphere of influence are in your own minds. We have presented several proposals in this matter.'

'As far as the territories of Earth are concerned, Mr. Secretary, a definition has been given.'

'But surely you must see that this is unsatisfactory. The boundaries of Earth and your lands are nowhere in contact. So far, you have done nothing but state this fact. While true, the mere statement is not satisfying.'

'We do not completely understand. Would you have us discuss the boundaries between ourselves and such independent human kingdoms as that of Vega?'

'Why, yes.'

'That cannot be done, sir. Surely, you realize that any relations between ourselves and the sovereign realm of Vega cannot possibly be any concern of Earth. They can be discussed only with Vega.'

'Then you will negotiate a hundred times with the hundred human world systems?'

'It is necessary. I would point out, however, that the necessity is imposed not by us but by the nature of your human organization.'

'Then that limits our field of discussion drastically.' The Secretary seemed abstracted. He was listening, not exactly to the Diaboli opposite, but, rather, it would seem, to something at a distance.

And now there was a faint commotion, barely heard from outside the Secretariat. The babble of distant voices, the brisk crackle of energy-guns muted by distance to nearly nothingness, and the hurried click-clacking of police hoppers.

The Diaboli showed no indication of hearing, nor was this simply another affectation of politeness. If their capacity for receiving supersonic sound waves was far more delicate and acute than almost anything human ingenuity had ever invented, their reception for ordinary sound waves was rather dull.

The Diabolus was saying, 'We beg leave to state our surprise. We were of the opinion that all this was known to you.'

A man in police uniform appeared in the doorway. The Secretary turned to him and, with the briefest of nods, the policeman departed.

The Secretary said suddenly and briskly, 'Quite. I merely wished to ascertain once again that this was the case. I trust you will be ready ot resume negotiations tomorrow?'

'Certainly, sir.'

One by one, slowly, with a dignity befitting the heirs of the universe, the Diaboli left.

An Earthman said, 'I'm glad they refused to eat with us.'

'I knew they couldn't accept,' said the Secretary, thoughtfully. 'They're vegetarian. They sicken thoroughly at the very thought of eating meat. I've seen them eat, you know. Not many humans have. They resemble our cattle in the business of eating. They bolt their food and then stand solemnly about in circles, chewing their cuds in a great community of thought. Perhaps they intercommunicate by a method we are unaware of. The huge lower jaw rotates horizontally in a slow, grinding process –'

The policeman had once more appeared in the doorway.

The Secretary broke off, and called, 'You have them all?'

'Yes, sir.'

'Do you have Altmayer?'

'Yes, sir.'

'Good.'

The crowd had gathered again when the five Diaboli emerged from the Secretariat. The schedule was strict. At 3 : 00 P.M. each day they left their suite and spent five minutes walking to the Secretariat. At 3 : 35, they emerged therefrom once again and returned to their suite, the way being kept clear by the police. They marched stolidly, almost mechanically, along the broad avenue.

Halfway in their trek there came the sounds of shouting men. To most of the crowd, the words were not clear but there was the crackle of an energy-gun and the pale blue fluorescence split the air overhead. Police wheeled, their own energy-guns drawn, hoppers springing seven feet into the air, landing delicately in the midst of groups of people, touching none of them, jumping again almost instantly. People scattered and their voices were joined to the general uproar.

Through it all, the Diaboli, either through defective hearing or excessive dignity, continued marching as mechanically as ever.

At the other end of the gathering, almost diametrically opposing the region of excitement, Richard Sayana Altmayer stroked his nose in a moment of satisfaction. The strict chronology of the Diaboli had made a split-second plan possible. The first diversionary disturbance was only to attract the attention of the police. It was now –

And he fired a harmless sound pellet into the air.

Instantly, from four directions, concussion pellets split the air. From the roofs of buildings lining the way, snipers fired.

Each of the Diaboli, torn by the shells, shuddered and exploded as the pellets detonated within them. One by one, they toppled.

And from nowhere, the police were at Altmayer's side. He stared at them with some surprise.

Gently, for in twenty years he had lost his fury and learned to be gentle, he said, 'You come quickly, but even so you come too late.' He gestured in the direction of the shattered Diaboli.

The crowd was in simple panic now. Additional squadrons of police, arriving in record time, could do nothing more than herd them off into harmless directions.

The policeman, who now held Altmayer in a firm grip, taking the sound gun from him and inspecting him quickly for further weapons, was a captain by rank. He said, stiffly, 'I think you've made a mistake, Mr. Altmayer. You'll notice you've drawn no blood.' And he, too, waved toward where the Diaboli lay motionless.

Altmayer turned, startled. The creatures lay there on their sides, some in pieces, tattered skin shredding away, frames distorted and bent, but the police captain was correct. There was no blood, no flesh. Altmayer's lips, pale and stiff, moved soundlessly.

The police captain interpreted the motion accurately enough. He said, 'You are correct, sir, they are robots.'

And from the great doors of the Secretariat of Defense, the true Diaboli emerged. Clubbing policemen cleared the way, but another way, so that they need not pass the sprawled travesties of plastic and aluminium which for three minutes had played the role of living creatures.

The police captain said, 'I'll ask you to come without trouble, Mr. Altmayer. The Secretary of Defense would like to see you.'

'I am coming, sir.' A stunned frustration was only now beginning to overwhelm him.

Geoffrey Stock and Richard Altmayer faced one another for the first time in almost a quarter of a century, there in the Defense Secretary's private office. It was a rather strait-laced office: a desk, an armchair, and two additional chairs. All were a dull brown in color, the chairs being topped by brown foamite which yielded to the body enough for comfort, not enough for luxury. There was a micro-viewer on the desk and a little cabinet big enough to hold several dozen opto-spools. On the wall opposite the desk was a trimensional view of the old *Dauntless,* the Secretary's first command.

Stock said, 'It is a little ridiculous meeting like this after so many years. I find I am sorry.'

'Sorry about what, Jeff?' Altmayer tried to force a smile, 'I am sorry about nothing but that you tricked me with those robots.'

'You were not difficult to trick,' said Stock, 'and it was an excellent opportunity to break your party. I'm sure it will be quite discredited after this. The pacifist tries to force war; the apostle of gentleness tries assassination.'

'War against the true enemy,' said Altmayer sadly. 'But you are right. It is a sign of desperation that this was forced on me.' – Then, 'How did you know my plans?'

'You still overestimate humanity, Dick. In any conspiracy the weakest points are the people that compose it. You had twenty-five co-conspirators. Didn't it occur to you that at least one of them might be an informer, or even an employee of mine?'

A dull red burned slowly on Altmayer's high cheekbones. 'Which one?' he said.

'Sorry. We may have to use him again.'

Altmayer sat back in his chair wearily. 'What have you gained?'

'What have *you* gained? You are as impractical now as on that last day I saw you; the day you decided to go to jail rather than report for induction. You haven't changed.'

Altmayer shook his head, 'The truth doesn't change.'

Stock said impatiently, 'If it is truth, why does it always fail? Your stay in jail accomplished nothing. The war went on. Not one life was saved. Since then, you've started a political party; and every cause it has backed has failed. Your conspiracy has failed. You're nearly fifty, Dick, and what have you accomplished? Nothing.'

Altmayer said, 'And you went to war, rose to command a ship, then to a place in the Cabinet. They say you will be the next Coordinator. You've accomplished a great deal. Yet success and failure do not exist in themselves. Success in what? Success in working the ruin of humanity. Failure in what? In a good cause, there are no failures; there are only delayed successes.'

'Even if you are executed for this day's work?'

'Even if I am executed. There will be someone else to carry on, and his success will be my success.'

'How do you envisage this success? Can you really see a union of worlds, a Galactic Federation? Do you want Santanni running our affairs? Do you want a Vegan telling you what to do? Do you want Earth to decide its own destiny or to be at the mercy of any random combination of powers?'

'We would be at their mercy no more than they would be at ours.'

'Except that we are the richest. We would be plundered for the sake of the depressed worlds of the Sirius Sector.'

'And pay the plunder out of what we would save in the wars that would no longer occur.'

'Do you have answers for all questions, Dick?'

'In twenty years we have been asked all questions, Jeff.'

'Then answer this one. How would you force this union of yours on unwilling humanity?'

'That is why I wanted to kill the Diaboli.' For the first time, Altmayer showed agitation. 'It would mean war with them, but all humanity would unite against the common enemy. Our own political and ideological differences would fade in the face of that.'

'You really believe that? Even when the Diaboli have never harmed us? They cannot live on our worlds. They must remain on their own worlds of sulfide atmosphere and oceans which are sodium sulfate solutions.'

'Humanity knows better, Jeff. They are spreading from world

to world like an atomic explosion. They block space-travel into regions where there are unoccupied oxygen worlds, the kind *we* could use. They are planning for the future: making room for uncounted future generations of Diaboli, while we are being restricted to one corner of the Galaxy, and fighting ourselves to death. In a thousand years we will be their slaves; in ten thousand we will be extinct. Oh, yes, they are the common enemy. Mankind knows that. You will find that out sooner than you think, perhaps.'

The Secretary said, 'Your party members speak a great deal of ancient Greece of the preatomic age. They tell us that the Greeks were a marvelous people, the most culturally advanced of their time, perhaps of all times. They set mankind on the road it has never yet left entirely. They had only one flaw. They could not unite. They were conquered and eventually died out. And we follow in their footsteps now, eh?'

'You have learned your lesson well, Jeff.'

'But have you, Dick?'

'What do you mean?'

'Did the Greeks have no common enemy against whom they could unite?'

Altmayer was silent.

Stock said, 'The Greeks fought Persia, their great common enemy. Was it not a fact that a good proportion of the Greek states fought on the Persian side?'

Altmayer said finally, 'Yes. Because they thought Persian victory was inevitable and they wanted to be on the winning side.'

'Human beings haven't changed, Dick. Why do you suppose the Diaboli are here? What is it we are discussing?'

'I am not a member of the government.'

'No,' said Stock, savagely, 'but I am. The Vegan League has allied itself with the Diaboli.'

'I don't believe you. It can't be.'

'It can be and is. The Diaboli have agreed to supply them with five hundred ships at any time they happen to be at war with Earth. In return, Vega abandons all claims to the Nigellian star cluster. So if you had really assassinated the Diaboli, it would have been war, but with half of humanity probably fighting on the side of your so-called common enemy. We are trying to prevent that.'

Altmayer said slowly, 'I am ready for trial. Or am I to be executed without one?'

Stock said, 'You are still foolish. If we shoot you, Dick, we make a martyr. If we keep you alive and shoot only your subordinates, you will be suspected of having turned state's evidence. As a presumed traitor, you will be quite harmless in the future.'

And so, on September 5th, 2788, Richard Sayama Altmayer, after the briefest of secret trials, was sentenced to five years in prison. He served his full term. The year he emerged from prison, Geoffrey Stock was elected Coordinator of Earth.

3 – December 21, 2800

Simon Devoire was not at ease. He was a little man, with sandy hair and a freckled, ruddy face. He said, 'I'm sorry I agreed to see you, Altmayer. It won't do you any good. It might do me harm.'

Altmayer said, 'I am an old man. I won't hurt you.' And he was indeed a very old man somehow. The turn of the century found his years at two thirds of a century, but he was older than that, older inside and older outside. His clothes were too big for him, as if he were shrinking away inside them. Only his nose had not aged; it was still the thin, aristocratic, high-beaked Altmayer nose.

Devoire said, 'It's not you I'm afraid of.'

'Why not? Perhaps you think I betrayed the men of '88.'

'No, of course not. No man of sense believes that you did. But the days of the Federalists are over, Altmayer.'

Altmayer tried to smile. He felt a little hungry; he hadn't eaten that day – no time for food. Was the day of the Federalists over? It might seem so to others. The movement had died on a wave of ridicule. A conspiracy that fails, a 'lost cause', is often romantic. It is remembered and draws adherents for generations, *if* the loss is at least a dignified one. But to shoot at living creatures and find the mark to be robots; to be outmaneuvered and outfoxed; to be made ridiculous – that is deadly. It is deadlier than treason, wrong, and sin. Not many had believed Altmayer had bargained for his life by betraying his associates, but the universal laughter killed Federalism as effectively as though they had.

But Altmayer had remained stolidly stubborn under it all. He said, 'The day of the Federalists will never be over, while the human race lives.'

'Words,' said Devoire impatiently. 'They meant more to me when I was younger. I am a little tired now.'

'Simon, I need access to the subetheric system.'

Devoire's face hardened. He said, 'And you thought of me. I'm sorry, Altmayer, but I can't let you use my broadcasts for your own purposes.'

'You were a Federalist once.'

'Don't rely on that,' said Devoire. 'That's in the past. Now I am – nothing. I am a Devoirist, I suppose. I want to live.'

'Even if it is under the feet of the Diaboli? Do you want to live when they are willing; die when they are ready?'

'Words!'

'Do you approve of the all-Galactic conference?'

Devoire reddened past his usual pink level. He gave the sudden impression of a man with too much blood for his body. He said smolderingly, 'Well, why not? What does it matter how we go about establishing the Federation of Man? If you're still a Federalist, what have you to object to in a united humanity?'

'United under the Diaboli?'

'What's the difference? Humanity can't unite by itself. Let us be driven to it, as long as the fact is accomplished. I am sick of it all, Altmayer, sick of all our stupid history. I'm tired of trying to be an idealist with nothing to be idealistic over. Human beings are human beings and that's the nasty part of it. Maybe we've *got* to be whipped into line. If so, I'm perfectly willing to let the Diaboli do the whipping.'

Altmayer said gently, 'You're very foolish, Devoire. It won't be a real union, you know that. The Diaboli called this conference so that they might act as umpires on all current interhuman disputes to their own advantage, and remain the supreme court of judgment over us hereafter. You know they have no intention of establishing a real central human government. It will only be a sort of inter-locking directorate; each human government will conduct its own affairs as before and pull in various directions as before. It is simply that we will grow accustomed to running to the Diaboli with our little problems.'

'How do you know that will be the result?'

'Do you seriously think any other result is possible?'

Devoire chewed at his lower lip, 'Maybe not!'

'Then see through a pane of glass, Simon. Any true independence we now have will be lost.'

'A lot of good this independence has ever done us. — Besides,
what's the use? We can't stop this thing. Coordinator Stock is
probably no keener on the conference than you are, but that
doesn't help him. If Earth doesn't attend, the union will be formed without us, and then we will face war with the rest of humanity and the Diaboli. And that goes for any other government
that wants to back out.'

'What if *all* the governments back out? Wouldn't the conference break up completely?'

'Have you ever known all the human governments to do *anything* together? You never learn, Altmayer.'

'There are new facts involved.'

'Such as? I know I am foolish for asking, but go ahead.'

Altmayer said, 'For twenty years most of the Galaxy has been
shut to human ships. You know that. None of us has the
slightest notion of what goes on within the Diaboli sphere
of influence. And yet some human colonies exist within that
sphere.'

'So?'

'So occasionally, human beings escape into the small portion
of the Galaxy that remains human and free. The government of
Earth receives reports; reports which they don't dare make public. But not *all* officials of the government can stand the coward-
ice involved in such actions forever. One of them has been to see
me. I can't tell you which one, of course — So I have documents,
Devoire, official, reliable, and true.'

Devoire shrugged, 'About what?' He turned the desk chron-
ometer rather ostentatiously so that Altmayer could see its
gleaming metal face on which the red, glowing figures stood out
sharply. They read 22:31, and even as it was turned, the 1 faded
and the new glow of a 2 appeared.

Altmayer said, 'There is a planet called by its colonists Chu
Hsi. It did not have a large population; two million, perhaps.
Fifteen years ago the Diaboli occupied worlds on various sides
of it; and in all those fifteen years, no human ship ever landed
on the planet. Last year the Diaboli themselves landed. They
brought with them huge freight ships filled with sodium sulfate
and bacterial cultures that are native to their own worlds.'

'What? – You can't make me believe it.'

'Try,' said Altmayer, ironically. 'It is not difficult. Sodium sulfate will dissolve in the oceans of any world. In a sulfate ocean, their bacteria will grow, multiply, and produce hydrogen sulfide in tremendous quantities which will fill the oceans and the atmosphere. They can then introduce their plants and animals and eventually themselves. Another planet will be suitable for Diaboli life – and unsuitable for any human. It would take time, surely, but the Diaboli have time. They are a united people and ...'

'Now, look,' Devoire waved his hand in disgust, 'that just doesn't hold water. The Diaboli have more worlds than they know what to do with.'

'For their present purposes, yes, but the Diaboli are creatures that look toward the future. Their birth rate is high and eventually they will fill the Galaxy. And how much better off they would be if they were the only intelligence in the universe.'

'But it's impossible on purely physical grounds. Do you know how many millions of tons of sodium it would take to fill up the oceans to their requirements?'

'Obviously a planetary supply.'

'Well, then, do you suppose they would strip one of their own worlds to create a new one? Where is the gain?'

'Simon, Simon, there are millions of planets in the Galaxy which through atomspheric conditions, temperature, or gravity are forever uninhabitable either to humans or to Diaboli. Many of these are quite adequately rich in sulfur.'

Devoire considered, 'What about the human beings on the planet?'

'On Chu Hsi? Euthanasia – except for the few who escaped in time. Painless I suppose. The Diaboli are not needlessly cruel, merely efficient.'

Altmayer waited. Devoire's fist clenched and unclenched.

Altmayer said, 'Publish this news. Spread it out on the interstellar subetheric web. Broadcast the documents to the reception centers on the various worlds. You can do it, and when you do, the all-Galactic conference will fall apart.'

Devoire's chair tilted forward. He stood up. 'Where's your proof?'

'Will you do it?'

'I want to see your proof.'

Altmayer smiled, 'Come with me.'

They were waiting for him when he came back to the furnished room he was living in. He didn't notice them at first. He was completely unaware of the small vehicle that followed him at a slow pace and a prudent distance. He walked with his head bent, calculating the length of time it would take for Devoire to put the information through the reaches of Space; how long it would take for the receiving stations on Vega and Santanni and Centaurus to blast out the news; how long it would take to spread it over the entire Galaxy. And in this way he passed, unheeding, between the two plain-clothes men who flanked the entrance of the rooming house.

It was only when he opened the door to his own room that he stopped and turned to leave but the plain-clothes men were behind him now. He made no attempt at violent escape. He entered the room instead and sat down, feeling so old. He thought feverishly, I need only hold them off for an hour and ten minutes.

The man who occupied the darkness reached up and flicked the switch that allowed the wall lights to operate. In the soft wall glow, the man's round face and balding gray-fringed head were startlingly clear.

Altmayer said gently, 'I am honored with a visit by the Co-ordinator himself.'

And Stock said, 'We are old friends, you and I, Dick. We meet every once in a while.'

Altmayer did not answer.

Stock said, 'You have certain government papers in your possession, Dick.'

Altmayer said, 'If you think so, Jeff, you'll have to find them.'

Stock rose wearily to his feet. 'No heroics, Dick. Let me tell you what those papers contained. They were circumstantial reports of the sulfation of the planet, Chu Hsi. Isn't that true?'

Altmayer looked at the clock.

Stock said, 'If you are planning to delay us, to angle us as though we were fish, you will be disappointed. We know where you've been, we know Devoire has the papers, we know exactly what's he planning to do with them.'

Altmayer stiffened. The thin parchment of his cheeks trembled. He said, 'How long have you known?'

'As long as you have, Dick. You are a very predictable man. It is the very reason we decided to use you. Do you suppose the Recorder would really come to see you as he did, without our knowledge?'

'I don't understand.'

Stock said, 'The Government of Earth, Dick, is not anxious that the all-Galactic conference be continued. However, we are not Feralists; we know humanity for what it is. What do you suppose would happen if the rest of the Galaxy discovered that the Diaboli were in the process of changing a salt-oxygen world into a sulfate-sulfide one?

'No, don't answer. You are Dick Altmayer and I'm sure you'd tell me that with one fiery burst of indignation, they'd abandon the conference, join together in a loving and brotherly union, throw themselves at the Diaboli, and overwhelm them.'

Stock paused such a long time that for a moment it might have seemed he would say no more. Then he continued in half a whisper, 'Nonsense. The other worlds would say that the Government of Earth for purposes of its own had initiated a fraud, had forged documents in a deliberate attempt to disrupt the conference. The Diaboli would deny everything, and most of the human worlds would find it to their interests to believe the denial. They would concentrate on the iniquities of Earth and forget about the iniquities of the Diaboli. So you see, we could sponsor no such exposé.'

Altmayer felt drained, futile. 'Then you will stop Devoire. It is always that you are so sure of failure beforehand; that you believe the worst of your fellow man —'

'Wait! I said nothing of stopping Devoire. I said only that the government could not sponsor such an exposé and we will not. But the exposé will take place just the same, except that afterward we will arrest Devoire and yourself and denounce the whole thing as vehemently as will the Diaboli. The whole affair would then be changed. The Government of Earth will have dissociated itself from the claims. It will then seem to the rest of the human government that for our own selfish purposes we are trying to hide the actions of the Diaboli, that we have, perhaps, a special understanding with them. They will fear that special understanding and unite against us. But *then* to be against us will mean that they are also against the Diaboli. They will insist on believing the exposé to be the truth, the documents to be real – and the conference will break up.'

'It will mean war again,' said Altmayer hopelessly, 'and not against the real enemy. It will mean fighting among the humans and a victory all the greater for the Diaboli when it is all over.'

'No war,' said Stock. 'No government will attack Earth with the Diaboli on our side. The other governments will merely draw away from us and grind a permanent anti-Diaboli bias into their propaganda. Later, if there should be war between ourselves and the Diaboli, the other governments will at least remain neutral.'

He looks very old, thought Altmayer. We are all old, dying men. Aloud, he said, 'Why would you expect the Diaboli to back Earth? You may fool the rest of mankind by pretending to attempt suppression of the facts concerning the planet Chu Hsi, but you won't fool the Diaboli. They won't for a moment believe Earth to be sincere in its claim that it believes the documents to be forgeries.'

'Ah, but they will.' Geoffrey Stock stood up, 'You see, the documents *are* forgeries. The Diaboli may be planning sulfation of planets in the future, but to our knowledge, they have not tried it yet.'

On December 21, 2800, Richard Sayama Altmayer entered prison for the third and last time. There was no trial, no definite sentence, and scarcely a real imprisonment in the literal sense of the word. His movements were confined and only a few officials were allowed to communicate with him, but otherwise his comforts were looked to assiduously. He had no access to news, of course, so that he was not aware that in the second year of this third imprisonment of his, the war between Earth and the Diaboli opened with the surprise attack near Sirius by an Earth squadron upon certain ships of the Diaboli navy.

In 2802, Geoffrey Stock came to visit Altmayer in his confinement. Altmayer rose in surprise to greet him.

'You're looking well, Dick,' Stock said.

He himself was not. His complexion had grayed. He still wore his naval captain's uniform, but his body stooped slightly within it. He was to die within the year, a fact of which he was not completely unaware. It did not bother him much. He thought repeatedly, I have lived the years I've had to live.

Altmayer, who looked the older of the two, had yet more than nine years to live. He said, 'An unexpected pleasure, Jeff, but this time you can't have come to imprison me. I'm in prison already.'

'I've come to set you free, if you would like.'

'For what purpose, Jeff? Surely you have a purpose? A clever way of using me?'

Stock's smile was merely a momentary twitch. He said, 'A way of using you, truly, but this time you will approve. . . . We are at war.'

'With whom?' Altmayer was startled.

'With the Diaboli. We have been at war for six months.'

Altmayer brought his hands together, thin fingers interlacing nervously, 'I've heard nothing of this.'

'I know.' The Coordinator clasped his hands behind his back and was distantly surprised to find that they were trembling. He said, 'It's been a long journey for the two of us, Dick. We've had the same goal, you and I – No, let me speak. I've often wanted to explain my point of view to you, but you would never have understood. You weren't the kind of man to understand, until I had the results for you. – I was twenty-five when I first visited a Diaboli world, Dick. I knew then it was either they or we.'

'I said so,' whispered Altmayer, 'from the first.'

'Merely saying so was not enough. You wanted to force the human governments to unite against them and that notion was politically unrealistic and completely impossible. It wasn't even desirable. Humans are not Diaboli. Among the Diaboli, individual consciousness is low, almost nonexistent. Ours is almost overpowering. They have no such thing as politics; we have nothing else. They can never disagree, can have nothing but a single government. We can never agree; if we had a single island to live on, we would split it in three.

'*But our very disagreements are our strength!* Your Federalist party used to speak of ancient Greece a great deal once. Do you remember? But your people always missed the point. To be sure, Greece could never unite and was therefore ultimately conquered. But even in her state of disunion, she defeated the gigantic Persian Empire. Why?

'I would like to point out that the Greek city-states over centuries had fought with one another. They were forced to specialize in things military to an extent far beyond the Persians. Even the Persians themselves realized that, and in the last century of their imperial existence, Greek mercenaries formed the most valued parts of their armies.

'The same might be said of the small nation-states of pre-atomic Europe, which in centuries of fighting had advanced their military arts to the point where they could overcome and hold for two hundred years the comparatively gigantic empires of Asia.

'So it is with us. The Diaboli, with vast extents of galactic space, have never fought a war. Their military machine is massive, but untried. In fifty years, only such advances have been made by them as they have been able to copy from the various human navies. Humanity, on the other hand, has competed ferociously in warfare. Each government has raced to keep ahead of its neighbors in military science. They've had to! It was our own disunion that made the terrible race for survival necessary, so that in the end almost any one of us was a match for all the Diaboli, provided only that none of us would fight on their side in a general war.

'It was toward the prevention of such a development that all of Earth's diplomacy had been aimed. Until it was certain that in a war between Earth and the Diaboli, the rest of humanity would be at least neutral, there could be no war, and no union of human governments could be allowed, since the race for military perfection must continue. Once we were sure of neutrality, through the hoax that broke up the conference two years ago, we sought the war, and now we have it.'

Altmayer, through all this, might have been frozen. It was a long time before he could say anything.

Finally, 'What if the Diaboli are victorious after all?'

Stock said, 'They aren't. Two weeks ago, the main fleets joined action and theirs was annihilated with practically no loss to ourselves, although we were greatly outnumbered. We might have been fighting unarmed ships. We had stronger weapons of greater range and more accurate sighting. We had three times their effective speed since we had antiacceleration devices which they lacked. Since the battle a dozen of the other human governments have decided to join the winning side and have declared war on the Diaboli. Yesterday the Diaboli requested that negotiations for an armistice be opened. The war is practically over; and henceforward the Diaboli will be confined to their original planets with only such future expansions as we permit.'

Altmayer murmured incoherently.

Stock said, 'And now union becomes necessary. After the defeat of Persia by the Greek city-states, they were ruined because of their continued wars among themselves, so that first Macedon and then Rome conquered them. After Europe colonized the Americas, cut up Africa, and conquered Asia, a series of continued European wars led to European ruin.

'Disunion until conquest; union thereafter! But now union is easy. Let one subdivision succeed by itself and the rest will clamor to become part of that success. The ancient writer, Toynbee, first pointed out this difference between what he called a "dominant minority" and a "creative minority".

'We are a creative minority now. In an almost spontaneous gesture, various human governments have suggested the formation of a United Worlds organization. Over seventy governments are willing to attend the first sessions in order to draw up a Charter of Federation. The others will join later, I am sure. We would like you to be one of the delegates from Earth, Dick.'

Altmayer found his eyes flooding, 'I – I don't understand your purpose. Is this all true?'

'It is all exactly as I say. You were a voice in the wilderness, Dick, crying for union. Your words will carry much weight. What did you once say: "In a good cause, there are no failures".'

'No!' said Altmayer, with sudden energy. 'It seems your cause was the good one.'

Stock's face was hard and devoid of emotion, 'You were always a misunderstander of human nature, Dick. When the United Worlds is a reality and when generations of men and women look back to these days of war through their centuries of unbroken peace, they will have forgotten the purpose of my methods. To them they will represent war and death. *Your* calls for union, *your* idealism, will be remembered forever.'

He turned away and Altmayer barely caught his last words:

'And when they build their statues, they will build none for me.'

In the Great Court, which stands as a patch of untouched peace among the fifty busy square miles devoted to the towering buildings that are the pulse beat of the United Worlds of the Galaxy, stands a statue . . .

Easily the most frequently asked question put to any writer of science fiction stories is: 'Where do you get your ideas?'

I imagine the person who asks the question is sure that there is some mysterious kind of inspiration that can only be produced by odd and possibly illicit means, or that the writer goes through an eldritch ritual that may even involve calling up the devil.

But the answer is only, 'You can get an idea from anything if you are willing to think hard enough and long enough.'

That long-and-hard bit seems to disillusion people. Their admiration for you drops precipitously and you get the feeling you have exposed yourself as an impostor. After all, if long-and-hard is all it takes, anyone *can do it.*

Strange, then, that so few do.

Anyway, my wife once broke down and asked me that question even though she knows I dislike having it asked. We had moved to the Boston area in 1949, when I took my position with Boston University School of Medicine, and periodically we made a train trip back to New York to visit our respective families.

Once, on one of those train trips, perhaps out of boredom, she asked The Question. I said, 'From anything. I can probably get one out of this train trip, if I try.'

'Go ahead,' she said, naturally enough.

So I thought hard and told her the story of a train trip which, when I got back home, I typed up in permanent form and called 'What If –.'

The story is unusual for me in another respect, too. I am not strong on romance in my stories. Why that should be, I will leave to the parlor psychoanalyst. I merely state the fact.

Sometimes, I do have women in my stories. On rare occasions, as in 'Hostess', the woman is even the protagonist. But even then romance is a minor factor, if it appears at all.

In 'What If –,' however, the story is all romance. Each time I think of that, the fact startles me. I believe it is the only one of my many stories that is all serious (as opposed to ribald) romance. Heavens!

First appearance – Fantastic, Summer 1952. Copyright, 1952, by Ziff-Davis Publishing Company.

Norman and Livvy were late, naturally, since catching a train is always a matter of last-minute delays, so they had to take the only available seat in the coach. It was the one toward the front; the one with nothing before it but the seat that faced wrong way, with its back hard against the front partition. While Norman heaved the suitcase onto the rack, Livvy found herself chafing a little.

If a couple took the wrong-way seat before them, they would be staring self-consciously into each other's faces all the hours it would take to reach New York; or else, which was scarcely better, they would have to erect synthetic barriers of newspaper. Still, there was no use in taking a chance on there being another unoccupied double seat elsewhere in the train.

Norman didn't seem to mind, and that was a little disappointing to Livvy. Usually they held their moods in common. That, Norman claimed, was why he remained sure that he had married the right girl.

He would say, 'We fit each other, Livvy, and that's the key fact. When you're doing a jigsaw puzzle and one piece fits another, that's it. There are no other possibilities, and of course there are no other girls.'

And she would laugh and say, 'If you hadn't been on the streetcar that day, you would probably never have met me. What would you have done then?'

'Stayed a bachelor. Naturally. Besides, I would have met you through Georgette another day.'

'It wouldn't have been the same.'

'Sure it would.'

'No, it wouldn't. Besides, Georgette would never have introduced me. She was interested in you herself, and she's the type who knows better than to create a possible rival.'

'What nonsense.'

Livvy asked her favorite question: 'Norman, what if you had been one minute later at the streetcar corner and had taken the next car? What *do* you suppose would have happened?'

'And what if fish had wings and all of them flew to the top of the mountains? What would we have to eat on Fridays then?'

But they *had* caught the streetcar, and fish *didn't* have wings, so that now they had been married five years and ate fish on Fridays. And because they had been married five years, they were going to celebrate by spending a week in New York.

Then she remembered the present problem. 'I wish we could have found some other seat.'

Norman said, 'Sure. So do I. But no one has taken it yet, so we'll have relative privacy as far as Providence, anyway.'

Livvy was unconsoled, and felt herself justified when a plump little man walked down the central aisle of the coach. Now, where had he come from? The train was halfway between Boston and Providence, and if he had had a seat, why hadn't he kept it? She took out her vanity and considered her reflection. She had a theory that if she ignored the little man, he would pass by. So she concentrated on her light-brown hair which, in the rush of catching the train, had become disarranged just a little; at her blue eyes, and at her little mouth with the plump lips which Norman said looked like a permanent kiss.

Not bad, she thought.

Then she looked up, and the little man was in the seat opposite. He caught her eye and grinned widely. A series of lines curled about the edges of his smile. He lifted his hat hastily and put it down beside him on top of the little black box he had been carrying. A circle of white hair instantly sprang up stiffly about the large bald spot that made the center of his skull a desert.

She could not help smiling back a little, but then she caught sight of the black box again and the smile faded. She yanked at Norman's elbow.

Norman looked up from his newspaper. He had startlingly dark eyebrows that almost met above the bridge of his nose, giving him a formidable first appearance. But they and the dark eyes beneath bent upon her now with only the usual look of pleased and somewhat amused affection.

He said, 'What's up?' He did not look at the plump little man opposite.

Livvy did her best to indicate what she saw by a little unobtrusive gesture of her hand and head. But the little man was watching and she felt a fool, since Norman simply stared at her blankly.

Finally she pulled him closer and whispered, 'Don't you see what's printed on his box?'

She looked again as she said it, and there was no mistake. It was not very prominent, but the light caught it slantingly and it was a slightly more glistening area on a black background. In flowing script it said, 'What If.'

The little man was smiling again. He nodded his head rapidly and pointed to the words and then to himself several times over.

Norman said in an aside, 'Must be his name.'

Livvy replied, 'Oh, how could that be anybody's name?'

Norman put his paper aside. 'I'll show you.' He leaned over and said, 'Mr. If?'

The little man looked at him eagerly.

'Do you have the time, Mr. If?'

The little man took out a large watch from his vest pocket and displayed the dial.

'Thank you, Mr. If,' said Norman. And again in a whisper, 'See, Livvy.'

He would have returned to his paper, but the little man was opening his box and raising a finger periodically as he did so, to enforce their attention. It was just a slab of frosted glass that he removed — about six by nine inches in length and width and perhaps an inch thick. It had beveled edges, rounded corners, and was completely featureless. Then he took out a little wire stand on which the glass slab fitted comfortably. He rested the combination on his knees and looked proudly at them.

Livvy said, with sudden excitement, 'Heavens, Norman, it's a picture of some sort.'

Norman bent close. Then he looked at the little man. 'What's this? A new kind of television?'

The little man shook his head, and Livvy said, 'No, Norman, it's *us.*'

'What?'

'Don't you see? That's the streetcar we met on. There you are in the back seat wearing that old fedora I threw away three years ago. And that's Georgette and myself getting on. The fat lady's in the way. Now! Can't you see us?'

He muttered, 'It's some sort of illusion.'

'But you see it too, don't you? That's why he calls this "What If." It will *show* us what if. What if the streetcar hadn't swerved . . .'

She was sure of it. She was very excited and very sure of it. As she looked at the picture in the glass slab, the late afternoon sunshine grew dimmer and the inchoate chatter of the passengers around and behind them began fading.

How she remembered that day. Norman knew Georgette and had been about to surrender his seat to her when the car swerved and threw Livvy into his lap. It was such a ridiculously corny situation, but it had worked. She had been so embarrassed that he was forced first into gallantry and then into conversation. An introduction from Georgette was not even necessary. By the time they got off the streetcar, he knew where she worked.

She could still remember Georgette glowering at her, sulkily forcing a smile when they themselves separated. Georgette said, 'Norman seems to like you.'

Livvy replied, 'Oh, don't be silly! He was just being polite. But he is nice-looking, isn't he?'

It was only six months after that that they married.

And now here was that same streetcar again, with Norman and herself and Georgette. As she thought that, the smooth train noises, the rapid clack-clack of the wheels, vanished completely. Instead, she was in the swaying confines of the streetcar. She had just boarded it with Georgette at the previous stop.

Livvy shifted weight with the swaying of the streetcar, as did forty others, sitting and standing, all to the same monotonous and rather ridiculous rhythm. She said, 'Somebody's motioning at you, Georgette. Do you know him?'

'At me?' Georgette directed a deliberately casual glance over her shoulder. Her artificially long eyelashes flickered. She said, 'I know him a little. What do you suppose he wants?'

'Let's find out,' said Livvy. She felt pleased and a little wicked.

Georgette had a well-known habit of hoarding her male acquaintances, and it was rather fun to annoy her this way. And besides, this one seemed quite . . . interesting.

She snaked past the line of standees, and Georgette followed without enthusiasm. It was just as Livvy arrived opposite the young man's seat that the streetcar lurched heavily as it rounded a curve. Livvy snatched desperately in the direction of the straps. Her fingertips caught and she held on. It was a long moment before she could breathe. For some reason, it had seemed that there were no straps close enough to be reached. Somehow, she felt that by all the laws of nature she should have fallen.

The young man did not look at her. He was smiling at Georgette and rising from his seat. He had astonishing eyebrows that gave him a rather competent and self-confident appearance. Livvy decided that she definitely liked him.

Georgette was saying, 'Oh no, don't bother. We're getting off in about two stops.'

They did. Livvy said, 'I thought we were going to Sach's.'

'We are. There's just something I remember having to attend to here. It won't take but a minute.'

'Next stop, Providence!' the loud-speakers were blaring. The train was slowing and the world of the past had shrunk itself into the glass slab once more. The little man was still smiling at them.

Livvy turned to Norman. She felt a little frightened. 'Were you through all that, too?'

He said, 'What happened to the time? We can't be reaching Providence yet?' He looked at his watch. 'I guess we are.' Then, to Livvy, 'You didn't fall that time.'

'Then you did see it?' She frowned. 'Now, that's like Georgette. I'm sure there was no reason to get off the streetcar except to prevent my meeting you. How long had you known Georgette before then, Norman?'

'Not very long. Just enough to be able to recognize her at sight and to feel that I ought to offer her my seat.'

Livvy curled her lip.

Norman grinned, 'You can't be jealous of a might-have-been, kid. Besides, what difference would it have made? I'd have been sufficiently interested in you to work out a way of meeting you.'

'You didn't even look at me.'

'I hardly had the chance.'

'Then how would you have met me?'

'Some way. I don't know how. But you'll admit this is a rather foolish argument we're having.'

They were leaving Providence. Livvy felt a trouble in her mind. The little man had been following their whispered conversation, with only the loss of his smile to show that he understood. She said to him, 'Can you show us more?'

Norman interrupted, 'Wait now, Livvy. What are you going to try to do?'

She said, 'I want to see our wedding day. What it would have been if I had caught the strap.'

Norman was visibly annoyed. 'Now, that's not fair. We might not have been married on the same day, you know.'

But she said, 'Can you show it to me, Mr. If?' and the little man nodded.

The slab of glass was coming alive again, glowing a little. Then the light collected and condensed into figures. A tiny sound of organ music was in Livvy's ears, without there actually being sound.

Norman said with relief, 'Well, there I am. That's our wedding. Are you satisfied?'

The train sounds were disappearing again, and the last thing Livvy heard was her own voice saying, 'Yes, there *you* are. But where am *I*?'

Livvy was well back in the pews. For a while she had not expected to attend at all. In the past months she had drifted further and further away from Georgette, without quite knowing why. She had heard of her engagement only through a mutual friend, and, of course, it was to Norman. She remembered very clearly that day, six months before, when she had first seen him on the streetcar. It was the time Georgette had so quickly snatched her out of sight. She had met him since on several occasions, but each time Georgette was with him, standing between.

Well, she had no cause for resentment; the man was certainly none of hers. Georgette, she thought, looked more beautiful than she really was. And he was very handsome indeed.

She felt sad and rather empty, as though something had gone wrong – something that she could not quite outline in her mind. Georgette had moved up the aisle without seeming to see her, but earlier she had caught his eyes and smiled at him. Livvy thought he had smiled in return.

She heard the words distantly as they drifted back to her, 'I now pronounce you –'

The noise of the train was back. A woman swayed down the aisle, herding a little boy back to their seats. There were intermittent bursts of girlish laughter from a set of four teenage girls halfway down the coach. A conductor hurried past on some mysterious errand.

Livvy was frozenly aware of it all.

She sat there, staring straight ahead, while the trees outside blended into a fuzzy, furious green and the telephone poles galloped past.

She said, 'It was *she* you married.'

He stared at her for a moment and then one side of his mouth quirked a little. He said lightly, 'I didn't really, Olivia. You're still my wife, you know. Just think about it for a few minutes.'

She turned to him. 'Yes, you married me – because I fell in your lap. If I hadn't, you would have married Georgette. If she hadn't wanted you, you would have married someone else. You would have married anybody. So much for your jigsaw puzzle pieces.'

Norman said very slowly, 'Well – I'll – be – darned!' He put both hands to his head and smoothed down the straight hair over his ears where it had a tendency to tuft up. For the moment it gave him the appearance of trying to hold his head together. He said, 'Now, look here, Livvy, you're making a silly fuss over a stupid magician's trick. You can't blame me for something I haven't done.'

'You would have done it.'

'How do you know?'

'You've seen it.'

'I've seen a ridiculous piece of – of hypnotism, I suppose.' His voice suddenly raised itself into anger. He turned to the little man opposite. 'Off with you, Mr. If, or whatever your name is. Get out of here. We don't want you. Get out before I throw your little trick out the window and you after it.'

Livvy yanked at his elbow. 'Stop it. Stop it! You're in a crowded train.'

The little man shrank back into the corner of the seat as far as he could go and held his little black bag behind him. Norman looked at him, then at Livvy, then at the elderly lady across the way who was regarding him with patent disapproval.

He turned pink and bit back a pungent remark. They rode in frozen silence to and through New London.

Fifteen minutes past New London, Norman said, 'Livvy!'

She said nothing. She was looking out the window but saw nothing but the glass.

He said again, 'Livvy! Livvy! Answer me!'

She said dully, 'What do you want?'

He said, 'Look, this is all nonsense. I don't know how the fellow does it, but even granting it's legitimate, you're not being fair. Why stop where you did? Suppose I had married Georgette, do your suppose you would have stayed single? For all I know, you were already married at the time of my supposed wedding. Maybe that's why I married Georgette.'

'I wasn't married.'

'How do you know?'

'I would have been able to tell. I knew what my own thoughts were.'

'Then you would have been married within the next year.'

Livvy grew angrier. The fact that a sane remnant within her clamored at the unreason of her anger did not soothe her. It irritated her further, instead. She said, 'And if I did, it would be no business of yours, certainly.'

'Of course it wouldn't. But it would make the point that in the world of reality we can't be held responsible for the "what ifs".'

Livvy's nostrils flared. She said nothing.

Norman said, 'Look! You remember the big New Year's celebration at Winnie's place year before last?'

'I certainly do. You spilled a keg of alcohol all over me.'

'That's beside the point, and besides, it was only a cocktail shaker's worth. What I'm trying to say is that Winnie is just about your best friend and had been long before you married me.'

'What of it?'

'Georgette was a good friend of hers too, wasn't she?'

'Yes.'

'All right, then. You and Georgette would have gone to the party regardless of which one of you I had married. I would have had nothing to do with it. Let him show us the party as it would have been if I had married Georgette, and I'll bet you'd be there with either your fiancé or your husband.'

Livvy hesitated. She felt honestly afraid of just that.

He said, 'Are you afraid to take the chance?'

And that, of course, decided her. She turned on him furiously. 'No, I'm not! And I hope I am married. There's no reason I should pine for you. What's more, I'd like to see what happens when you spill the shaker all over Georgette. She'll fill both your ears for you, and in public, too. I know her. Maybe you'll see a certain difference in the jigsaw pieces then.' She faced forward and crossed her arms angrily and firmly across her chest.

Norman looked across at the little man, but there was no need to say anything. The glass slab was on his lap already. The sun slanted in from the west, and the white foam of hair that topped his head was edged with pink.

Norman said tensely, 'Ready?'

Livvy nodded and let the noise of the train slide away again.

Livvy stood, a little flushed with recent cold, in the doorway. She had just removed her coat, with its sprinkling of snow, and her bare arms were still rebelling at the touch of open air.

She answered the shouts that greeted her with 'Happy New Years' of her own, raising her voice to make herself heard over the squealing of the radio. Georgette's shrill tones were almost the first thing she heard upon entering, and now she steered toward her. She hadn't seen Georgette, or Norman, in weeks.

Georgette lifted an eyebrow, a mannerism she had lately culti-vated, and said, 'Isn't anyone with you, Olivia?' Her eyes swept the immediate surroundings and then returned to Livvy.

Livvy said indifferently, 'I think Dick will be around later. There was something or other he had to do first.' She felt as indifferent as she sounded.

Georgette smiled tightly. 'Well, Norman's here. That ought to keep you from being lonely, dear. At least, it's turned out that way before.'

And as she said so, Norman sauntered in from the kitchen. He had a cocktail shaker in his hand, and the rattling of ice cubes castanetted his words. 'Line up, you rioting revelers, and get a mixture that will really revel your riots – Why, Livvy!'

He walked toward her, grinning his welcome. 'Where've you been keeping yourself? I haven't seen you in twenty years, seems like. What's the matter? Doesn't Dick want anyone else to see you?'

'Fill my glass, Norman,' said Georgette sharply.

'Right away,' he said, not looking at her. 'Do you want one too, Livvy? I'll get you a glass.' He turned, and everything hap-pened at once.

Livvy cried. 'Watch out!' She saw it coming, even had a vague feeling that all this had happened before, but it played itself out inexorably. His heel caught the edge of the carpet; he lurched, tried to right himself, and lost the cocktail shaker. It seemed to jump out of his hands, and a pint of ice-cold liquor drenched Livvy from shoulder to hem.

She stood there, gasping. The noises muted about her, and for a few intolerable moments she made futile brushing gestures at her gown, while Norman kept repeating, 'Damnation!' in rising tones.

Georgette said coolly, 'It's too bad, Livvy. Just one of those things. I imagine the dress can't be very expensive.'

Livvy turned and ran. She was in the bedroom, which was at least empty and relatively quiet. By the light of the fringe-shaded lamp on the dresser, she poked among the coats on the bed, looking for her own.

Norman had come in behind her. 'Look, Livvy, don't pay any attention to what she said. I'm really devilishly sorry. I'll pay –'
There was something that was about to happen, I think.' He

'That's all right. It wasn't your fault.' She blinked rapidly and didn't look at him. 'I'll just go home and change.'

'Are you coming back?'

'I don't know. I don't think so.'

'Look, Livvy . . .' His warm fingers were on her shoulders –

Livvy felt a queer tearing sensation deep inside her, as though she were ripping away from clinging cobwebs and –

– and the train noises were back.

Something *did* go wrong with the time when she was in there – in the slab. It was deep twilight now. The train lights were on. But it didn't matter. She seemed to be recovering from the wrench inside her.

Norman was rubbing his eyes with thumb and forefinger. 'What happened?'

Livvy said, 'It just ended. Suddenly.'

Norman said uneasily, 'You know, we'll be putting into New Haven soon.' He looked at his watch and shook his head.

Livvy said wonderingly, 'You spilled it on me.'

'Well, so I did in real life.'

'But in real life I was your wife. You ought to have spilled it on Georgette this time. Isn't that queer?' But she was thinking of Norman pursuing her; his hands on her shoulders. . . .

She looked up at him and said with warm satisfaction, 'I wasn't married.'

'No, you weren't. But was that Dick Reinhardt you were going around with?'

'Yes.'

'You weren't planning to marry him, were you, Livvy?'

'Jealous, Norman?'

Norman looked confused. 'Of that? Of a slab of glass? Of course not.'

'I don't think I would have married him.'

Norman said, 'You know, I wish it hadn't ended when it did. There was something that was about to happen, I think.' He stopped, then added slowly, 'It was as though I would rather have done it to anybody else in the room.'

'Even to Georgette.'

'I wasn't giving two thoughts to Georgette. You don't believe me, I suppose.'

'Maybe I do.' She looked up at him. 'I've been silly, Norman. Let's – let's live our real life. Let's not play with all the things that just might have been.'

But he caught her hands. 'No, Livvy. One last time. Let's see what we would have been doing right now, Livvy! This very minute! If I had married Georgette.'

Livvy was a little frightened. 'Let's not, Norman.' She was thinking of his eyes, smiling hungrily at her as he held the shaker, while Georgette stood beside her, unregarded. She didn't *want* to know what happened afterward. She just wanted this life now, this good life.

New Haven came and went.

Norman said again, 'I want to try, Livvy.'

She said, 'If you want to, Norman.' She decided fiercely that it wouldn't matter. Nothing would matter. Her hands reached out and encircled his arm. She held it tightly, and while she held it she thought: 'Nothing in the make-believe can take him from me.'

Norman said to the little man, 'Set 'em up again.'

In the yellow light the process seemed to be slower. Gently the frosted slab cleared, like clouds being torn apart and dispersed by an unfelt wind.

Norman was saying, 'There's something wrong. That's just the two of us, exactly as we are now.'

He was right. Two little figures were sitting in a train on the

seats which were farthest toward the front. The field was en-
larging now – they were merging into it. Norman's voice was distant and fading.

'It's the same train,' he was saying. 'The window in back is
cracked just as –'

Livvy was blindingly happy. She said, 'I wish we were in
New York.'

He said, 'It will be less than an hour, darling.' Then he said,
'I'm going to kiss you.' He made a movement, as though he
were about to begin.

'Not here! Oh, Norman, people are looking.'

Norman drew back. He said, 'We should have taken a taxi.'

'From Boston to New York?'

'Sure. The privacy would have been worth it.'

She laughed. 'You're funny when you try to act ardent.'

'It isn't an act.' His voice was suddenly a little somber. 'It's
not just an hour, you know. I feel as though I've been waiting
five years.'

'I do, too.'

'Why couldn't I have met you first? It was such a waste.'

'Poor Georgette,' Livvy sighed.

Norman moved impatiently. 'Don't be sorry for her, Livvy.
We never really made a go of it. She was glad to get rid of me.'

'I know that. That's why I say "Poor Georgette." I'm just
sorry for her for not being able to appreciate what she had.'

'Well, see to it that *you* do,' he said. 'See to it that you're im-
mensely appreciative, infinitely appreciative – or more than that,
see that you're at least half as appreciative as I am of what *I've*
got.'

'Or else you'll divorce me, too?'

'Over my dead body,' said Norman.

Livvy said, 'It's all so strange. I keep thinking: "What if you
hadn't spilt the cocktails on me that time at the party?" You
wouldn't have followed me out; you wouldn't have told me;
I wouldn't have known. It would have been so different ...
everything.'

'Nonsense. It would have been just the same. It would have
all happened another time.'

'I wonder,' said Livvy softly.

Train noises merged into train noises. City lights flickered outside, and the atmosphere of New York was about them. The coach was astir with travelers dividing the baggage among themselves.

Livvy was an island in the turmoil until Norman shook her.

She looked at him and said, 'The jigsaw pieces fit after all.'

He said, 'Yes.'

She put a hand on his. 'But it wasn't good, just the same. I was very wrong. I thought that because we had each other, we should have all the *possible* each others. But all the possibles are none of our business. The real is enough. Do you know what I mean?'

He nodded.

She said, 'There are millions of other *what ifs*. I don't want to know what happened in any of them. I'll never say "What if" again.'

Norman said, 'Relax, dear. Here's your coat.' And he reached for the suitcases.

Livvy said with sudden sharpness, 'Where's Mr. If?'

Norman turned slowly to the empty seat that faced them. Together they scanned the rest of the coach.

'Maybe', Norman said, 'he went into the next coach.'

'But why? Besides, he wouldn't leave his hat.' And she bent to pick it up.

Norman said, 'What hat?'

And Livvy stopped her fingers hovering over nothingness. She said, 'It was here — I almost touched it.' She straightened and said, 'Oh, Norman, what if —'

Norman put a finger on her mouth. 'Darling . . .'

She said, 'I'm sorry. Here, let me help you with the suitcases.'

The train dived into the tunnel beneath Park Avenue, and the noise of the wheels rose to a roar.

As long as I mentioned the parlor psychoanalyst in the introduction to 'What If –,' I may as well go on to those fellows who analyze stories in Freudian fashion.

Given a Freudian cast of mind and sufficient ingenuity, it is possible, I think, to translate any collection of words (rational, irrational, or nonsensical) into sexual symbolism, and then prate learnedly about the writer's unconscious.

I have said this before and I'll say it again. I don't know what is in my unconscious mind and I don't care. I don't even know for sure that I have one.

I am told that the contents of one's unconscious may so distort his personality that he can only straighten out by a close study of those hidden mental factors under the guidance of an analyst.

Maybe so, but the only thing about myself that I consider to be severe enough to warrant psychoanalytic treatment is my compulsion to write. Perhaps if I vacuumed my mentality and got rid of the compulsion, I could spend more time sleeping in the sun and playing golf, or whatever it is that people do who have nothing better to do.

But I don't want to, thank you. I know all about my compulsion and I like it and intend to keep it. Someone else can have my ticket for sleeping in the sun and playing golf.

So I hope no one ever has the impulse to psychoanalyze my stories and come to me with a complete explanation of my compulsions and hangups and neuroses and expect me to be tearfully grateful. I'm not in the market. Nor am I interested in the hidden meanings of my stories. If you find them, keep them.

Which brings me to 'Sally'. It is well known that the average American male loves his car with a pseudosexual passion, and who am I to be un-American?

Anyone reading 'Sally' can sense that I feel strongly attracted to the heroine of the story and that this probably reflects something of my own life. Toward the end of the story, in fact, Sally does something which will allow the amateur Freudian a field day. (Oh, find it for yourself; it won't be hard.) The sexual symbolism is blatant and the parlor psychoanalyst can chuckle himself to death with what he will be sure exists in my unconscious mind.

Except that he will be quite wrong, because none of that was

*put in by my unconscious mind. It was all carefully and de-
liberately inserted by my conscious mind, because I wanted to.*

First appearance – Fantastic, May–June, 1953. Copyright,
1953, by Ziff-Davis Publishing Company.

SALLY

Sally was coming down the lake road, so I waved to her and
called her by name. I always liked to see Sally. I liked all of them,
you understand, but Sally's the prettiest one of the lot. There
just isn't any question about it.

She moved a little faster when I waved to her. Nothing undig-
nified. She was never that. She moved just enough faster to
show that she was glad to see me, too.

I turned to the man standing beside me. 'That's Sally,' I said.

He smiled at me and nodded.

Mrs. Hester had brought him in. She said, 'This is Mr. Gellhorn, Jake. You remember he sent you the letter asking for an
appointment.'

That was just talk, really. I have a million things to do around
the Farm, and one thing I just can't waste my time on is mail.
That's why I have Mrs. Hester around. She lives pretty close
by, she's good at attending to foolishness without running to
me about it, and most of all, she likes Sally and the rest. Some
people don't.

'Glad to see you, Mr. Gellhorn,' I said.

'Raymond J. Gellhorn,' he said, and gave me his hand, which
I shook and gave back.

He was a largish fellow, half a head taller than I and wider,
too. He was about half my age, thirtyish. He had black hair,
plastered down slick, with a part in the middle, and a thin mustache, very neatly trimmed. His jawbones got big under his ears
and made him look as if he had a slight case of mumps. On

video he'd be a natural to play the villain, so I assumed he was a nice fellow. It goes to show that video can't be wrong all the time.

'I'm Jacob Folkers,' I said. 'What can I do for you?'

He grinned. It was a big, wide, white-toothed grin. 'You can tell me a little about your Farm here, if you don't mind.'

I heard Sally coming up behind me and I put out my hand. She slid right into it and the feel of the hard, glossy enamel of her fender was warm in my palm.

'A nice automatobile,' said Gellhorn.

That's one way of putting it. Sally was a 2045 convertible with a Hennis-Carleton positronic motor and an Armat chassis. She had the cleanest, finest lines I've ever seen on any model, bar none. For five years, she'd been my favorite, and I'd put everything into her I could dream up. In all that time, there'd never been a human being behind her wheel.

Not once.

'Sally,' I said, patting her gently, 'meet Mr. Gellhorn.'

Sally's cylinder-purr keyed up a little. I listened carefully for any knocking. Lately, I'd been hearing motor-knock in almost all the cars and changing the gasoline hadn't done a bit of good. Sally was as smooth as her paint job this time, however.

'Do you have names for all your cars?' asked Gellhorn.

He sounded amused, and Mrs. Hester doesn't like people to sound as though they were making fun of the Farm. She said, sharply, 'Certainly. The cars have real personalities, don't they, Jake? The sedans are all males and the convertibles are females.'

Gellhorn was smiling again. 'And do you keep them in separate garages, ma'am?'

Mrs. Hester glared at him.

Gellhorn said to me, 'And now I wonder if I can talk to you alone, Mr. Folkers?'

'That depends,' I said. 'Are you a reporter?'

'No, sir. I'm a sales agent. Any talk we have is not for publication. I assure you I am interested in strict privacy.'

'Let's walk down the road a bit. There's a bench we can use.'

We started down. Mrs. Hester walked away. Sally nudged along after us.

I said, 'You don't mind if Sally comes along, do you?'

'Not at all. She can't repeat what we say, can she?' He laughed at his own joke, reached over and rubbed Sally's grille.

Sally raced her motor and Gellhorn's hand drew away quickly.

'She's not used to strangers,' I explained.

We sat down on the bench under the big oak tree where we could look across the small lake to the private speedway. It was the warm part of the day and the cars were out in force, at least thirty of them. Even at this distance I could see that Jeremiah was pulling his usual stunt of sneaking up behind some staid older model, then putting on a jerk of speed and yowling past with deliberately squealing brakes. Two weeks before he had crowded old Angus off the asphalt altogether, and I had turned off his motor for two days.

It didn't help though, I'm afraid, and it looks as though there's nothing to be done about it. Jeremiah is a sports model to begin with and that kind is awfully hot-headed.

'Well, Mr. Gellhorn,' I said. 'Could you tell me why you want the information?'

But he was just looking around. He said, 'This *is* an amazing place, Mr. Folkers.'

'I wish you'd call me Jake. Everyone does.'

'All right, Jake. How many cars do you have here?'

'Fifty-one. We get one or two new ones every year. One year we got five. We haven't lost one yet. They're all in perfect running order. We even have a '15 model Mat-O-Mot in working order. One of the original automatics. It was the first car here.'

Good old Matthew. He stayed in the garage most of the day now, but then he was the granddaddy of all positronic-motored cars. Those were the days when blind war veterans, paraplegics and heads of state were the only ones who drove automatics. But Samson Harridge was my boss and he was rich enough to be able to get one. I was his chauffeur at the time.

The thought makes me feel old. I can remember when there wasn't an automobile in the world with brains enough to find its own way home. I chauffeured dead lumps of machines that needed a man's hand at their controls every minute. Every year machines like that used to kill tens of thousands of people.

The automatics fixed that. A positronic brain can react much faster than a human one, of course, and it paid people to keep hands off the controls. You got in, punched your destination and let it go its own way.

We take it for granted now, but I remember when the first laws came out forcing the old machines off the highways and limiting travel to automatics. Lord, what a fuss. They called it everything from communism to fascism, but it emptied the highways and stopped the killing, and still more people get around more easily the new way.

Of course, the automatics were ten to a hundred times as expensive as the hand-driven ones, and there weren't many that could afford a private vehicle. The industry specialized in turning out omnibus-automatics. You could always call a company and have one stop at your door in a matter of minutes and take you where you wanted to go. Usually, you had to drive with others who were going your way, but what's wrong with that?

Samson Harridge had a private car though, and I went to him the minute it arrived. The car wasn't Matthew to me then. I didn't know it was going to be the dean of the Farm some day. I only knew it was taking my job away and I hated it.

I said, 'You won't be needing me any more, Mr. Harridge?'

He said, 'What are you dithering about, Jake? You don't think I'll trust myself to a contraption like that, do you? You stay right at the controls.'

I said, 'But it works by itself, Mr. Harridge. It scans the road, reacts properly to obstacles, humans, and other cars, and remembers routes to travel.'

'So they say. So they say. Just the same, you're sitting right behind the wheel in case anything goes wrong.'

Funny how you can get to like a car. In no time I was calling it Matthew and was spending all my time keeping it polished and humming. A positronic brain stays in condition best when it's got control of its chassis at all times, which means it's worth keeping the gas tank filled so that the motor can turn over slowly day and night. After a while, it got so I could tell by the sound of the motor how Matthew felt.

In his own way, Harridge grew fond of Matthew, too. He had no one else to like. He'd divorced or outlived three wives and outlived five children and three grandchildren. So when he died, maybe it wasn't surprising that he had his estate converted into a Farm for Retired Automobiles, with me in charge and Matthew the first member of a distinguished line.

It's turned out to be my life. I never got married. You can't get married and still tend to automatics the way you should.

The newspapers thought it was funny, but after a while they stopped joking about it. Some things you can't joke about. Maybe you've never been able to afford an automatic and maybe you never will, either, but take it from me, you get to love them. They're hard-working and affectionate. It takes a man with no heart to mistreat one or to see one mistreated.

It got so that after a man had an automatic for a while, he would make provisions for having it left to the Farm, if he didn't have an heir he could rely on to give it good care.

I explained that to Gellhorn.

He said, 'Fifty-one cars! That represents a lot of money.'

'Fifty thousand minimum per automatic, original investment,' I said. 'They're worth a lot more now. I've done things for them.'

'It must take a lot of money to keep up the Farm.'

'You're right there. The Farm's a non-profit organization, which gives us a break on taxes and, of course, new automatics that come in usually have trust funds attached. Still, costs are always going up. I have to keep the place landscaped; I keep laying down new asphalt and keeping the old in repair; there's gasoline, oil, repairs, and new gadgets. It adds up.'

'And you've spent a long time at it.'

'I sure have, Mr. Gellhorn. Thirty-three years.'

'You don't seem to be getting much out of it yourself.'

'I don't? You surprise me, Mr. Gellhorn. I've got Sally and fifty others. Look at her.'

I was grinning. I couldn't help it. Sally was so clean, it almost hurt. Some insect must have died on her windshield or one speck of dust too many had landed, so she was going to work. A little tube protruded and spurted Tergosol over the glass. It spread quickly over the silicone surface film and squeegees snapped into place instantly, passing over the windshield and forcing the water into the little channel that led it, dripping, down to the ground. Not a speck of water got onto her glistening apple-green hood. Squeegee and detergent tube snapped back into place and disappeared.

Gellhorn said, 'I never saw an automatic do that.'

'I guess not,' I said. 'I fixed that up specially on our cars. They're clean. They're always scrubbing their glass. They like it. I've even got Sally fixed up with wax jets. She polishes herself every night till you can see your face in any part of her and shave by it. If I can scrape up the money, I'd be putting it on the rest of the girls. Convertibles are very vain.'

'I can tell you how to scrape up the money, if that interests you.'

'That always does. How?'

'Isn't it obvious, Jake? Any of your cars is worth fifty thousand minimum, you said. I'll bet most of them top six figures.'

'So?'

'Ever think of selling a few?'

I shook my head. 'You don't realize it, I guess, Mr. Gellhorn, but I can't sell any of these. They belong to the Farm, not to me.'

'The money would go to the Farm.'

'The incorporation papers of the Farm provide that the cars receive perpetual care. They can't be sold.'

'What about the motors, then?'

'I don't understand you.'

Gellhorn shifted position and his voice got confidential. 'Look here, Jake, let me explain the situation. There's a big market for private automatics if they could only be made cheaply enough. Right?'

'That's no secret.'

'And ninety-five per cent of the cost is the motor. Right? Now, I know where we can get a supply of bodies. I also know where we can sell automatics at a good price – twenty or thirty thousand for the cheaper models, maybe fifty or sixty for the better ones. All I need are the motors. You see the solution?'

'I don't, Mr. Gellhorn.' I did, but I wanted him to spell it out.

'It's right here. You've got fifty-one of them. You're an expert automatobile mechanic, Jake. You must be. You could unhook a motor and place it in another car so that no one would know the difference.'

'It wouldn't be exactly ethical.'

'You wouldn't be harming the cars. You'd be doing them a favor. Use your older cars. Use that old Mat-O-Mot.'

'Well, now, wait a while, Mr. Gellhorn. The motors and bodies aren't two separate items. They're a single unit. Those motors are used to their own bodies. They wouldn't be happy in another car.'

'All right, that's a point. That's a very good point, Jake. It would be like taking your mind and putting it in someone else's skull. Right? You don't think you would like that?'

'I don't think I would. No.'

'But what if I took your mind and put it into the body of a young athlete. What about that, Jake? You're not a youngster anymore. If you had the chance, wouldn't you enjoy being twenty again? That's what I'm offering some of your positronic motors. They'll be put into new '57 bodies. The latest construction.'

I laughed. 'That doesn't make much sense, Mr. Gellhorn. Some of our cars may be old, but they're well-cared for. Nobody drives them. They're allowed their own way. They're *retired*, Mr. Gellhorn. I wouldn't want a twenty-year-old body if it meant I had to dig ditches for the rest of my new life and never have enough to eat. . . . What do you think, Sally?'

Sally's two doors opened and then shut with a cushioned slam.

'What that?' said Gellhorn.

'That's the way Sally laughs.'

Gellhorn forced a smile. I guess he thought I was making a bad joke. He said, 'Talk sense, Jake. Cars are made to be driven. They're probably not happy if you don't drive them.'

I said, 'Sally hasn't been driven in five years. She looks happy to me.'

'I wonder.'

He got up and walked toward Sally slowly. 'Hi, Sally, how'd you like a drive?'

Sally's motor reved up. She backed away.

'Don't push her, Mr. Gellhorn,' I said. 'She's liable to be a little skittish.'

Two sedans were about a hundred yards up the road. They had stopped. Maybe, in their own way, they were watching. I didn't bother about them. I had my eyes on Sally, and I kept them there.

Gellhorn said, 'Steady now, Sally.' He lunged out and seized the door handle. It didn't budge, of course.

He said, 'It opened a minute ago.'

I said, 'Automatic lock. She's got a sense of privacy, Sally has.'

He let go, then said, slowly and deliberately, 'A car with a sense of privacy shouldn't go around with its top down.'

He stepped back three or four paces, then quickly, so quickly I couldn't take a step to stop him, he ran forward and vaulted into the car. He caught Sally completely by surprise, because as he came down, he shut off the ignition before she could lock it in place.

For the first time in five years, Sally's motor was dead.

I think I yelled, but Gellhorn had the switch on 'Manual' and locked that in place, too. He kicked the motor into action. Sally was alive again but she had no freedom of action.

He started up the road. The sedans were still there. They turned and drifted away, not very quickly. I suppose it was all a puzzle to them.

One was Giuseppe, from the Milan factories, and the other was Stephen. They were always together. They were both new at the Farm, but they'd been here long enough to know that our cars just didn't have drivers.

Gellhorn went straight on, and when the sedans finally got it through their heads that Sally wasn't going to slow down, that she *couldn't* slow down, it was too late for anything but desperate measures.

They broke for it, one to each side, and Sally raced between them like a streak. Steve crashed through the lakeside fence and rolled to a halt on the grass and mud not six inches from the water's edge. Giuseppe bumped along the land side of the road to a shaken halt.

I had Steve back on the highway and was trying to find out what harm, if any, the fence had done him, when Gellhorn came back.

Gellhorn opened Sally's door and stepped out. Leaning back, he shut off the ignition a second time.

'There,' he said. 'I think I did her a lot of good.'

I held my temper. 'Why did you dash through the sedans? There was no reason for that.'

'I kept expecting them to turn out.'

'They did. One went through a fence.'

'I'm sorry, Jake,' he said. 'I thought they'd move more quickly. You know how it is. I've been in lots of buses, but I've only been in a private automatic two or three times in my life, and this is the first time I ever drove one. That just shows you, Jake. It got me, driving one, and I'm pretty hard-boiled. I tell you, we don't have to go more than twenty per cent below list price to reach a good market, and it would be ninety per cent profit.'

'Which we would split?'

'Fifty-fifty. And I take all the risks, remember.'

'All right. I listened to you. Now you listen to me.' I raised my voice because I was just too mad to be polite anymore. 'When you turn off Sally's motor, you hurt her. How would you like to be kicked unconscious? That's what you do to Sally, when you turn her off.'

'You're exaggerating, Jake. The automatobuses get turned off every night.'

'Sure, that's why I want none of my boys or girls in your fancy '57 bodies, where I won't know what treatment they'll get. Buses need major repairs in their positronic circuits every couple of years. Old Matthew hasn't had his circuits touched in twenty years. What can you offer him compared with that?'

'Well, you're excited now. Suppose you think over my proposition when you've cooled down and get in touch with me.'

'I've thought it over all I want to. If I ever see you again, I'll call the police.'

His mouth got hard and ugly. He said, 'Just a minute, old-timer.'

I said, 'Just a minute, you. This is private property and I'm ordering you off.'

He shrugged. 'Well, then, good-bye.'

I said, 'Mrs. Hester will see you off the property. Make that good-bye permanent.'

But it wasn't permanent. I saw him again two days later. Two and a half days, rather, because it was about noon when I saw him first and a little after midnight when I saw him again.

I sat up in bed when he turned the light on, blinking blindly till I made out what was happening. Once I could see, it didn't take much explaining. In fact, it took none at all. He had a gun in his right fist, the nasty little needle barrel just visible between two fingers. I knew that all he had to do was to increase the pressure of his hand and I would be torn apart.

He said, 'Put on your clothes, Jake.'

I didn't move. I just watched him.

He said, 'Look, Jake, I know the situation. I visited you two days ago, remember. You have no guards on this place, no electrified fences, no warning signals. Nothing.'

I said, 'I don't need any. Meanwhile there's nothing to stop you from leaving, Mr. Gellhorn. I would if I were you. This place can be very dangerous.'

He laughed a little. 'It is, for anyone on the wrong side of a fist gun.'

'I see it,' I said. 'I know you've got one.'

'Then get a move on. My men are waiting.'

'No, sir, Mr. Gellhorn. Not unless you tell me what you want, and probably not then.'

'I made you a proposition day before yesterday.'

'The answer's still no.'

There's more to the proposition now. I've come here with some men and an automatobus. You have your chance to come with me and disconnect twenty-five of the positronic motors. I don't care which twenty-five you choose. We'll load them on the bus and take them away. Once they're disposed of, I'll see to it that you get your fair share of the money.'

'I have your word on that, I suppose.'

He didn't act as if he thought I was being sarcastic. He said, 'You have.'

I said, 'No.'

'If you insist on saying no, we'll go about it in our own way. I'll disconnect the motors myself, only I'll disconnect all fifty-one. Every one of them.'

'It isn't easy to disconnect positronic motors, Mr. Gellhorn. Are you a robotics expert? Even if you are, you know, these motors have been modified by me.'

'I know that, Jake. And to be truthful, I'm not an expert. I may ruin quite a few motors trying to get them out. That's why I'll have to work over all fifty-one if you don't cooperate. You see, I may only end up with twenty-five when I'm through. The first few I'll tackle will probably suffer the most. Till I get the hang of it, you see. And if I go it myself, I think I'll put Sally first in line.'

I said, 'I can't believe you're serious, Mr. Gellhorn.'

He said, 'I'm serious, Jake.' He let it all dribble in. 'If you want to help, you can keep Sally. Otherwise, she's liable to be hurt very badly. Sorry.'

I said, 'I'll come with you, but I'll give you one more warning. You'll be in trouble, Mr. Gellhorn.'

He thought that was very funny. He was laughing very quietly as we went down the stairs together.

There was an automatobus waiting outside the driveway to

the garage apartments. The shadows of three men waited beside it, and their flash beams went on as we approached.

Gellhorn said in a low voice, 'I've got the old fellow. Come on. Move the truck up the drive and let's get started.'

One of the others leaned in and punched the proper instructions on the control panel. We moved up the driveway with the bus following submissively.

'It won't go inside the garage,' I said. 'The door won't take it. We don't have buses here. Only private cars.'

'All right,' said Gellhorn. 'Pull it over onto the grass and keep it out of sight.'

I could hear the thrumming of the cars when we were still ten yards from the garage.

Usually they quieted down if I entered the garage. This time they didn't. I think they knew that strangers were about, and once the faces of Gellhorn and the others were visible they got noisier. Each motor was a warm rumble, and each motor was knocking irregularly until the place rattled.

The lights went up automatically as we stepped inside. Gelhorn didn't seem bothered by the car noise, but the three men with him looked surprised and uncomfortable. They had the look of the hired thug about them, a look that was not compounded of physical features so much as of a certain wariness of eye and hang-dogness of face. I knew the type and I wasn't worried.

One of them said, 'Damn it, they're burning gas.'

'My cars always do,' I replied stiffly.

'Not tonight,' said Gellhorn. 'Turn them off.'

'It's not that easy, Mr. Gellhorn,' I said.

'Get started!' he said.

I stood there. He had his fist gun pointed at me steadily. I said, 'I told you, Mr. Gellhorn, that my cars have been well-treated while they've been at the Farm. They're used to being treated that way, and they resent anything else.'

'You have one minute,' he said. 'Lecture me some other time.'

'I'm trying to explain something. I'm trying to explain that my cars can understand what I say to them. A positronic motor will learn to do that with time and patience. My cars have learned. Sally understood your proposition two days ago. You'll remember she laughed when I asked her opinion. She also knows what you did to her and so do the two sedans you scattered. And the rest know what to do about trespassers in general.'

'Look, you crazy old fool –'

'All I have to say is –' I raised my voice. 'Get them!'

One of the men turned pasty and yelled, but his voice was drowned completely in the sound of fifty-one horns turned loose at once. They held their notes, and within the four walls of the garage the echoes rose to a wild, metallic call. Two cars rolled forward, not hurriedly, but with no possible mistake as to their target. Two cars fell in line behind the first two. All the cars were stirring in their separate stalls.

The thugs stared, then backed.

I shouted, 'Don't get up against a wall.'

Apparently, they had that instinctive thought themselves. They rushed madly for the door of the garage.

At the door one of Gellhorn's men turned, brought up a fist gun of his own. The needle pellet tore a thin, blue flash toward the first car. The car was Giuseppe.

A thin line of paint peeled up Giuseppe's hood, and the right half of his windshield crazed and splintered but did not break through.

The men were out the door, running, and two by two the cars crunched out after them into the night, their horns calling the charge.

I kept my hand on Gellhorn's elbow, but I don't think he could have moved in any case. His lips were trembling.

I said, 'That's why I don't need electrified fences or guards. My property protects itself.'

Gellhorn's eyes swiveled back and forth in fascination as, pair by pair, they whizzed by. He said, 'They're killers!'

'Don't be silly. They won't kill your men.'

'They're killers!'

'They'll just give your men a lesson. My cars have been special-ly trained for cross-country pursuit for just such an occasion; I think what your men will get will be worse than an outright quick kill. Have you ever been chased by an automatobile?'

Gellhorn didn't answer.

I went on. I didn't want him to miss a thing. 'They'll be shadows going no faster than your men, chasing them here, blocking them there, blaring at them, dashing at them, missing with a screech of brake and a thunder of motor. They'll keep it up till your men drop, out of breath and half-dead, waiting for the wheels to crunch over their breaking bones. The cars won't do that. They'll turn away. You can bet, though, that your men will never return here in their lives. Not for all the money you or ten like you could give them. Listen —'

I tightened my hold on his elbow. He strained to hear.

I said, 'Don't you hear car doors slamming?'

It was faint and distant, but unmistakable.

I said, 'They're laughing. They're enjoying themselves.'

His face crumpled with rage. He lifted his hand. He was still holding his fist gun.

I said, 'I wouldn't. One automatocar is still with us.'

I don't think he had noticed Sally till then. She had moved up so quietly. Though her right front fender nearly touched me, I couldn't hear her motor. She might have been holding her breath.

Gellhorn yelled.

I said, 'She won't touch you, as long as I'm with you. But if you kill me. . . . You know, Sally doesn't like you.'

Gellhorn turned the gun in Sally's direction.

'Her motor is shielded,' I said, 'and before you could ever squeeze the gun a second time she would be on top of you.'

'All right, then,' he yelled, and suddenly my arm was bent behind my back and twisted so I could hardly stand. He held me between Sally and himself, and his pressure didn't let up. 'Back out with me and don't try to break loose, old-timer, or I'll tear your arm out of its socket.'

I had to move. Sally nudged along with us, worried, uncertain what to do. I tried to say something to her and couldn't. I could only clench my teeth and moan.

Gellhorn's automatobus was still standing outside the garage. I was forced in. Gellhorn jumped in after me, locking the doors.

He said, 'All right, now. We'll talk sense.'

I was rubbing my arm, trying to get life back into it, and even as I did I was automatically and without any conscious effort studying the control board of the bus.

I said, 'This is a rebuilt job.'

'So?' he said caustically. 'It's a sample of my work. I picked up a discarded chassis, found a brain I could use and spliced me a private bus. What of it?'

I tore at the repair panel, forcing it aside.

He said, 'What the hell. Get away from that.' The side of his palm came down numbingly on my left shoulder.

I struggled with him. 'I don't want to do this bus any harm. What kind of a person do you think I am? I just want to take a look at some of the motor connections.'

It didn't take much of a look. I was boiling when I turned to him. I said, 'You're a hound and a bastard. You had no right installing this motor yourself. Why didn't you get a robotics man?'

He said, 'Do I look crazy?'

'Even if it was a stolen motor, you had no right to treat it so. I wouldn't treat a man the way you treated that motor. Solder, tape, and pinch clamps! It's brutal!'

'It works, doesn't it?'

'Sure it works, but it must be hell for the bus. You could live with migraine headaches and acute arthritis, but it wouldn't be much of a life. This car is *suffering*.'

'Shut up!' For a moment he glanced out the window at Sally, who had rolled up as close to the bus as she could. He made sure the doors and windows were locked.

He said, 'We're getting out of here now, before the other cars come back. We'll stay away.'

'How will that help you?'

'Your cars will run out of gas someday, won't they? You haven't got them fixed up so they can tank up on their own, have you? We'll come back and finish the job.'

'They'll be looking for me,' I said. 'Mrs. Hester will call the police.'

He was past reasoning with. He just punched the bus in gear. It lurched forward. Sally followed.

He giggled. 'What can she do if you're here with me?'

Sally seemed to realize that, too. She picked up speed, passed us and was gone. Gellhorn opened the window next to him and spat through the opening.

The bus lumbered on over the dark road, its motor rattling unevenly. Gellhorn dimmed the periphery light until the phosphorescent green stripe down the middle of the highway, sparkling in the moonlight, was all that kept us out of the trees. There was virtually no traffic. Two cars passed ours, going the other way, and there was none at all on our side of the highway, either before or behind.

I heard the door-slamming first. Quick and sharp in the silence, first on the right and then on the left. Gellhorn's hands quivered as he punched savagely for increased speed. A beam of light shot out from among a scrub of trees, blinding us. Another beam plunged at us from behind the guard rails on the other side. At a crossover, four hundred yards ahead, there was a sque-e-e-e-e as a car darted across our path.

'Sally went for the rest,' I said. 'I think you're surrounded.'

'So what? What can they do?'

He hunched over the controls, peering through the windshield.

'And don't *you* try anything, old-timer,' he muttered.

I couldn't. I was bone-weary; my left arm was on fire. The motor sounds gathered and grew closer. I could hear the motors missing in odd patterns; suddenly it seemed to me that my cars were speaking to one another.

A medley of horns came from behind. I turned and Gellhorn looked quickly into the rear-view mirror. A dozen cars were following in both lanes.

Gellhorn yelled and laughed madly.

I cried, 'Stop! Stop the car!'

Because not a quarter of a mile ahead, plainly visible in the light beams of two sedans on the roadside was Sally, her trim body plunked square across the road. Two cars shot into the opposite lane to our left, keeping perfect time with us and preventing Gellhorn from turning out.

But he had no intention of turning out. He put his finger on the full-speed-ahead button and kept it there.

He said, 'There'll be no bluffing here. This bus outweighs her five to one, old-timer, and we'll just push her off the road like a dead kitten.'

I knew he could. The bus was on manual and his finger was on the button. I knew he would.

I lowered the window, and stuck my head out. 'Sally,' I screamed. 'Get out of the way. *Sally!*'

It was drowned out in the agonized squeal of maltreated brake-bands. I felt myself thrown forward and heard Gellhorn's breath puff out of his body.

I said, 'What happened?' It was a foolish question. We had stopped. That was what had happened. Sally and the bus were five feet apart. With five times her weight tearing down on her, she had not budged. The guts of her.

Gellhorn yanked at the Manual toggle switch. 'It's got to,' he kept muttering. 'It's got to.'

I said, 'Not the way you hooked up the motor, expert. Any of the circuits could cross over.'

He looked at me with a tearing anger and growled deep in his throat. His hair was matted over his forehead. He lifted his fist.

'That's all the advice out of you there'll ever be, old-timer.'

And I knew the needle gun was about to fire.

I pressed back against the bus door, watching the fist come up, and when the door opened I went over backward and out, hitting the ground with a thud. I heard the door slam closed again.

I got to my knees and looked up in time to see Gellhorn struggle uselessly with the closing window, then aim his fist gun quickly through the glass. He never fired. The bus got under way with a tremendous roar, and Gellhorn lurched backward.

Sally wasn't in the way any longer, and I watched the bus's rear lights flicker away down the highway.

I was exhausted. I sat down right there, right on the highway, and put my head down in my crossed arms, trying to catch my breath.

I heard a car stop gently at my side. When I looked up, it was Sally. Slowly – lovingly, you might say – her front door opened.

No one had driven Sally for five years – except Gellhorn, of course – and I know how valuable such freedom was to a car. I appreciated the gesture, but I said, 'Thanks, Sally, but I'll take one of the newer cars.'

I got up and turned away, but skillfully and neatly as a pirouette, she wheeled before me again. I couldn't hurt her feelings. I got in. Her front seat had the fine, fresh scent of an automatobile that kept itself spotlessly clean. I lay down across it, thankfully, and with even, silent, and rapid efficiency, my boys and girls brought me home.

Mrs. Hester brought me the copy of the radio transcript the next evening with great excitement.

'It's Mr. Gellhorn,' she said. 'The man who came to see you.'

'What about him?'

I dreaded her answer.

'They found him dead,' she said. 'Imagine that. Just lying dead in a ditch.'

'It might be a stranger altogether,' I mumbled.

'Raymond J. Gellhorn,' she said, sharply. 'There can't be two, can there? The description fits, too. Lord, what a way to die? They found tire marks on his arms and body. Imagine! I'm glad it turned out to be a bus; otherwise they might have come poking around here.'

'Did it happen near here?' I asked, anxiously.

'No ... Near Cooksville. But, goodness, read about it yourself if you – What happened to Giuseppe?'

I welcomed the diversion. Giuseppe was waiting patiently for me to complete the repaint job. His windshield had been replaced.

After she left, I snatched up the transcript. There was no doubt about it. The doctor reported he had been running and was in a state of totally spent exhaustion. I wondered for how many miles the bus had played with him before the final lunge. The transcript had no notion of anything like that, of course.

They had located the bus and identified it by the tire tracks. The police had it and were trying to trace its ownership.

There was an editorial in the transcript about it. It had been the first traffic fatality in the state for that year and the paper warned strenuously against manual driving after night.

There was no mention of Gellhorn's three thugs and for that, at least, I was grateful. None of our cars had been seduced by the pleasure of the chase into killing.

That was all. I let the paper drop. Gellhorn had been a criminal. His treatment of the bus had been brutal. There was no question in my mind he deserved death. But still I felt a bit queasy over the manner of it.

A month has passed now and I can't get it out of my mind.

My cars talk to one another. I have no doubt about it anymore. It's as though they've gained confidence; as though they're not bothering to keep it secret anymore. Their engines rattle and knock continuously.

And they don't talk among themselves only. They talk to the cars and buses that come into the Farm on business. How long have they been doing that?

They must be understood, too. Gellhorn's bus understood

them, for all it hadn't been on the grounds more than an hour. I can close my eyes and bring back that dash along the highway, with our cars flanking the bus on either side, clacking their motors at it till it understood, stopped, let me out, and ran off with Gellhorn.

Did my cars tell him to kill Gellhorn? Or was that his idea?

Can cars have such ideas? The motor designers say no but they mean under ordinary conditions. Have they foreseen *everything*?

Cars get ill-used, you know.

Some of them enter the Farm and observe. They get told things. They find out that cars exist whose motors are never stopped, whom no one ever drives, whose every need is supplied.

Then maybe they go out and tell others. Maybe the word is spreading quickly. Maybe they're going to think that the Farm way should be the way all over the world. They don't understand. You couldn't expect them to understand about legacies and the whims of rich men.

There are millions of automatobiles on Earth, tens of millions. If the thought gets rooted in them that they're slaves; that they should do something about it . . . If they begin to think the way Gellhorn's bus did. . . .

Maybe it won't be till after my time. And then they'll have to keep a few of us to take care of them, won't they? They wouldn't kill us all.

And maybe they would. Maybe they wouldn't understand about how someone would have to care for them. Maybe they won't wait.

Every morning I wake up and think, Maybe today. . . .

I don't get as much pleasure out of my cars as I used to. Lately, I notice that I'm even beginning to avoid Sally.

In late 1949, a new magazine appeared on the newsstands: The Magazine of Fantasy. By the second issue it had expanded its name to The Magazine of Fantasy and Science Fiction, and it is universally known by the initials F & SF.

I found F & SF daunting at first. It stressed style, it seemed to me, even more than idea, and I wasn't at all sure that I could manage style, or that I even knew what style might be. It was only a few months ago, indeed, that a reviewer, referring to me in her review of one of my books, said, 'He is no stylist.' I wrote at once to ask what a stylist was, but she never answered, so it looks as though I'll never find out.

As it happened, though, Anthony Boucher, the co-editor of the magazine, wrote me a letter after the appearance of 'Hostess' – the first communication on record between us. In 'Hostess,' I had spoken of the 'the paler emotional surges of the late thirties,' and Tony wrote in mild expostulation, having himself just turned forty at the time. (I had just turned thirty.) He told me that I had a delightful surprise ahead of me, and he was entirely right.

This initiated a pleasant correspondence and I lost some of my fear of F & SF. I thought I would try a story that stressed style but since I didn't (either then or now) know what style was, or how one went about getting it, I hadn't the faintest idea whether I had succeeded or not. I guess I did, though, for it was 'Flies' I wrote and Mr. Boucher accepted and published it.

I had no way of telling it at the time, but this began what turned out to be the happiest of all my associations with science fiction magazines. I have no complaints about Astounding, Galaxy, or any of the rest, heaven knows, but F & SF has become something special to me, and it is only honest of me to say so.

By the way, if anyone thinks I am so arrogant that I can never accept any editorial correction, he is quite wrong. I don't enjoy editorial correction (no writer does) but I accept it quite often. (This, actually, is intended for my brother, who is a newspaper editor and who seems to think that all writers are fiendishly anti-editor out of sheer malevolent stupidity.)

Anyway, here is my example of how sweetly compliant I can be. When I first wrote 'Flies', I named it 'King Lear, IV, i, 36–37.' Mr. Boucher wrote me, somewhat in horror, and asked if I insisted on the title because nobody would look it up and it would be meaningless.

I thought it over and decided he was right and renamed the story 'Flies'. After you read the story, however, you're welcome to look it up. You'll find out what started the train of thought that ended in this particular story.

First appearance – The Magazine of Fantasy and Science Fiction, *June 1953. Copyright, 1953, by Fantasy House, Inc.*

FLIES

'Flies!' said Kendell Casey, wearily. He swung his arm. The fly circled, returned and nestled on Casey's shirt-collar.

From somewhere there sounded the buzzing of a second fly.

Dr. John Polen covered the slight uneasiness of his chin by moving his cigarette quickly to his lips.

He said, 'I didn't expect to meet you, Casey. Or you, Winthrop. Or ought I call you Reverend Winthrop?'

'Ought I call you Professor Polen?' said Winthrop, carefully striking the proper vein of rich-toned friendship.

They were trying to snuggle into the cast-off shell of twenty years back, each of them. Squirming and cramming and not fitting.

Damn, thought Polen fretfully, why do people attend college re-unions?

Casey's hot blue eyes were still filled with the aimless anger of the college sophomore who has discovered intellect, frustration, and the tag-ends of cynical philosophy all at once.

Casey! Bitter man of the campus!

He hadn't outgrown that. Twenty years later and it was Casey, bitter ex-man of the campus! Polen could see that in the way his finger tips moved aimlessly and in the manner of his spare body.

As for Winthrop? Well, twenty years older, softer, rounder. Skin pinker, eyes milder. Yet no nearer the quiet certainty he would never find. It was all there in the quick smile he never entirely abandoned, as though he feared there would be nothing to take its place, that its absence would turn his face into a smooth and featureless flesh.

Polen was tired of reading the aimless flickering of a muscle's end; tired of usurping the place of his machines; tired of the too much they told him.

Could they read him as he read them? Could the small restlessness of his own eyes broadcast the fact that he was damp with the disgust that had bred mustily within him?

Damn, thought Polen, why didn't I stay away?

They stood there, all three, waiting for one another to say something, to flick something from across the gap and bring it, quivering, into the present.

Polen tried it. He said, 'Are you still working in chemistry, Casey?'

'In my own way, yes,' said Casey, gruffly. 'I'm not the scientist you're considered to be. I do research on insecticides for E. J. Link at Chatham.'

Winthrop said, 'Are you really? You said you would work on insecticides. Remember, Polen? And with all that, the flies dare still be after you, Casey?'

Casey said, 'Can't get rid of them. I'm the best proving ground in the labs. No compound we've made keeps them away when I'm around. Someone once said it was my odor. I attract them.'

Polen remembered the someone who had said that.

Winthrop said, 'Or else –'

Polen felt it coming. He tensed.

'Or else,' said Winthrop, 'it's the curse, you know.' His smile intensified to show that he was joking, that he forgave past grudges.

Damn, thought Polen, they haven't even changed the words. And the past came back.

'Flies,' said Casey, swinging his arm, and slapping. 'Ever see such a thing? Why don't they light on you two?'

Johnny Polen laughed at him. He laughed often then. 'It's something in your body odor, Casey. You could be a boon to science. Find out the nature of the odorous chemical, concentrate it, mix it with DDT, and you've got the best fly-killer in the world.'

'A fine situation. What do I smell like? A lady fly in heat? It's a shame they have to pick on me when the whole damned world's a dung heap.'

Winthrop frowned and said with a faint flavor of rhetoric, 'Beauty is not the only thing, Casey, in the eye of the beholder.'

Casey did not deign a direct response. He said to Polen, 'You know what Winthrop told me yesterday? He said those damned flies were the curse of Beelzebub.'

'I was joking,' said Winthrop.

'Why Beelzebub?' asked Polen.

'It amounts to a pun,' said Winthrop. 'The ancient Hebrews used it as one of their many terms of derision for alien gods. It comes from *Ba'al*, meaning *lord* and *zevuv*, meaning *fly*. The lord of flies.'

Casey said, 'Come on, Winthrop, don't say you don't believe in Beelzebub.'

'I believe in the existence of evil,' said Winthrop, stiffly.

'I mean Beelzebub. Alive. Horns. Hooves. A sort of competition deity.'

'Not at all.' Winthrop grew stiffer. 'Evil is a short-term affair. In the end it must lose —'

Polen changed the subject with a jar. He said, 'I'll be doing graduate work for Venner, by the way. I talked with him day before yesterday, and he'll take me on.'

'No! That's wonderful.' Winthrop glowed and leaped to the subject-change instantly. He held out a hand with which to pump Polen's. He was always conscientiously eager to rejoice in another's good fortune. Casey often pointed that out.

Casey said, 'Cybernetics Venner? Well, if you can stand him, I suppose he can stand you.'

Winthrop went on. 'What did he think of your idea? Did you tell him your idea?'

'What idea?' demanded Casey.

Polen had avoided telling Casey so far. But now Venner had considered it and had passed it with a cool, 'Interesting!' How could Casey's dry laughter hurt it now?

Polen said, 'It's nothing much. Essentially, it's just a notion that emotion is the common bond of life, rather than reason or intellect. It's practically a truism, I suppose. You can't tell what a baby thinks or even *if* it thinks, but it's perfectly obvious that it can be angry, frightened or contented even when a week old. See?

'Same with animals. You can tell in a second if a dog is happy or if a cat is afraid. The point is that their emotions are the same as those we would have under the same circumstances.'

'So?' said Casey. 'Where does it get you?'

'I don't know yet. Right now, all I can say is that emotions are universals. Now suppose we could properly analyze all the actions of men and certain familiar animals and equate them with the visible emotion. We might find a tight relationship. Emotion A might always involve Motion B. Then we could apply it to animals whose emotions we couldn't guess at by common sense alone. Like snakes, or lobsters.'

'Or flies,' said Casey, as he slapped viciously at another and flicked its remains off his wrist in furious triumph.

He went on. 'Go ahead, Johnny. I'll contribute the flies and you study them. We'll establish a science of flychology and labor to make them happy by removing their neuroses. After all, we want the greatest good of the greatest number, don't we? And there are more flies than men.'

'Oh, well,' said Polen.

Casey said, 'Say, Polen, did you ever follow up that weird idea of yours? I mean, we all know you're a shining cybernetic light, but I haven't been reading your papers. With so many ways of wasting time, something has to be neglected, you know.'

'What idea?' asked Polen, woodenly.

'Come on. You know. Emotions of animals and all that sort of guff. Boy, those were the days. I used to know madmen. Now I only come across idiots.'

Winthrop said, 'That's right, Polen. I remember it very well. Your first year in graduate school you were working on dogs and rabbits. I believe you even tried some of Casey's flies.'

Polen said, 'It came to nothing in itself. It gave rise to certain new principles of computing, however, so it wasn't a total loss.'

Why did they talk about it?

Emotions! What right had anyone to meddle with emotions? Words were invented to conceal emotions. It was the dreadfulness of raw emotion that had made language a basic necessity.

Polen knew. His machines had by-passed the screen of verbalization and dragged the unconscious into the sunlight. The boy and the girl, the son and the mother. For that matter, the cat and the mouse or the snake and the bird. The data rattled together in its universality and it had all poured into and through Polen until he could no longer bear the touch of life.

In the last few years he had so painstakingly schooled his thoughts in other directions. Now these two came, dabbling in his mind, stirring up its mud.

Casey batted abstractedly across the tip of his nose to dislodge a fly. 'Too bad,' he said. 'I used to think you could get some-fascinating things out of, say, rats. Well, maybe not fascinating, but then not as boring as the stuff you would get out of our somewhat-human beings. I used to think –'

Polen remembered what he used to think.

Casey said, 'Damn this DDT. The flies feed on it, I think. You know, I'm going to do graduate work in chemistry and then get a job on insecticides. So help me. I'll personally get something that *will* kill the vermin.'

They were in Casey's room, and it had a somewhat keroseny odor from the recently applied insecticide.

Polen shrugged and said, 'A folded newspaper will always kill.'

Casey detected a non-existent sneer and said instantly, 'How would you summarize your first year's work, Polen? I mean aside from the true summary any scientist could state if he dared, by which I mean: "Nothing".'

'Nothing,' said Polen. 'There's your summary.'

'Go on,' said Casey. 'You use more dogs than the physiologists do and I bet the dogs mind the physiological experiments less. I would.'

'Oh, leave him alone,' said Winthrop. 'You sound like a piano with 87 keys eternally out of order. You're a bore!'

You couldn't say that to Casey.

He said, with sudden liveliness, looking carefully away from Winthrop, 'I'll tell you what you'll probably find in animals, if you look closely enough. Religion.'

'What the dickens!' said Winthrop, outraged. 'That's a fool-ish remark.'

Casey smiled. 'Now, now, Winthrop. *Dickens* is just a eu-phemism for *devil* and you don't want to be swearing.'

'Don't teach me morals. And don't be blasphemous.'

'What's blasphemous about it? Why shouldn't a flea consider the dog as something to be worshipped? It's the source of warmth, food, and all that's good for a flea.'

'I don't want to discuss it.'

'Why not? Do you good. You could even say that to an ant, an anteater is a higher order of creation. He would be too big for them to comprehend, too mighty to dream of resisting. He would move among them like an unseen, inexplicable whirlwind, visiting them with destruction and death. But that wouldn't spoil things for the ants. They would reason that destruction was simply their just punishment for evil. And the anteater wouldn't even know he was a deity. Or care.'

Winthrop had gone white. He said, 'I know you're saying this only to annoy me and I am sorry to see you risking your soul for a moment's amusement. Let me tell you this,' his voice trembled a little, 'and let me say it very seriously. The flies that torment you are your punishment in this life. Beelzebub, like all the forces of evil, may think he does evil, but it's only the ultimate good after all. The curse of Beelzebub is on you for *your* good. Perhaps it will succeed in getting you to change your way of life before it's too late.'

He ran from the room.

Casey watched him go. He said, laughing, 'I told you Winthrop believed in Beelzebub. It's funny the respectable names you can give to superstition.' His laughter died a little short of its natural end.

There were two flies in the room, buzzing through the vapors toward him.

Polen rose and left in heavy depression. One year had taught him little, but it was already too much, and his laughter was thinning. Only his machines could analyze the emotions of animals properly, but he was already guessing too deeply concerning the emotions of men.

He did not like to witness wild murder-yearnings where others could see only a few words of unimportant quarrel.

Casey said, suddenly, 'Say, come to think of it, you did try some of my flies, the way Winthrop says. How about that?

'Did I? after twenty years, I scarcely remember,' murmured Polen.

Winthrop said, 'You must. We were in your laboratory and you complained that Casey's flies followed him even there. He suggested you analyze them and you did. You recorded their motions and buzzings and wing-wiping for half an hour or more. You played with a dozen different flies.'

Polen shrugged.

'Oh, well,' said Casey. 'It doesn't matter. It was good seeing you, old man.' The hearty hand-shake, the thump on the shoulder, the broad grin – to Polen it all translated into sick disgust on Casey's part that Polen was a 'success' after all.

Polen said, 'Let me hear from you sometimes.'

The words were dull thumps. They meant nothing. Casey knew that. Polen knew that. Everyone knew that. But words were meant to hide emotion and when they failed, humanity loyally maintained the pretense.

Winthrop's grasp of the hand was gentler. He said, 'This brought back old times, Polen. If you're ever in Cincinnati, why don't you stop in at the meeting-house? You'll always be welcome.'

To Polen, it all breathed of the man's relief at Polen's obvious depression. Science, too, it seemed, was not the answer, and Winthrop's basic and ineradicable insecurity felt pleased at the company.

'I will,' said Polen. It was the usual polite way of saying, I won't.

He watched them thread separately to other groups.

Winthrop would never know. Polen was sure of that. He wondered if Casey knew. It would be the supreme joke if Casey did not.

He *had* run Casey's flies, of course, not that once alone, but many times. Always the same answer! Always the same unpublishable answer.

With a cold shiver he could not quite control, Polen was suddenly conscious of a single fly loose in the room, veering aimlessly for a moment, then beating strongly and reverently in the direction Casey had taken a moment before.

Could Casey *not* know? Could it be the essence of the primal punishment that he never learn he was Beelzebub?

Casey! Lord of the Flies!

I suppose that one of those stock phrases for which everyone is responsible at one time or another is: 'Well, whatever does he see in her?' Or, 'Well, whatever does she see in him?'

It's a ridiculous question because the sort of thing that he sees in her or she sees in him that isn't visible to the general population is probably you-know-very-well-what.

Just the same, I'm as prone to sneer as the next fellow and when I see a movie in which the girl falls in love with a fellow who has no visible advantages outside of being tall, lean, strong, fearless, and incredibly handsome, I am naturally disgusted. 'Whatever does she see in him?' I ask.

Pressed for a reason for the sneer, I can point out that this tall, lean, strong, fearless, and incredibly handsome fellow almost invariably has the brain capacity of a gnat. He speaks in an occasional grunt and views the world with dim eyes backed by a lackluster brain. He is known to all and sundry, and particularly to the girl who is trying to mask her mad passion for him, as a 'big lug', or, possibly, as a 'big galoot'.

These lugs or galoots are particularly impervious to even subhuman understanding of feminine psychology and the more they display this the more desperately they are loved.

I tell you I can't stand it. The fact that I know darned well that if I ever tried to compete for a girl with one of these tall, lean cretins, I would lose out, makes it worse. So I took my revenge; I decided never to write a big lug into one of my stories.

As far as I knew I never did. As of yesterday, I would have sworn to that, and backed the oath with any sum of money. Yet when I read over 'Nobody Here But—' just now, prior to writing a fitting introduction, I realized with sinking heart and disbelieving mind that here was a story with a galoot.

Good Lord!

First appearance – Star Science Fiction Stories, 1953. Copyright, 1953, by Ballantine Books, Inc.

You see, it wasn't our fault. We had no idea anything was wrong until I called Cliff Anderson and spoke to him when he wasn't there. What's more, I wouldn't have known he wasn't there, if it wasn't that he walked in while I was talking to him.

No, no, no, *no* –

I never seem to be able to tell this straight. I get too excited. – Look, I might as well begin at the beginning. I'm Bill Billings; my friend is Cliff Anderson. I'm an electrical engineer, he's a mathematician, and we're on the faculty of Midwestern Institute of Technology. Now you know who we are.

Ever since we got out of uniform, Cliff and I have been working on calculating machines. You know what they are. Norbert Wiener popularized them in his book, *Cybernetics*. If you've seen pictures of them, you know that they're great big things. They take up a whole wall and they're very complicated; also expensive.

But Cliff and I had ideas. You see, what makes a thinking machine so big and expensive is that it has to be full of relays and vacuum tubes just so that microscopic electric currents can be controlled and made to flicker on and off, here and there. Now the really important things are those little electric currents, so –

I once said to Cliff, 'Why can't we control the currents without all the salad dressing?'

Cliff said, 'Why not, indeed,' and started working on the mathematics.

How we got where we did in two years is no matter. It's what we got after we finished that made the trouble. It turned out that we ended with something about this high and maybe so wide and just about this deep –

No, no. I forget that you can't see me. I'll give you the figures. It was about three feet high, six feet long, and two feet deep. Got that? It took two men to carry it but it could be carried and that was the point. And still, mind you, it could do anything the wall-size calculators could. Not as fast, maybe, but we were still working.

We had big ideas about that thing, the very biggest. We could put it on ships or airplanes. After a while, if we could make it small enough, an automobile could carry one.

We were especially interested in the automobile angle. Suppose you had a little thinking machine on the dashboard, hooked to the engine and battery and equipped with photo-electric eyes. It could choose an ideal course, avoid cars, stop at red lights, pick the optimum speed for the terrain. Everybody could sit in the back seat and automobile accidents would vanish.

All of it was fun. There was so much excitement to it, so many thrills every time we worked out another consolidation, that I could still cry when I think of the time I picked up the telephone to call our lab and tumbled everything into the discard.

I was at Mary Ann's house that evening – Or have I told you about Mary Ann yet? No. I guess I haven't.

Mary Ann was the girl who would have been my fiancée but for two ifs. One, if she were willing, and two, if I had the nerve to ask her. She has red hair and crams something like two tons of energy into about 110 pounds of body which fills out very nicely from the ground to five and a half feet up. I was dying to ask her, you understand, but each time I'd see her coming into sight, setting a match to my heart with every movement, I'd just break down.

It's not that I'm not good-looking. People tell me I'm adequate. I've got all my hair; I'm nearly six feet tall; I can even dance. It's just that I've nothing to offer. I don't have to tell you what college teachers make. With inflation and taxes, it amounts to just about nothing. Of course, if we got the basic patents rolled up on our little thinking machine, things would be different. But I couldn't ask her to wait for that, either. Maybe, after it was all set –

Anyway, I just stood there, wishing, that evening, as she came into the living room. My arm was groping blindly for the phone.

Mary Ann said, 'I'm all ready, Bill. Let's go.'

I said, 'Just a minute. I want to ring up Cliff.'

She frowned a little, 'Can't it wait?'

'I was supposed to call him two hours ago,' I explained.

It only took two minutes. I rang the lab. Cliff was putting in an evening of work and so he answered. I asked something, then he said something, I asked some more and he explained. The details don't matter, but as I said, he's the mathematician of the combination. When I build the circuits and put things together in what look like impossible ways, he's the guy who shuffles the symbols and tells me whether they're really impossible. Then, just as I finished and hung up, there was a ring at the door.

For a minute, I thought Mary Ann had another caller and got sort of stiff-backed as I watched her go to the door. I was scribbling down some of what Cliff had just told me while I watched. But then she opened the door and it was only Cliff Anderson after all.

He said, 'I thought I'd find you here – Hello, Mary Ann. Say, weren't you going to ring me at six? You're as reliable as a cardboard chair.' Cliff is short and plump and always willing to start a fight, but I know him and pay no attention.

I said, 'Things turned up and it slipped my mind. But I just called, so what's the difference?'

'Called? Me? When?'

I started to point to the telephone and gagged. Right then, the bottom fell out of things. Exactly five seconds before the doorbell had sounded I had been on the phone talking to Cliff in the lab, and the lab was six miles away from Mary Ann's house.

I said, 'I – just spoke to you.'

I wasn't getting across. Cliff just said, 'To me?' again.

I was pointing to the phone with both hands now, 'On the phone. I called the lab. On this phone here! Mary Ann heard me. Mary Ann, wasn't I just talking to –'

Mary Ann said, 'I don't know whom you were talking to. – Well, shall we go?' That's Mary Ann. She's a stickler for honesty.

I sat down. I tried to be very quiet and clear. I said, 'Cliff, I dialed the lab's phone number, you answered the phone, I asked you if you had the details worked out, you said, yes, and gave them to me. Here they are. I wrote them down. Is this correct or not?'

I handed him the paper on which I had written the equations.

Cliff looked at them. He said, 'They're correct. But where could you have gotten them? You didn't work them out yourself, did you?'

'I just told you. You gave them to me over the phone.'

Cliff shook his head. 'Bill, I haven't been in the lab since seven fifteen. There's nobody there.'

'I spoke to somebody, I tell you.'

Mary Ann was fiddling with her gloves. 'We're getting late.' she said.

I waved my hands at her to wait a bit, and said to Cliff, 'Look, are you sure —'

'There's nobody there, unless you want to count Junior.' Junior was what we called our pint-sized mechanical brain.

We stood there, looking at one another. Mary Ann's toe was still hitting the floor like a time bomb waiting to explode.

Then Cliff laughed. He said, 'I'm thinking of a cartoon I saw, somewhere. It shows a robot answering the phone and saying, "Honest, boss, there's nobody here but us complicated thinking machines."'

I didn't think that was funny. I said, 'Let's go to the lab.'

Mary Ann said, 'Hey! We won't make the show.'

I said, 'Look, Mary Ann, this is very important. It's just going to take a minute. Come along with us and we'll go straight to the show from there.'

She said, 'The show starts —' And then she stopped talking, because I grabbed her wrist and we left.

That just shows how excited I was. Ordinarily, I wouldn't ever have dreamed of shoving her around. I mean, Mary Ann is quite the lady. It's just that I had so many things on my mind. I don't even really remember grabbing her wrist, come to think of it. It's just that the next thing I knew, I was in the auto and so was Cliff and so was she, and she was rubbing her wrist and muttering under her breath about big gorillas.

I said, 'Did I hurt you, Mary Ann?'

She said, 'No, of course not. I have my arm yanked out of its socket every day, just for fun.' Then she kicked me in the shin.

She only does things like that because she has red hair. Actually, she has a very gentle nature, but she tries very hard to live up to the redhead mythology. I see right through that, of course, but I humor her, poor kid.

We were at the laboratory in twenty minutes.

The Institute is empty at night. It's emptier than a building would ordinarily be. You see, it's designed to have crowds of students rushing through the corridors and when they aren't there, it's unnaturally lonely. Or maybe it was just that I was afraid to see what might be sitting in our laboratory upstairs. Either way, footsteps were uncomfortably loud and the self-service elevator was downright dingy.

I said to Mary Ann, 'This won't take long.' But she just sniffed and looked beautiful.

She can't help looking beautiful.

Cliff had the key to the laboratory and I looked over his shoulder when he opened the door. There was nothing to see. Junior was there, sure, but he looked just as he had when I saw him last. The dials in front registered nothing and except for that, there was just a large box, with a cable running back into the wall socket.

Cliff and I walked up on either side of Junior. I think we were planning to grab it if/it made a sudden move. But then we stopped because Junior just wasn't doing anything. Mary Ann was looking at it, too. In fact, she ran her middle finger along its top and then looked at the finger tip and twiddled it against her thumb to get rid of the dust.

I said, 'Mary Ann, don't you go near it. Stay at the other end of the room.'

She said, 'It's just as dirty there.'

She'd never been in our lab before, and of course she didn't realize that a laboratory wasn't the same thing as a baby's bedroom, if you know what I mean. The janitor comes in twice a day and all he does is empty the wastebaskets. About once a week, he comes in with a dirty mop, makes mud on the floor, and shoves it around a little.

Cliff said, 'The telephone isn't where I left it.'

I said, 'How do you know?'

'Because I left it there.' He pointed. 'And now it's here.'

If he were right, the telephone had moved closer to Junior. I swallowed and said, 'Maybe you don't remember right.' I tried to laugh without sounding very natural and said, 'Where's the screw driver?'

'What are you going to do?'

'Just take a look inside. For laughs.'

Mary Ann said, 'You'll get yourself all dirty.' So I put on my lab coat. She's a very thoughtful girl, Mary Ann.

I got to work with a screw driver. Of course, once Junior was really perfected, we were going to have models manufactured in welded, one-piece cases. We were even thinking of molded plastic in colors, for home use. In the lab model, though, we held it together with screws so that we could take it apart and put it together as often as we wanted to.

Only the screws weren't coming out. I grunted and yanked and said, 'Some joker was putting his weight on these when he screwed these things in.'

Cliff said, 'You're the only one who ever touches the thing.'

He was right, too, but that didn't make it any easier. I stood up and passed the back of my hand over my forehead. I held out the screw driver to him, 'Want to try?'

He did, and didn't get any further than I did. He said, 'That's funny.'

I said, 'What's funny?'

He said, 'I had a screw turning just now. It moved about an eighth of an inch and then the screw driver slipped.'

'What's funny about that?'

Cliff backed away and put down the screw driver with two fingers, 'What's funny is that I saw the screw move back an eighth of an inch and tighten up again.'

Mary Ann was fidgeting again. She said, 'Why don't your scientific minds think of a blowtorch, if you're so anxious.' There was a blowtorch on one of the benches and she was pointing to it.

Well, ordinarily, I wouldn't think any more of using a blowtorch on Junior than on myself. But I was thinking something and Cliff was thinking something and we were both thinking the same thing. *Junior didn't want to be opened up.*

Cliff said, 'What do you think, Bill?'

And I said, 'I don't know, Cliff.'

Mary Ann said, 'Well, hurry up, lunkhead, we'll miss the show.'

So I picked up the blowtorch and adjusted the gauge on the oxygen cylinder. It was going to be like stabbing a friend.

But Mary Ann stopped the proceedings by saying, 'Well, how stupid can men be? These screws are loose. You must have been turning the screw driver the wrong way.'

Now there isn't much chance of turning a screw driver the wrong way. Just the same, I don't like to contradict Mary Ann, so I just said, 'Mary Ann, don't stay too close to Junior. Why don't you wait by the door.'

But she just said, 'Well, look!' And there was a screw in her hand and an empty hole in the front of Junior's case. She had removed it by hand.

Cliff said, 'Holy Smoke!'

They were turning, all dozen screws. They were doing it by themselves, like little forms crawling out of their holes, turning round and round, then dropping out. I scrabbled them up and only one was left. It hung on for a while, the front panel sagging from it, till I reached out. Then the last screw dropped and the panel fell gently into my arms. I put it to one side.

Cliff said, 'It did that on purpose. It heard us mention the blowtorch and gave up.' His face is usually pink, but it was white then.

I was feeling a little queer myself. I said, 'What's it trying to hide?'

'I don't know.'

We bent before its open insides and for a while we just looked. I could hear Mary Ann's toe begin to tap the floor again. I looked at my wrist watch and I had to admit to myself we didn't have much time. In fact, we didn't have any time left.

And then I said, 'It's got a diaphragm.'

Cliff said, 'Where?' and bent closer.

I pointed, 'And a loud speaker.'

'You didn't put them in?'

'Of course I didn't put them in. I ought to know what I put in. If I put it in, I'd remember.'

'Then how did it get in?'

We were squatting and arguing. I said, 'It made them itself, I suppose. Maybe it grows them. Look at that.'

I pointed again. Inside the box at two different places, were coils of something that looked like thin garden hose, except that they were of metal. They spiraled tightly so that they lay flat. At the end of each coil, the metal divided into five or six thin filaments that were in little sub-spirals.

'You didn't put those in either?'

'No, I didn't put those in either.'

'What are they?'

He knew what they were and I knew what they were. Something had to reach out to get materials for Junior to make parts for itself; something had to snake out for the telephone. I picked up the front panel and looked at it again. There were two circular bits of metal cut out and hinged so that they could swing forward and leave a hole for something to come through.

I poked a finger through one and held it up for Cliff to see, and said, 'I didn't put this in either.'

Mary Ann was looking over my shoulder now, and without warning she reached out. I was wiping my fingers with a paper towel to get off the dust and grease and didn't have time to stop her. I should have known Mary Ann, though; she's always so anxious to help.

Anyway, she reached in to touch one of the – well, we might as well say it – tentacles. I don't know if she actually touched them or not. Later on she claimed she hadn't. But anyway, what happened then was that she let out a little yell and suddenly sat down and began rubbing her arm.

'The same one,' she whimpered. 'First you, and then *that*.'

I helped her up. 'It must have been a loose connection, Mary Ann. I'm sorry, but I told you –'

Cliff said, 'Nuts! That was no loose connection. Junior's just protecting itself.'

I had thought the same thing, myself. I had thought lots of things. Junior was a new kind of machine. Even the mathematics that controlled it were different from anything anybody had worked with before. Maybe it had something no machine previously had ever had. Maybe it felt a desire to stay alive and grow. Maybe it would have a desire to make more machines until there were millions of them all over the earth, fighting with human beings for control.

I opened my mouth and Cliff must have known what I was going to say, because he yelled, 'No. No, don't say it!'

But I couldn't stop myself. It just came out and I said, 'Well, look, let's disconnect Junior – What's the matter?'

Cliff said bitterly, 'Because he's listening to what we say, you jackass. He heard about the blowtorch, didn't he? I was going to sneak up behind it, but now it will probably electrocute me if I try.'

Mary Ann was still brushing at the back of her dress and saying how dirty the floor was, even though I kept telling her I had nothing to do with that. I mean, it's the janitor that makes the mud.

Anyway, she said, 'Why don't you put on rubber gloves and yank the cord out?'

I could see Cliff was trying to think of reasons why that wouldn't work. He didn't think of any, so he put on the rubber gloves and walked towards Junior.

I yelled, 'Watch out!'

It was a stupid thing to say. He *had* to watch out; he had no choice. One of the tentacles moved and there was no doubt what they were now. It whirled out and drew a line between Cliff and the power cable. It remained there, vibrating a little with its six finger-tendrils splayed out. Tubes inside Junior were beginning to glow. Cliff didn't try to go past that tentacle. He backed away and after a while, it spiraled inward again. He took off his rubber gloves.

'Bill,' he said, 'we're not going to get anywhere. That's a smarter gadget than we dreamed we could make. It was smart enough to use my voice as a model when it built its diaphragm. It may become smart enough to learn how to –' He looked over his shoulder, and whispered, 'how to generate its own power and become self-contained.

'Bill, we've got to stop it, or someday someone will telephone the planet Earth and get the answer, "Honest, boss, there's nobody here anywhere but us complicated thinking machines"!'

'Let's get in the police,' I said. 'We'll explain. A grenade, or something –'

Cliff shook his head, 'We can't have anyone else find out. They'll build other Juniors and it looks like we don't have enough answers for that kind of a project after all.'

'Then what do we do?'

'I don't know.'

I felt a sharp blow on my chest. I looked down and it was Mary Ann, getting ready to spit fire. She said, 'Look, lunkhead, if we've got a date, we've got one, and if we haven't, we haven't. Make up your mind.'

I said, 'Now, Mary Ann –'

She said, 'Answer me. I never heard such a ridiculous thing. Here I get dressed to go to a play, and you take me to a dirty laboratory with a foolish machine and spend the rest of the evening twiddling dials.'

'Mary Ann, I'm not –'

She wasn't listening; she was talking. I wish I could remember what she said after that. Or maybe I don't; maybe it's just as well I can't remember, since none of it was very complimentary. Every once in a while I would manage a 'But, Mary Ann –' and each time it would get sucked under and swallowed up.

Actually, as I said, she's a very gentle creature and it's only when she gets excited that she's ever talkative or unreasonable. Of course, with red hair, she feels she ought to get excited rather often. That's my theory, anyway. She just feels she has to live up to her red hair.

Anyway, the next thing I *do* remember clearly is Mary Ann finishing with a stamp on my right foot and then turning to leave. I ran after her, trying once again, 'But, Mary Ann –'

Then Cliff yelled at us. Generally, he doesn't pay any attention to us, but this time he was shouting. 'Why don't you ask her to marry you, you lunkhead?'

Mary Ann stopped. She was in the doorway by then but she didn't turn around. I stopped too, and felt the words get thick and clogged up in my throat. I couldn't even manage a 'But, Mary Ann –'

Cliff was yelling in the background. I heard him as though he were a mile away. He was shouting, 'I got it! I got it!' over and over again.

Then Mary Ann turned and she looked so beautiful – Did I tell you that she's got green eyes with a touch of blue in them? Anyway she looked so beautiful that all the words in my throat jammed together very tightly and came out in that funny sound you make when you swallow.

She said, 'Were you going to say something, Bill?'

Well, Cliff had put it in my head. My voice was hoarse and I said, 'Will you marry me, Mary Ann?'

The minute I said it, I wished I hadn't, because I thought she would never speak to me again. Then two minutes after that I was glad I had, because she threw her arms around me and reached up to kiss me. It was a while before I was quite clear what was happening, and then I began to kiss back. This went on for quite a long time, until Cliff's banging on my shoulder managed to attract my attention.

I turned and said, snappishly, 'What the devil do you want?' It was a little ungrateful. After all, he had started this.

He said, 'Look!'

In his hand, he held the main lead that had connected Junior to the power supply.

I had forgotten about Junior, but now it came back. I said, 'He's disconnected, then.'

'Cold!'

'*How did you do it?*'

He said, 'Junior was so busy watching you and Mary Ann fight that I managed to sneak up on it. Mary Ann put on one good show.'

I didn't like that remark because Mary Ann is a very dignified and self-contained sort of girl and doesn't put on 'shows'. However, I had too much in hand to take issue with him.

I said to Mary Ann, 'I don't have much to offer, Mary Ann; just a school teacher's salary. Now that we've dismantled Junior, there isn't even any chance of –'

Mary Ann said, 'I don't care, Bill. I just gave up on you, you lunkheaded darling. I've tried practically everything –'

'You've been kicking my shins and stamping on my toes.'

'I'd run out of everything else. I was desperate.'

The logic wasn't quite clear, but I didn't answer because I remembered about the show. I looked at my watch and said, 'Look, Mary Ann, if we hurry we can still make the second act.'

She said, 'Who wants to see the show?'

So I kissed her some more; and we never did get to see the show at all.

There's only one thing that bothers me now. Mary Ann and I are married, and we're perfectly happy. I just had a promotion; I'm an associate professor now. Cliff keeps working away at plans for building a controllable Junior and he's making progress.

None of that's it.

You see, I talked to Cliff the next evening, to tell him Mary Ann and I were going to marry and to thank him for giving me the idea. And after staring at me for a minute, he swore he hadn't said it; he hadn't shouted for me to propose marriage.

Of course, there was something else in the room with Cliff's voice.

I keep worrying Mary Ann will find out. She's the gentlest

girl I know, but she *has* got red hair. She can't help trying to live up to that, or have I said that already?

Anyway, what will she say if she ever finds out that I didn't have the sense to propose till a *machine* told me to?

We all have our lovable eccentricities and I have a few that are all my own.

For instance, I hate nice days. Show me a day in which the temperature is just 78, and a light breeze has the lush foliage of June, or the just turning leaves of September, rustling with a soft murmur; a day in which there is a drowsy softness over the landscape, and a sweet freshness to the air, and a general peacefulness over the world, and I'll show you one unhappy fellow – namely, me.

There's a reason for it, a good one. (You don't think I'm irrational, do you?) As I said in the preface to 'Sally', I am a compulsive writer. That means that my idea of a pleasant time is to go up to my attic, sit at my electric typewriter (as I am doing right now), and bang away, watching the words take shape like magic before my eyes. To minimize distractions, I keep the window-shades down at all times and work exclusively by artificial light.

No one has any particular objection to this as long as we have the sleet of a typical New England late fall day darting through the air, or the blustering wind of a typical New England early spring day, or the leaden weight of Gulf air that splats out over New England in the summer, or the dancing flakes of that third foot of snow that blankets New England in the winter. Everyone says, 'Boy, you're lucky you don't have to go out in that weather.'

And I agree with them.

But then comes a beautiful day in May–June or September– October and everyone says to me, 'What are you doing indoors on a day like this, you creep?' Sometimes out of sheer indignation they pick me up and throw me out the window so I can enjoy the nice day.

The niceness of being a writer, of course, is that you can take all your frustrations and annoyances and spread them out on paper. This prevents them from building up to dangerous levels and explains why writers in general are such lovable, normal people and are a joy to all who know them.

For instance, I wrote a novel in 1953 which pictured a world in which everyone lived in underground cities, comfortably enclosed away from the open air.

People would say, 'How could you imagine such a nightmarish situation?'

And I would answer in astonishment, 'What nightmarish situation?'

But with me everything becomes a challenge. Having made my pitch in favor of enclosure, I wondered if I could reverse the situation.

So I wrote 'It's Such a Beautiful Day' – and did such a good job at convincing myself, that very often these days, sometimes twice in one week, when I feel I've put in a good day's work, I go out in the late afternoon and take a walk through the neighborhood.

But I don't know. That thing you people have up there in the sky. It's got quite a glare to it.

First appearance – Star Science Fiction Stories 3. Copyright, 1954, by Ballantine Books, Inc.

IT'S SUCH A BEAUTIFUL DAY

On April 12, 2117, the field-modulator brake-valve in the Door belonging to Mrs. Richard Hanshaw depolarized for reasons unknown. As a result, Mrs. Hanshaw's day was completely upset and her son, Richard, Jr., first developed his strange neurosis.

It was not the type of thing you would find listed as a neurosis in the usual textbooks and certainly young Richard behaved, in most respects, just as a well-brought-up twelve-year-old in prosperous circumstances ought to behave.

And yet from April 12 on, Richard Hanshaw, Jr., could only with regret ever persuade himself to go through a Door.

Of all this, on April 12, Mrs. Hanshaw had no premonition. She woke in the morning (an ordinary morning) as her mekkano slithered gently into her room, with a cup of coffee on a small tray. Mrs. Hanshaw was planning a visit to New York in the afternoon and she had several things to do first that could not quite be trusted to a mekkano, so after one or two sips, she stepped out of bed.

The mekkano backed away, moving silently along the diamagnetic field that kept its oblong body half an inch above the floor, and moved back to the kitchen, where its simple computer was quite adequate to set the proper controls on the various kitchen appliances in order that an appropriate breakfast might be prepared.

Mrs. Hanshaw, having bestowed the usual sentimental glance upon the cubograph of her dead husband, passed through the stages of her morning ritual with a certain contentment. She could hear her son across the hall clattering through his, but she knew she need not interfere with him. The mekkano was well adjusted to see to it, as a matter of course, that he was showered, that he had on a change of clothing, and that he would eat a nourishing breakfast. The tergo-shower she had had installed the year before made the morning wash and dry so quick and pleasant that, really, she felt certain Dickie would wash even without supervision.

On a morning like this, when she was busy, it would certainly not be necessary for her to do more than deposit a casual peck on the boy's cheek before he left. She heard the soft chime the mekkano sounded to indicate approaching school time and she floated down the force-lift to the lower floor (her hair-style for the day only sketchily designed, as yet) in order to perform that motherly duty.

She found Richard standing at the door, with his text-reels and pocket projector dangling by their strap and a frown on his face.

'Say, Mom,' he said, looking up, 'I dialed the school's co-ords but nothing happens.'

She said, almost automatically, 'Nonsense, Dickie. I never heard of such a thing.'

'Well, you try.'

Mrs. Hanshaw tried a number of times. Strange, the school door was always set for general reception. She tried other co-ordinates. Her friends' Doors might not be set for reception, but there would be a signal at least, and then she could explain.

But nothing happened at all. The Door remained an inactive gray barrier despite all her manipulations. It was obvious that

the Door was out of order – and only five months after its an-
nual fall inspection by the company.

She was quite angry about it.

It *would* happen on a day when she had so much planned.
She thought petulantly of the fact that a month earlier she had
decided against installing a subsidiary Door on the ground that
it was an unnecessary expense. How was she to know that Doors
were getting to be so *shoddy*?

She stepped to the visiphone while the anger still burned in
her and said to Richard, 'You just go down the road, Dickie,
and use the Williamsons' Door.'

Ironically, in view of later developments, Richard balked.
'Aw, gee, Mom, I'll get dirty. Can't I stay home till the Door is
fixed?'

And, as ironically, Mrs. Hanshaw insisted. With her finger on
the combination board of the phone, she said, 'You won't get
dirty if you put flexies on your shoes, and don't forget to brush
yourself well before you go into their house.'

'But, golly –'

'No back-talk, Dickie. You've got to be in school. Just let me
see you walk out of here. And quickly, or you'll be late.'

The mekkano, an advanced model and very responsive, was
already standing before Richard with flexies in one appendage.

Richard pulled the transparent plastic shields over his shoes
and moved down the hall with visible reluctance. 'I don't even
know how to work this thing, Mom.'

'You just push that button,' Mrs. Hanshaw called. 'The red
button. Where it says "For Emergency Use". And don't dawdle.
Do you want the mekkano to go along with you?'

'Gosh, no,' he called back, morosely, 'what do you think I
am? A baby? Gosh!' His muttering was cut off by a slam.

With flying fingers, Mrs. Hanshaw punched the appropriate
combination on the phone board and thought of the things she
intended saying to the Company about this.

Joe Bloom, a reasonable young man, who had gone through
technology school with added training in force-field mechanics,
was at the Hanshaw residence in less than half an hour. He was
really quite competent, though Mrs. Hanshaw regarded his
youth with deep suspicion

She opened the movable house-panel when he first signaled
and her sight of him was as he stood there, brushing at himself

vigorously to remove the dust of the open air. He took off his flexies and dropped them where he stood. Mrs. Hanshaw closed the house-panel against the flash of raw sunlight that had entered. She found herself irrationally hoping that the step-by-step trip from the public Door had been an unpleasant one. Or perhaps that the public Door itself had been out of order and the youth had had to lug his tools even farther than the necessary two hundred yards. She wanted the Company, or its representative at least, to suffer a bit. It would teach them what broken Doors meant.

But he seemed cheerful and unperturbed as he said, 'Good morning, ma'am. I came to see about your Door.'

'I'm glad someone did,' said Mrs. Hanshaw, ungraciously. 'My day is quite ruined.'

'Sorry, ma'am. What seems to be the trouble?'

'It just won't work. Nothing at all happens when you adjust co-ords,' said Mrs. Hanshaw. 'There was no warning at all. I had to send my son out to the neighbors through that – that thing.'

She pointed to the entrance through which the repair man had come.

He smiled and spoke out of the conscious wisdom of his own specialized training in Doors. 'That's a door, too, ma'am. You don't give that kind a capital letter when you write it. It's a hand-door, sort of. It used to be the only kind once.'

'Well, at least it works. My boy's had to go out in the dirt and germs.'

'It's not bad outside today, ma'am,' he said, with the connoisseur-like air of one whose profession forced him into the open nearly every day. 'Sometimes it *is* real unpleasant. But I guess you want I should fix this here Door, ma'am, so I'll get on with it.'

He sat down on the floor, opened the large tool case he had brought in with him and in half a minute, by use of a point-demagnetizer, he had the control panel removed and a set of intricate vitals exposed.

He whistled to himself as he placed the fine electrodes of the field-analyzer on numerous points, studying the shifting needles on the dials. Mrs. Hanshaw watched him, arms folded.

Finally, he said, 'Well, here's something,' and with a deft twist, he disengaged the brake-valve.

He tapped it with a fingernail and said, 'This here brake-valve is depolarized, ma'am. There's your whole trouble.' He ran his finger along the little pigeonholes in his tool case and lifted out a duplicate of the object he had taken from the door mechanism. 'These things just go all of a sudden. Can't predict it.'

He put the control panel back and stood up. 'It'll work now, ma'am.'

He punched a reference combination, blanked it, then punched another. Each time, the dull gray of the Door gave way to a deep, velvety blackness. He said, 'Will you sign here, ma'am? and put down your charge number, too, please? Thank you, ma'am.'

He punched a new combination, that of his home factory, and with a polite touch of finger to forehead, he stepped through the Door. As his body entered the blackness, it cut off sharply. Less and less of him was visible and the tip of his tool case was the last thing that showed. A second after he had passed through completely, the Door turned back to dull gray.

Half an hour later, when Mrs. Hanshaw had finally completed her interrupted preparations and was fuming over the misfortune of the morning, the phone buzzed annoyingly and her real troubles began.

Miss Elizabeth Robbins was distressed. Little Dick Hanshaw had always been a good pupil. She hated to report him like this. And yet, she told herself, his actions were certainly queer. And she would talk to his mother, not to the principal.

She slipped out to the phone during the morning study period, leaving a student in charge. She made her connection and found herself staring at Mrs. Hanshaw's handsome and somewhat formidable head.

Miss Robbins quailed, but it was too late to turn back. She said, diffidently, 'Mrs. Hanshaw, I'm Miss Robbins.' She ended on a rising note.

Mrs. Hanshaw looked blank, then said, 'Richard's teacher?' That, too, ended on a rising note.

'That's right. I called you, Mrs. Hanshaw,' Miss Robbins plunged right into it, 'to tell you that Dick was quite late to school this morning.'

'He *was?* But that couldn't be. I saw him leave.'

Miss Robbins looked astonished. She said, 'You mean you saw him use the Door?'

Mrs. Hanshaw said quickly, 'Well, no. Our Door was temporarily out of order. I sent him to a neighbor and he used that Door.'

'Are you sure?'

'Of course I'm sure. I wouldn't lie to you.'

'No, no, Mrs. Hanshaw. I wasn't implying that at all. I meant are you sure he found the way to the neighbor? He might have got lost.'

'Ridiculous. We have the proper maps, and I'm sure Richard knows the location of every house in District A-3.' Then, with the quiet pride of one who knows what is her due, she added, 'Not that he ever needs to know, of course. The co-ords are all that are necessary at any time.'

Miss Robbins, who came from a family that had always had to economize rigidly on the use of its Doors (the price of power being what it was) and who had therefore run errands on foot until quite an advanced age, resented the pride. She said, quite clearly, 'Well, I'm afraid, Mrs. Hanshaw, that Dick did not use the neighbor's Door. He was over an hour late to school and the condition of his flexies made it quite obvious that he tramped cross-country. They were *muddy*.'

'*Muddy*?' Mrs. Hanshaw repeated the emphasis on the word. 'What did he say? What was his excuse?'

Miss Robbins couldn't help but feel a little glad at the discomfiture of the other woman. She said, 'He wouldn't talk about it. Frankly, Mrs. Hanshaw, he seems ill. That's why I called you. Perhaps you might want to have a doctor look at him.'

'Is he running a temperature?' The mother's voice went shrill.

'Oh, no. I don't mean physically ill. It's just his attitude and the look in his eyes.' She hesitated, then said with every attempt at delicacy, 'I thought perhaps a routine checkup with a psychic probe –'

She didn't finish. Mrs. Hanshaw, in a chilled voice and with what was as close to a snort as her breeding would permit, said, 'Are you implying that Richard is *neurotic*?'

'Oh, no, Mrs. Hanshaw, but –'

'It certainly sounded so. The idea! He has always been perfectly healthy. I'll take this up with him when he gets home.

I'm sure there's a perfectly normal explanation which he'll give *me*.'

The connection broke abruptly, and Miss Robbins felt hurt and uncommonly foolish. After all she had only tried to help, to fulfill what she considered an obligation to her students.

She hurried back to the classroom with a glance at the metal face of the wall clock. The study period was drawing to an end. English Composition next.

But her mind wasn't completely on English Composition. Automatically, she called the students to have them read selections from their literary creations. And occasionally she punched one of those selections on tape and ran it through the small vocalizer to show the students how English *should* be read.

The vocalizer's mechanical voice, as always, dripped perfection, but, again as always, lacked character. Sometimes, she wondered if it was wise to try to train the students into a speech that was divorced from individuality and geared only to a mass-average accent and intonation.

Today, however, she had no thought for that. It was Richard Hanshaw she watched. He sat quietly in his seat, quite obviously indifferent to his surroundings. He was lost deep in himself and just not the same boy he had been. It was obvious to her that he had had some unusual experience that morning and, really, she was right to call his mother, although perhaps she ought not to have made the remark about the probe. Still it was quite the thing these days. All sorts of people got probed. There wasn't any disgrace attached to it. Or there shouldn't be, anyway.

She called on Richard, finally. She had to call twice, before he responded and rose to his feet.

The general subject assigned had been: 'If you had your choice of traveling on some ancient vehicle, which would you choose, and why?' Miss Robbins tried to use the topic every semester. It was a good one because it carried a sense of history with it. It forced the youngster to think about the manner of living of people in past ages.

She listened while Richard Hanshaw read in a low voice.

'If I had my choice of ancient vehicles,' he said, pronouncing the 'h' in vehicles, 'I would choose the stratoliner. It travels slow like all vehicles but it is clean. Because it travels in the stratosphere, it must be all enclosed so that you are not likely to catch disease. You can see the stars if it is night time almost as good as in a planetarium. If you look down you can see the Earth like a map or maybe see clouds –' He went on for several hundred more words.

She said brightly when he had finished reading, 'It's pronounced vee-ick-ulls, Richard. No "h". Accent on the first syllable. And you don't say "travels slow" or "see good". What do you say, class?'

There was a small chorus of responses and she went on, 'That's right. Now what is the difference between an adjective and an adverb? Who can tell me?'

And so it went. Lunch passed. Some pupils stayed to eat; some went home. Richard stayed. Miss Robbins noted that, as usually he didn't.

The afternoon passed, too, and then there was the final bell and the usual upsurging hum as twenty-five boys and girls rattled their belongings together and took their leisurely place in line.

Miss Robbins clapped her hands together. 'Quickly, children. Come, Zelda, take your place.'

'I dropped my tape-punch, Miss Robbins,' shrilled the girl, defensively.

'Well, pick it up, pick it up. Now children, be brisk, be brisk.'

She pushed the button that slid a section of the wall into a recess and revealed the gray blankness of a large Door. It was not the usual Door that the occasional student used in going home for lunch, but an advanced model that was one of the prides of this well-to-do private school.

In addition to its double width, it possessed a large and impressively gear-filled 'automatic serial finder' which was capable of adjusting the door for a number of different co-ordinates at automatic intervals.

At the beginning of the semester, Miss Robbins always had to spend an afternoon with the mechanic, adjusting the device for the co-ordinates of the homes of the new class. But then, thank goodness, it rarely needed attention for the remainder of the term.

The class lined up alphabetically, first girls, then boys. The Door went velvety black and Hester Adams waved her hand and stepped through. 'By-y-y –'

The 'bye' was cut off in the middle, as it almost always was.

The Door went gray, then black again, and Theresa Cant-rocchi went through. Gray, black, Zelda Charlowicz. Gray, black Patricia Coombs. Gray, black, Sara May Evans.

The line grew smaller as the Door swallowed them one by one, depositing each in her home. Of course, an occasional mother forgot to leave the house Door on special reception at the appropriate time and then the school Door remained gray. Automatically, after a minute-long wait, the Door went on to the next combination in line and the pupil in question had to wait till it was all over, after which a phone call to the forgetful parent would set things right. This was always bad for the pupils involved, especially the sensitive ones who took seriously the implication that they were little thought of at home. Miss Robbins always tried to impress this on visiting parents, but it happened at least once every semester just the same.

The girls were all through now. John Abramowitz stepped through and then Edwin Byrne –

Of course, another trouble, and a more frequent one was the boy or girl who got into line out of place. They *would* do it despite the teacher's sharpest watch, particularly at the beginning of the term when the proper order was less familiar to them.

When that happened, children would be popping into the wrong houses by the half-dozen and would have to be sent back. It always meant a mixup that took minutes to straighten out and parents were invariably irate.

Miss Robbins was suddenly aware that the line had stopped. She spoke sharply to the boy at the head of the line.

'Step through, Samuel. What are you waiting for?'

Samuel Jones raised a complacent countenance and said, 'It's not my combination, Miss Robbins.'

'Well, whose is it?' She looked impatiently down the line of five remaining boys. Who was out of place?

'It's Dick Hanshaw's, Miss Robbins.'

'Where is he?'

Another boy answered, with the rather repulsive tone of self-righteousness all children automatically assume in reporting the deviations of their friends to elders in authority, 'He went through the fire door, Miss Robbins.'

'What?'

The schoolroom Door had passed on to another combination

and Samuel Jones passed through. One by one, the rest followed.

Miss Robbins was alone in the classroom. She stepped to the fire door. It was a small affair, manually operated, and hidden behind a bend in the wall so that it would not break up the uniform structure of the room.

She opened it a crack. It was there as a means of escape from the building in case of fire, a device which was enforced by an anachronistic law that did not take into account the modern methods of automatic fire-fighting that all public buildings used. There was nothing outside, but the – outside. The sunlight was harsh and a dusty wind was blowing.

Miss Robbins closed the door. She was glad she had called Mrs. Hanshaw. She had done her duty. More than ever, it was obvious that something was wrong with Richard. She suppressed the impulse to phone again.

Mrs. Hanshaw did not go to New York that day. She remained home in a mixture of anxiety and an irrational anger, the latter directed against the impudent Miss Robbins.

Some fifteen minutes before school's end, her anxiety drove her to the Door. Last year she had had it equipped with an automatic device which activated it to the school's co-ordinates at five of three and kept it so, barring manual adjustment, until Richard arrived.

Her eyes were fixed on the Door's dismal gray (why couldn't an inactive force-field be any other color, something more lively and cheerful?) and waited. Her hands felt cold as she squeezed them together.

The Door turned black at the precise second but nothing happened. The minutes passed and Richard was late. Then quite late. Then very late.

It was a quarter of four and she was distracted. Normally, she would have phoned the school, but she couldn't, she couldn't. Not after that teacher had deliberately cast doubts on Richard's mental well-being. How could she?

Mrs. Hanshaw moved about restlessly, lighting a cigarette with fumbling fingers, then smudging it out. Could it be something quite normal? Could Richard be staying after school for some reason? Surely he would have told her in advance. A gleam of light struck her; he knew she was planning to go

to New York and might not be back till late in the evening –
No, he would surely have told her. Why fool herself?

Her pride was breaking. She would have to call the school, or
even (she closed her eyes and teardrops squeezed through between the lashes) the police.

And when she opened her eyes, Richard stood before her,
eyes on the ground and his whole bearing that of someone waiting for a blow to fall.

'Hello, Mom.'

Mrs. Hanshaw's anxiety transmuted itself instantly (in a
manner known only to mothers) into anger. 'Where have you
been, Richard?'

And then, before she could go further into the refrain concerning careless, unthinking sons and broken-hearted mothers,
she took note of his appearance in greater detail, and gasped in
utter horror.

She said, 'You've been in the open.'

Her son looked down at his dusty shoes (minus flexies), at
the dirt marks that streaked his lower arms and at the small,
but definite tear in his shirt. He said, 'Gosh, Mom, I just thought
I'd –' and he faded out.

She said, 'Was there anything wrong with the school Door?'

'No, Mom.'

'Do you realize I've been worried sick about you?' She waited
vainly for an answer. 'Well, I'll talk to you afterward, young
man. First, you're taking a bath, and every stitch of your clothing is being thrown out. Mekkano!'

But the mekkano had already reacted properly to the phrase
'taking a bath' and was off to the bathroom in its silent glide.

'You take your shoes off right here,' said Mrs. Hanshaw,
'then march after mekkano.'

Richard did as he was told with a resignation that placed him
beyond futile protest.

Mrs Hanshaw picked up the soiled shoes between thumb and
forefinger and dropped them down the disposal chute which
hummed in faint dismay at the unexpected load. She dusted
her hands carefully on a tissue which she allowed to float down
the chute after the shoes.

She did not join Richard at dinner but let him eat in the
worse-than-lack-of-company of the mekkano. this, she
thought, would be an active sign of her displeasure and would

do more than any amount of scolding or punishment to make him realize that he had done wrong. Richard, she frequently told herself, was a sensitive boy.

But she went up to see him at bedtime.

She smiled at him and spoke softly. She thought that would be the best way. After all, he had been punished already.

She said, 'What happened today, Dickie-boy?' She had called him that when he was a baby and just the sound of the name softened her nearly to tears.

But he only looked away and his voice was stubborn and cold. 'I just don't like to go through those darn Doors, Mom.'

'But why ever not?'

He shuffled his hands over the filmy sheet (fresh, clean, anti-septic and, of course, disposable after each use) and said, 'I just don't like them.'

'But then how do you expect to go to school, Dickie?'

'I'll get up early,' he mumbled.

'But there's nothing wrong with Doors.'

'Don't like 'em.' He never once looked up at her.

She said, despairingly, 'Oh, well, you have a good sleep and tomorrow morning you'll feel much better.'

She kissed him and left the room, automatically passing her hand through the photo-cell beam and in that manner dimming the room-lights.

But she had trouble sleeping herself that night. Why should Dickie dislike Doors so suddenly? They had never bothered him before. To be sure, the Door had broken down in the morning but that should make him appreciate them all the more.

Dickie was behaving so unreasonably.

Unreasonably? That reminded her of Miss Robbins and her diagnosis and Mrs. Hanshaw's soft jaw set in the darkness and privacy of her bedroom. Nonsense! The boy was upset and a night's sleep was all the therapy he needed.

But the next morning when she arose, her son was not in the house. The Mekkano could not speak but it could answer questions with gestures of its appendages equivalent to a yes or no, and it did not take Mrs. Hanshaw more than half a minute to ascertain that the boy had arisen thirty minutes earlier than usual, skimped his shower, and darted out of the house.

But not by way of the Door.

Out the other way – through the door. Small 'd'.

Mrs. Hanshaw's visiphone signaled genteelly at 3:10 p.m. that day. Mrs. Hanshaw guessed the caller and having activated the receiver, saw that she had guessed correctly. A quick glance in the mirror to see that she was properly calm after a day of abstracted concern and worry and then she keyed in her own transmission.

'Yes, Miss Robbins,' she said coldly.

Richard's teacher was a bit breathless. She said, 'Mrs. Hanshaw, Richard has deliberately left through the fire door although I told him to use the regular Door. I do not know where he went.'

Mrs. Hanshaw said, carefully, 'He left to come home.'

Miss Robbins looked dismayed, 'Do you approve of this?'

Pale-faced, Mrs. Hanshaw set about putting the teacher in her place. 'I don't think it is up to you to criticize. If my son does not choose to use the Door, it is his affair and mine. I don't think there is any school ruling that would force him to use the Door, is there?' Her bearing quite plainly intimated that if there were she would see to it that it was changed.

Miss Robbins flushed and had time for one quick remark before contact was broken. She said, 'I'd have him probed. I really would.'

Mrs. Hanshaw remained standing before the quartzinium plate, staring blindly at its blank face. Her sense of family placed her for a few moments quite firmly on Richard's side. Why *did* he have to use the Door if he chose not to? And then she settled down to wait and pride battled the gnawing anxiety that something after all was wrong with Richard.

He came home with a look of defiance on his face, but his mother, with a strenuous effort at self-control, met him as though nothing were out of the ordinary.

For weeks, she followed that policy. It's nothing, she told herself. It's a vagary. He'll grow out of it.

It grew into an almost normal state of affairs. Then, too, every once in a while, perhaps three days in a row, she would come down to breakfast to find Richard waiting sullenly at the Door, then using it when school time came. She always refrained from commenting on the matter.

Always, when he did that, and especially when he followed it up by arriving home via the Door, her heart grew warm and she thought, 'Well, it's over.' But always with the passing of one day, two or three, he would return like an addict to his drug and drift silently out by the door – small 'd' – before she woke.

And each time she thought despairingly of psychiatrists and probes, and each time the vision of Miss Robbins' low-bred satisfaction at (possibly) learning of it, stopped her, although she was scarcely aware that that was the true motive.

Meanwhile, she lived with it and made the best of it. The mekkano was instructed to wait at the door – small 'd' – with a Tergo kit and a change of clothing. Richard washed and changed without resistance. His underthings, socks and flexies were disposable in any case, and Mrs. Hanshaw bore uncomplainingly the expense of daily disposal of shirts. Trousers she finally allowed to go a week before disposal on condition of rigorous nightly cleansing.

One day she suggested that Richard accompany her on a trip to New York. It was more a vague desire to keep him in sight than part of any purposeful plan. He did not object. He was even happy. He stepped right through the Door, unconcerned. He didn't hesitate. He even lacked the look of resentment he wore on those mornings he used the Door to go to school.

Mrs. Hanshaw rejoiced. This could be a way of weaning him back into Door usage, and she racked her ingenuity for excuses to make trips with Richard. She even raised her power bill to quite unheard-of heights by suggesting, and going through with, a trip to Canton for the day in order to witness a Chinese festival.

That was on a Sunday, and the next morning Richard marched directly to the hole in the wall he always used. Mrs. Hanshaw, having wakened particularly early, witnessed that. For once, badgered past endurance, she called after him plaintively, 'Why not the Door, Dickie?'

He said, briefly, 'It's all right for Canton,' and stepped out of the house.

So that plan ended in failure. And then, one day, Richard came home soaking wet. The mekkano hovered about him uncertainly and Mrs. Hanshaw, just returned from a four-hour visit with her sister in Iowa, cried, 'Richard Hanshaw!'

He said, hang-dog fashion, 'It started raining. All of a sudden, it started raining.'

For a moment, the word didn't register with her. Her own school days and her studies of geography were twenty years in the past. And then she remembered and caught the vision of water pouring recklessly and endlessly down from the sky – a mad cascade of water with no tap to turn off, no button to push, no contact to break.

She said, 'And you stayed out in it?'

He said, 'Well, gee, Mom, I came home fast as I could. I didn't know it was going to rain.'

Mrs. Hanshaw had nothing to say. She was appalled and the sensation filled her too full for words to find a place.

Two days later, Richard found himself with a running nose, and a dry, scratchy throat. Mrs. Hanshaw had to admit that the virus of disease had found a lodging in her house, as though it were a miserable hovel of the Iron Age.

It was over that that her stubbornness and pride broke and she admitted to herself that, after all, Richard had to have psychiatric help.

Mrs. Hanshaw chose a psychiatrist with care. Her first impulse was to find one at a distance. For a while, she considered stepping directly into the San Francisco Medical Center and choosing one at random.

And then it occurred to her that by doing that she would become merely an anonymous consultant. She would have no way of obtaining any greater consideration for herself than would be forthcoming to any public-Door user of the city slums. Now if she remained in her own community, her word would carry weight –

She consulted the district map. It was one of that excellent series prepared by Doors, Inc., and distributed free of charge to their clients. Mrs. Hanshaw couldn't quite suppress that little thrill of civic pride as she unfolded the map. It wasn't a fine-print directory of Door co-ordinates only. It was an actual map, with each house carefully located.

And why not? District A-3 was a name of moment in the world, a badge of aristocracy. It was the first community on the planet to have been established on a completely Doored basis. The first, the largest, the wealthiest, the best-known. It needed no factories, no stores. It didn't even need roads. Each house was a little secluded castle, the Door of which had entry anywhere the world over where other Doors existed.

Carefully, she followed down the keyed listing of the five

thousand families of District A-3. She knew it included several psychiatrists. The learned professions were well represented in A-3.

Doctor Hamilton Sloane was the second name she arrived at and her finger lingered upon the map. His office was scarcely two miles from the Hanshaw residence. She liked his name. The fact that he lived in A-3 was evidence of worth. And he was a neighbor, practically a neighbor. He would understand that it was a matter of urgency – and confidential.

Firmly, she put in a call to his office to make an appointment.

Doctor Hamilton Sloane was a comparatively young man, not quite forty. He was of good family and he had indeed heard of Mrs. Hanshaw.

He listened to her quietly and then said, 'And this all began with the Door breakdown.'

'That's right, doctor.'

'Does he show any fear of the Doors?'

'Of course not. What an idea!' She was plainly startled.

'It's possible, Mrs. Hanshaw, it's possible. After all, when you stop to think of how a Door works it is rather a frightening thing, really. You step into a Door, and for an instant your atoms are converted into field-energies, transmitted to another part of space and reconverted into matter. For that instant you're not alive.'

'I'm sure no one thinks of such things.'

'But your son may. He witnessed the breakdown of the Door. He may be saying to himself, "What if the Door breaks down just as I'm half-way through?" '

'But that's nonsense. He still uses the Door. He's even been to Canton with me; Canton, China. And as I told you, he uses it for school about once or twice a week.'

'Freely? Cheerfully?'

'Well,' said Mrs. Hanshaw, reluctantly, 'he does seem a bit put out by it. But really, Doctor, there isn't much use talking about it, is there? If you would do a quick probe, see where the trouble was,' and she finished on a bright note, 'why, that would be all. I'm sure it's quite a minor thing.'

Dr. Sloane sighed. He detested the word 'probe' and there was scarcely any word he heard oftener.

'Mrs. Hanshaw,' he said patiently, 'there is no such thing as a quick probe. Now I know the mag-strips are full of it and it's a rage in some circles, but it's much overrated.'

'Are you serious?'

'Quite. The probe is very complicated and the theory is that it traces mental circuits. You see, the cells of the brains are inter-connected in a large variety of ways. Some of those inter-connected paths are more used than others. They represent habits of thought, both conscious and unconscious. Theory has it that these paths in any given brain can be used to diagnose mental ills early and with certainty.'

'Well, then?'

'But subjection to the probe is quite a fearful thing, especially to a child. It's a traumatic experience. It takes over an hour. And even then, the results must be sent to the Central Psycho-analytical Bureau for analysis, and that could take weeks. And on top of all that, Mrs. Hanshaw, there are many psychiatrists who think the theory of probe-analyses to be most uncertain.'

Mrs. Hanshaw compressed her lips. 'You mean nothing can be done.'

Dr. Sloane smiled. 'Not at all. There were psychiatrists for centuries before there were probes. I suggest that you let me talk to the boy.'

'Talk to him? Is that all?'

'I'll come to you for background information when neces-sary, but the essential thing, I think, is to talk to the boy.'

'Really, Dr. Sloane, I doubt if he'll discuss the matter with you. He won't talk to me about it and I'm his mother.'

'That often happens,' the psychiatrist assured her. 'A child will sometimes talk more readily to a stranger. In any case, I cannot take the case otherwise.'

Mrs. Hanshaw rose, not at all pleased. 'When can you come, Doctor?'

'What about this coming Saturday? The boy won't be in school. Will you be busy?'

'We will be ready.'

She made a dignified exit. Dr. Sloane accompanied her through the small reception room to his office Door and waited while she punched the co-ordinates of her house. He watched her pass through. She became a half-woman, a quarter-woman, an isolated elbow and foot, a nothing.

It *was* frightening.

Did a Door ever break down during passage, leaving half a body here and half there? He had never heard of such a case, but he imagined it could happen.

He returned to his desk and looked up the time of his next appointment. It was obvious to him that Mrs. Hanshaw was annoyed and disappointed at not having arranged for a psychic probe treatment.

Why, for God's sake? Why should a thing like the probe, an obvious piece of quackery in his own opinion, get such a hold on the general public? It must be part of this general trend toward machines. Anything man can do, machines can do better. Machines! More machines! Machines for anything and everything! O tempora! O mores!

Oh, hell!

His resentment of the probe was beginning to bother him. Was it a fear of technological unemployment, a basic insecurity on his part, a mechanophobia, if that was the word –

He made a mental note to discuss this with his own analyst.

Dr. Sloane had to feel his way. The boy wasn't a patient who had come to him, more or less anxious to talk, more or less anxious to be helped.

Under the circumstances it would have been best to keep his first meeting with Richard short and noncommittal. It would have been sufficient merely to establish himself as something less than a total stranger. The next time he would be someone Richard had seen before. The time after he would be an acquaintance, and after that a friend of the family.

Unfortunately, Mrs. Hanshaw was not likely to accept a long-drawn-out process. She would go searching for a probe and, of course, she would find it.

And harm the boy. He was certain of that.

It was for that reason he felt he must sacrifice a little of the proper caution and risk a small crisis.

An uncomfortable ten minutes had passed when he decided he must try. Mrs. Hanshaw was smiling in a rather rigid way, eyeing him narrowly, as though she expected verbal magic from him. Richard wriggled in his seat, unresponsive to Dr. Sloane's tentative comments, overcome with boredom and unable not to show it.

Dr. Sloane said, with casual suddenness, 'Would you like to take a walk with me, Richard?'

The boy's eyes widened and he stopped wriggling. He looked directly at Dr. Sloane. 'A walk, sir?'

'I mean, outside.'

'Do you go – outside?'

'Sometimes. When I feel like it.'

Richard was on his feet, holding down a squirming eagerness. 'I didn't think anyone did.'

'I do. And I like company.'

The boy sat down, uncertainly. 'Mom? –'

Mrs. Hanshaw had stiffened in her seat, her compressed lips radiating horror, but she managed to say, 'Why certainly, Dickie. But watch yourself.'

And she managed a quick and baleful glare at Dr. Sloane.

In one respect, Dr. Sloane had lied. He did *not* go outside 'sometimes'. He hadn't been in the open since early college days. True, he had been athletically inclined (still was to some extent) but in his time the indoor ultra-violet chambers, swimming pools and tennis courts had flourished. For those with the price, they were much more satisfactory than the outdoor equivalents, open to the elements as they were, could possibly be. There was no occasion to go outside.

So there was a crawling sensation about his skin when he felt wind touch it, and he put down his flexied shoes on bare grass with a gingerly movement.

'Hey, look at that.' Richard was quite different now, laughing, his reserve broken down.

Dr. Sloane had time only to catch a flash of blue that ended in a tree. Leaves rustled and he lost it.

'What was it?'

'A bird,' said Richard. 'A blue kind of bird.'

Dr. Sloane looked about him in amazement. The Hanshaw residence was on a rise of ground, and he could see for miles. The area was only lightly wooded and between clumps of trees, grass gleamed brightly in the sunlight.

Colors set in deeper green made red and yellow patterns. They were flowers. From the books he had viewed in the course of his lifetime and from the old video shows, he had learned enough so that all this had an eerie sort of familiarity.

And yet the grass was so trim, the flowers so patterned. Dimly, he realized he had been expecting something wilder. He said, 'Who takes care of all this?'

Richard shrugged. 'I dunno. Maybe the mekkanos do it.'

'Mekkanos?'

'There's loads of them around. Sometimes they got a sort of atomic knife they hold near the ground. It cuts the grass. And they're always fooling around with the flowers and things. There's one of them over there.'

It was a small object, half a mile away. Its metal skin cast back highlights as it moved slowly over the gleaming meadow, engaged in some sort of activity that Dr. Sloane could not identify.

Dr. Sloane was astonished. Here it was a perverse sort of estheticism, a kind of conspicuous consumption –

'What's that?' he asked suddenly.

Richard looked. He said, 'That's a house. Belongs to the Froehlichs. Co-ordinates, A-3, 23, 461. That little pointy building over there is the public Door.'

Dr. Sloane was staring at the house. Was that what it looked like from the outside? Somehow he had imagined something much more cubic, and taller.

'Come along,' shouted Richard, running ahead.

Dr. Sloane followed more sedately. 'Do you know all the houses about here?'

'Just about.'

'Where is A-23, 26, 475?' It was his own house, of course.

Richard looked about. 'Let's see. Oh, sure, I know where it is – you see that water there?'

'Water?' Dr. Sloane made out a line of silver curving across the green.

'Sure. Real water. Just sort of running over rocks and things. It keeps running all the time. You can get across it if you step on the rocks. It's called a river.'

More like a creek, thought Dr. Sloane. He had studied geography, of course, but what passed for the subject these days was really economic and cultural geography. Physical geography was almost an extinct science except among specialists. Still, he knew what rivers and creeks were, in a theoretical sort of way.

Richard was still talking. 'Well, just past the river, over that hill with the big clump of trees and down the other side a way is A-23, 26, 475. It's a light green house with a white roof.'

'It is?' Dr. Sloane was genuinely astonished. He hadn't known it was green.

Some small animal disturbed the grass in its anxiety to avoid the oncoming feet. Richard looked after it and shrugged. 'You can't catch them. I tried.'

A butterfly flitted past, a wavering bit of yellow. Dr. Sloane's eyes followed it.

There was a low hum that lay over the fields, interspersed with an occasional harsh, calling sound, a rattle, a twittering, a chatter that rose, then fell. As his ear accustomed itself to listening, Dr. Sloane heard a thousand sounds, and none were man-made.

A shadow fell upon the scene, advancing toward him, covering him. It was suddenly cooler and he looked upward, startled.

Richard said, 'It's just a cloud. It'll go away in a minute – look at these flowers. They're the kind that smell.'

They were several hundred yards from the Hanshaw residence. The cloud passed and the sun shone once more. Dr. Sloane looked back and was appalled at the distance they had covered. If they moved out of sight of the house and if Richard ran off, would he be able to find his way back?

He pushed the thought away impatiently and looked out toward the line of water (nearer now) and past it to where his own house must be. He thought wonderingly: Light green?

He said, 'You must be quite an explorer.'

Richard said, with a shy pride, 'When I go to school and come back, I always try to use a different route and see new things.'

'But you don't go outside every morning, do you? Sometimes you use the Doors, I imagine.'

'Oh, sure.'

'Why is that, Richard?' Somehow, Dr. Sloane felt there might be significance in that point.

But Richard quashed him. With his eyebrows up and a look of astonishment on his face, he said, 'Well, gosh, some mornings it rains and I *have* to use the Door. I hate that, but what can you do? About two weeks ago, I got caught in the rain and I –' he looked about him automatically, and his voice sank to a whisper '– caught a cold, and wasn't Mom upset, though.'

Dr. Sloane sighed. 'Shall we go back now?'

There was a quick disappointment on Richard's face. 'Aw, what for?'

'You remind me that your mother must be waiting for us.'

'I guess so.' The boy turned reluctantly.

They walked slowly back. Richard was saying, chattily, 'I wrote a composition at school once about how if I could go on some ancient vehicle' (he pronounced it with exaggerated care) 'I'd go in a stratoliner and look at stars and clouds and things. Oh, boy, I was sure nuts.'

'You'd pick something else now?'

'You bet. I'd go in an aut'm'bile, real show. Then I'd see everything there was.'

Mrs. Hanshaw seemed troubled, uncertain. 'You don't think it's abnormal, then, doctor?'

'Unusual, perhaps; but not abnormal. He likes the outside.'

'But how can he? It's so dirty, so unpleasant.'

'That's a matter of individual taste. A hundred years ago our ancestors were all outside most of the time. Even today, I dare say there are a million Africans who have never seen a Door.'

'But Richard's always been taught to behave himself the way a decent person in District A-3 is supposed to behave,' said Mrs. Hanshaw, fiercely, 'Not like an African or – or an ancestor.'

'That may be part of the trouble, Mrs. Hanshaw. He feels this urge to go outside and yet he feels it to be wrong. He's ashamed to talk about it to you or to his teacher. It forces him into sullen retreat and it could eventually be dangerous.'

'Then how can we persuade him to stop?'

Dr. Sloane said, 'Don't try. Channel the activity instead. The day your Door broke down, he was forced outside, found he liked it, and that set a pattern. He used the trip to school and back as an excuse to repeat that first exciting experience. Now suppose you agree to let him out of the house for two hours on Saturdays and Sundays. Suppose he gets it through his head that after all he can go outside without necessarily having to go anywhere in the process. Don't you think he'll be willing to use the Door to go to school and back thereafter? And don't you think that will stop the trouble he's now having with his teacher and probably with his fellow-pupils?'

'But then will matters remain so? Must they? Won't he ever be normal again?'

Dr. Sloane rose to his feet. 'Mrs. Hanshaw, he's as normal as need be right now. Right now, he's tasting the joys of the forbidden. If you co-operate with him, show that you don't disapprove, it will lose some of its attraction right there. Then, as he grows older, he will become more aware of the expectations and demands of society. He will learn to conform. After all, there is a little of the rebel in all of us, but it generally dies down as we grow old and tired. Unless, that is, it is unreasonably suppressed and allowed to build up pressure. Don't do that. Richard will be all right.'

He walked to the Door.

Mrs. Hanshaw said, 'And you don't think a probe will be necessary, doctor?'

He turned and said vehemently, 'No, definitely not! There is nothing about the boy that requires it. Understand? Nothing.'

His fingers hesitated an inch from the combination board and the expression on his face grew lowering.

'What's the matter, Dr. Sloane?' asked Mrs. Hanshaw.

But he didn't hear her because he was thinking of the Door and the psychic probe and all the rising, choking tide of machinery. There is a little of the rebel in all of us, he thought.

So he said in a soft voice, as his hand fell away from the board and his feet turned away from the Door, 'You know, it's such a beautiful day that I think I'll walk.'

Surprises work both ways, I explained in my introduction to 'Nightfall' that its success had been completely unexpected. Well, in the case of 'Strikebreaker', I thought I had a block-buster. It seemed to me to be fresh and original; I felt it contained a stirring sociological theme, with lots of meaning, and with considerable pathos. Yet, as nearly as I can make out, it dropped silently into the sea of audience reaction without as much as marking out a single circular ripple on its surface.

But I can be stubborn about such things. If I like a story, I like it, and I include it here to give the audience a second chance.

This is one of those stories where I can remember the exact occasion that put it into my mind. It involved one of my periodic trips to New York which have, more and more, become a kind of highlight to my life. They are the only occasions on which I can stop writing for as much as three or four days at a time without feeling either guilty or restless.

Naturally, anything that would tend to interfere with one of my trips would ruffle my otherwise imperturbable sang-froid. Actually, I would throw a fit. It was bad enough when something enormous would get in my way – a hurricane or a blizzard, for instance. But a subway strike? And not of all the subway employees, but only a few key men, say thirty-five. They would stall the entire subway system and, with that, the entire city. And if the strike came to pass, I could scarcely venture into a stalled city.

'Where will this all end?' I apostrophized the heavens in my best tragical manner, one fist raised high and the other clenched in my hair. 'A mere handful of men can paralyze an entire megalopolis. Where will it end?'

My gesture remained frozen as, in thought, I carried the situation to its logical extreme. I carefully unhooked the gesture, went upstairs, and wrote 'Strikebreaker.'

The happy ending is that the threatened strike did not come to pass, and I went to New York.

One more point about this story. It represents my personal record for stupid title changes. The editor of the magazine in which this story first appeared was Robert W. Lowndes, as sweet and as erudite a man as I have ever known. He had nothing to do with it. Some idiot in the higher echelons decided to call the story 'Male Strikebreaker'.

Why 'Male'? What possible addition to the sense of the title can be made by that adjective? What illumination? What improvement? Heavens, I can understand (though not approve) a ridiculous title change which the publisher felt would imply something salacious and thus increase sales, but the modified title doesn't even do that.

Oh, well – I'll just change it back.

First appearance – The Original Science Fiction Stories, *January 1957, under the title 'Male Strikebreaker'. Copyright, 1956, by Columbia Publications, Inc.*

STRIKEBREAKER

Elvis Blei rubbed his plump hands and said, 'Self-containment is the word.' He smiled uneasily as he helped Steven Lamorak of Earth to a light. There was uneasiness all over his smooth face with its small wide-set eyes.

Lamorak puffed smoke appreciatively and crossed his lanky legs.

His hair was powdered with gray and he had a large and powerful jawbone. 'Home grown?' he asked, staring critically at the cigarette. He tried to hide his own disturbance at the other's tension.

'Quite,' said Blei.

'I wonder,' said Lamorak, 'that you have room on your small world for such luxuries.'

(Lamorak thought of his first view of Elsevere from the spaceship visiplate. It was a jagged, airless planetoid, some hundred miles in diameter – just a dust-gray rough-hewn rock, glimmering dully in the light of its sun, 200,000,000 miles distant. It was the only object more than a mile in diameter that circled that sun, and now men had burrowed into that miniature world and constructed a society in it. And he himself, as a sociologist, had come to study the world and see how humanity had made itself fit into that queerly specialized niche.)

Blei's polite fixed smile expanded a hair. He said, 'We are not a small world, Dr. Lamorak; you judge us by two-dimensional standards. The surface area of Elsevere is only three quarters that of the State of New York, but that's irrelevant. Remember, we can occupy, if we wish, the entire interior of Elsevere. A sphere of 50 miles radius has a volume of well over half a million cubic miles. If all of Elsevere were occupied by levels 50 feet apart, the total surface area within the planetoid would be 56,000,000 square miles, and that is equal to the total land area of Earth. And none of these square miles, Doctor, would be unproductive.'

Lamorak said, 'Good Lord,' and stared blankly for a moment. 'Yes, of course you're right. Strange I never thought of it that way. But then, Elsevere is the only thoroughly exploited planetoid world in the Galaxy; the rest of us simply can't get away from thinking of two-dimensional surfaces, as you pointed out. Well, I'm more than ever glad that your Council has been so cooperative as to give me a free hand in this investigation of mine.'

Blei nodded conclusively at that.

Lamorak frowned slightly and thought: He acts for all the world as though he wished I had not come. Something's wrong.

Blei said, 'Of course, you understand that we are actually much smaller than we could be; only minor portions of Elsevere have as yet been hollowed out and occupied. Nor are we particularly anxious to expand, except very slowly. To a certain extent we are limited by the capacity of our pseudo-gravity engines and Solar energy converters.'

'I understand. But tell me, Councillor Blei – as a matter of personal curiosity, and not because it is of prime importance to my project – could I view some of your farming and herding levels first? I am fascinated by the thought of fields of wheat and herds of cattle inside a planetoid.'

'You'll find the cattle small by your standards, Doctor, and we don't have much wheat. We grow yeast to a much greater extent. But there will be some wheat to show you. Some cotton and tobacco, too. Even fruit trees.'

'Wonderful. As you say, self-containment. You recirculate everything, I imagine.'

Lamorak's sharp eyes did not miss the fact that this last remark twinged Blei. The Elseverian's eyes narrowed to slits that hid his expression.

He said, 'We must recirculate, yes. Air, water, food, minerals – everything that is used up – must be restored to its original state; waste products are reconverted to raw materials. All that is needed is energy, and we have enough of that. We don't manage with one hundred per cent efficiency, of course; there is a certain seepage. We import a small amount of water each year; and if our needs grow, we may have to import some coal and oxygen.'

Lamorak said, 'When can we start our tour, Councillor Blei?'

Blei's smile lost some of its negligible warmth. 'As soon as we can, Doctor. There are some routine matters that must be arranged.'

Lamorak nodded, and having finished his cigarette, stubbed it out.

Routine matters? There was none of this hesitancy during the preliminary correspondence. Elsevere had seemed proud that its unique planetoid existence had attracted the attention of the Galaxy.

He said, 'I realize I would be a disturbing influence in a tightly-knit society,' and watched grimly as Blei leaped at the explanation and made it his own.

'Yes,' said Blei, 'we feel marked off from the rest of the Galaxy. We have our own customs. Each individual Elseverian fits into a comfortable niche. The appearance of a stranger without fixed caste is unsettling.'

'The caste system does involve a certain inflexibility.'

'Granted,' said Blei quickly; 'but there is also a certain self-assurance. We have firm rules of intermarriage and rigid inheritance of occupation. Each man, woman and child knows his place, accepts it, and is accepted in it; we have virtually no neurosis or mental illness.'

'And are there no misfits?' asked Lamorak.

Blei shaped his mouth as though to say no, then clamped it suddenly shut, biting the word into silence; a frown deepened on his forehead. He said, at length, 'I will arrange for the tour, Doctor. Meanwhile, I imagine you would welcome a chance to freshen up and to sleep.'

They rose together and left the room, Blei politely motioning the Earthman to precede him out the door.

Larnorak felt oppressed by the vague feeling of crisis that had pervaded his discussion with Blei.

The newspaper reinforced that feeling. He read it carefully before getting into bed, with what was at first merely a clinical interest. It was an eight-page tabloid of synthetic paper. One quarter of its items consisted of 'personals': births, marriages, deaths, record quotas, expanding habitable volume (not area! three dimensions!). The remainder included scholarly essays, educational material, and fiction. Of news, in the sense to which Lamorak was accustomed, there was virtually nothing.

One item only could be so considered and that was chilling in its incompleteness.

It said, under a small headline: *DEMANDS UN-CHANGED: There has been no change in his attitude of yesterday. The Chief Councillor, after a second interview, announced that his demands remain completely unreasonable and cannot be met under any circumstances.*

Then, in parenthesis, and in different type, there was the statement: *The editors of this paper agree that Elsevere cannot and will not jump to his whistle, come what may.*

Lamorak read it over three times. *His* attitude. *His* demands. *His* whistle.

Whose?

He slept uneasily, that night.

He had no time for newspapers in the days that followed; but spasmodically, the matter returned to his thoughts.

Blei, who remained his guide and companion for most of the tour, grew ever more withdrawn.

On the third day (quite artificially clock-set in an Earthlike twenty-four hour pattern), Blei stopped at one point, and said, 'Now this level is devoted entirely to chemical industries. That section is not important –'

But he turned away a shade too rapidly and Lamorak seized his arm. 'What are the products of that section?'

'Fertilizers. Certain organics,' said Blei stiffly.

Lamorak held him back, looking for what sight Blei might be evading. His gaze swept over the close-by horizons of lined rock and the buildings squeezed and layered between the levels.

Lamorak said, 'Isn't that a private residence there?'

Blei did not look in the indicated direction.

Lamorak said, 'I think that's the largest one I've seen yet. Why is it here on a factory level?' That alone made it noteworthy. He had already seen that the levels on Elsevere were divided rigidly among the residential, the agricultural and the industrial.

He looked back and called, 'Councillor Blei!'

The councillor was walking away and Lamorak pursued him with hasty steps. 'Is there something wrong, sir?'

Blei muttered, 'I am rude, I know. I am sorry. There are matters that prey on my mind –' He kept up his rapid pace.

'Concerning *his* demands.'

Blei came to a full halt. 'What do *you* know about that?'

'No more than I've said. I read that much in the newspaper.'

Blei muttered something to himself.

Lamorak said, 'Ragusnik? What's that?'

Blei sighed heavily. 'I suppose you ought to be told. It's humiliating, deeply embarrassing. The Council thought that matters would certainly be arranged shortly and that your visit need not be interfered with, that you need not know or be concerned. But it is almost a week now. I don't know what will happen and, appearances notwithstanding, it might be best for you to leave. No reason for an Outworlder to risk death.'

The Earthman smiled incredulously. 'Risk death? In this little world, so peaceful and busy. I can't believe it.'

The Elseverian councillor said, 'I can explain. I think it best I should.' He turned his head away. 'As I told you, everything on Elsevere must recirculate. You understand that.'

'Yes.'

'That includes – uh, human wastes.'

'I assumed so,' said Lamorak.

'Water is reclaimed from it by distillation and absorption. What remains is converted into fertilizer for yeast use; some of it is used as a source of fine organics and other by-products. These factories you see are devoted to this.'

'Well?' Lamorak had experienced a certain difficulty in the drinking of water when he first landed on Elsevere, because he had been realistic enough to know what it must be reclaimed from; but he had conquered the feeling easily enough. Even on Earth, water was reclaimed by natural processes from all sorts of unpalatable substances.

Blei, with increasing difficulty, said, 'Igor Ragusnik is the man who is in charge of the industrial processes immediately involving the wastes. The position has been in his family since Elsevere was first colonized. One of the original settlers was Mikhail Ragusnik and he – he –'

'Was in charge of waste reclamation.'

'Yes. Now that residence you singled out is the Ragusnik residence; it is the best and most elaborate on the planetoid. Ragusnik gets many privileges the rest of us do not have; but, after all –' Passion entered the Councillor's voice with great suddenness, 'we cannot *speak* to him.'

'What?'

'He demands full social equality. He wants his children to mingle with ours, and our wives to visit – Oh!' It was a groan of utter disgust.

Lamorak thought of the newspaper item that could not even bring itself to mention Ragusnik's name in print, or to say anything specific about his demands. He said, 'I take it he's an outcast because of his job.'

'Naturally. Human wastes and –' words failed Blei. After a pause, he said more quietly, 'As an Earthman, I suppose you don't understand.'

'As a sociologist, I think I do.' Lamorak thought of the Untouchables in ancient India, the ones who handled corpses. He thought of the position of swineherds in ancient Judea.

He went on, 'I gather Elsevere will not give in to those demands.'

'Never,' said Blei, energetically. 'Never.'

'And so?'

'Ragusnik has threatened to cease operations.'

'Go on strike, in other words.'

'Yes.'

'Would that be serious?'

'We have enough food and water to last quite a while; reclamation is not essential in that sense. But the wastes would accumulate; they would infect the planetoid. After generations of careful disease control, we have low natural resistance to germ diseases. Once an epidemic started – and one would – we would drop by the hundred.'

'Is Ragusnik aware of this?'

'Yes, of course.'

'Do you think he is likely to go through with his threat, then?'

'He is mad. He has already stopped working; there has been no waste reclamation since the day before you landed.' Blei's bulbous nose sniffed at the air as though it already caught the whiff of excrement.

Lamorak sniffed mechanically at that, but smelled nothing.

Blei said, 'So you see why it might be wise for you to leave. We are humiliated, of course, to have to suggest it.'

But Lamorak said, 'Wait; not just yet. Good Lord, this is a matter of great interest to me professionally. May I speak to the Ragusnik?'

'On no account,' said Blei, alarmed.

'But I would like to understand the situation. The sociological conditions here are unique and not to be duplicated elsewhere. In the name of science –'

'How do you mean, speak? Would image-reception do?'

'Yes.'

'I will ask the Council,' muttered Blei.

They sat about Lamorak uneasily, their austere and dignified expressions badly marred with anxiety. Blei, seated in the midst of them, studiously avoided the Earthman's eyes.

The Chief Councillor, gray-haired, his face harshly wrinkled, his neck scrawny, said in a soft voice, 'If in any way you can persuade him, sir, out of your own convictions, we will welcome that. In no case, however, are you to imply that we will, in any way, yield.'

A gauzy curtain fell between the Council and Lamorak. He could make out the individual councillors still, but now he turned sharply toward the receiver before him. It glowed to life.

A head appeared in it, in natural color and with great realism. A strong dark head, with massive chin faintly stubbled, and thick, red lips set into a firm horizontal line.

The image said, suspiciously, 'Who are you?'

Lamorak said, 'My name is Steven Lamorak; I am an Earthman.'

'An Outworlder?'

'That's right. I am visiting Elsevere. You are Ragusnik?'

'Igor Ragusnik, at your service,' said the image, mockingly.

'Except that there is no service and will be none until my family and I are treated like human beings.'

Lamorak said, 'Do you realize the danger that Elsevere is in? The possibility of epidemic disease?'

'In twenty-four hours, the situation can be made normal, if they allow me humanity. The situation is theirs to correct.'

'You sound like an educated man, Ragusnik.'

'So?'

'I am told you're denied of no material comforts. You are housed and clothed and fed better than anyone on Elsevere. Your children are the best educated.'

'Granted. But all by servo-mechanism. And motherless girl-babies are sent us to care for until they grow to be our wives. And they die young for loneliness. Why?' There was sudden passion in his voice. 'Why must we live in isolation as if we were all monsters, unfit for human beings to be near? Aren't we human beings like others, with the same needs and desires and feelings. Don't we perform an honorable and useful function –?'

There was a rustling of sighs from behind Lamorak. Ragusnik heard it, and raised his voice. 'I see you of the Council behind there. Answer me: Isn't it an honorable and useful function? It is *your* waste made into food for *you*. Is the man who purifies corruption worse than the man who produces it? – Listen, Councillors, I will *not* give in. Let all of Elsevere die of disease – including myself and my son, if necessary – but I will not give in. My family will be better dead of disease, than living as now.'

Lamorak interrupted. 'You've led this life since birth, haven't you?'

'And if I have?'

'Surely you're used to it.'

'Never. Resigned, perhaps. My father was resigned, and I was resigned for a while; but I have watched my son, my only son, with no other little boy to play with. My brother and I had each other, but my son will never have anyone, and I am no longer resigned. I am through with Elsevere and through with talking.'

The receiver went dead.

The Chief Councillor's face had paled to an aged yellow. He and Blei were the only ones of the group left with Lamorak.

The Chief Councillor said, 'The man is deranged; I do not know how to force him.'

He had a glass of wine at his side; as he lifted it to his lips, he spilled a few drops that stained his white trousers with purple splotches.

Lamorak said, 'Are his demands so unreasonable? Why can't he be accepted into society?'

There was momentary rage in Blei's eyes. 'A dealer in excrement.' Then he shrugged. 'You are from Earth.'

Incongruously, Lamorak thought of another unacceptable, one of the numerous classic creations of the medieval cartoonist, Al Capp. The variously-named 'inside man at the skonk works.'

He said, 'Does Ragusnik really deal with excrement? I mean, is there physical contact? Surely, it is all handled by automatic machinery.'

'Of course,' said the Chief Councillor.

'Then exactly what is Ragusnik's function?'

'He manually adjusts the various controls that assure the proper functioning of the machinery. He shifts units to allow repairs to be made; he alters functional rates with the time of day; he varies end production with demand.' He added sadly, 'If we had the space to make the machinery ten times as complex, all this could be done automatically; but that would be such needless waste.'

'But even so,' insisted Lamorak, 'all Ragusnik does he does simply by pressing buttons or closing contacts or things like that.'

'Yes.'

'Then his work is no different from any Elseverian's.'

Blei said, stiffly, 'You don't understand.'

'And for that you will risk the death of your children?'

'We have no other choice,' said Blei. There was enough agony in his voice to assure Lamorak that the situation was torture for him, but that he had no other choice indeed.

Lamorak shrugged in disgust. 'Then break the strike. Force him.'

'How?' said the Chief Councillor. 'Who would touch him or go near him? And if we kill him by blasting from a distance, how will that help us?'

Lamorak said, thoughtfully, 'Would you know how to run his machinery?'

The Chief Councillor came to his feet. 'I?' he howled.

'I don't mean *you*,' cried Lamorak at once. 'I used the pronoun in its indefinite sense. Could *someone* learn how to handle Ragusnik's machinery?'

Slowly, the passion drained out of the Chief Councillor. 'It is in the handbooks, I am certain – though I assure you I have never concerned myself with it.'

'Then couldn't someone learn the procedure and substitute for Ragusnik until the man gives in?'

Blei said, 'Who would agree to do such a thing? Not I, under any circumstances.'

Lamorak thought fleetingly of Earthly taboos that might be almost as strong. He thought of cannibalism, incest, a pious man cursing God. He said, 'But you must have made provision for vacancy in the Ragusnik job. Suppose he died.'

'Then his son would automatically succeed to his job, or his nearest other relative,' said Blei.

'What if he had no adult relatives? What if all his family died at once?'

'That has never happened; it will never happen.'

The Chief Councillor added, 'If there were danger of it, we might, perhaps, place a baby or two with the Ragusniks and have it raised to the profession.'

'Ah. And how would you choose that baby?'

'From among children of mothers who died in childbirth, as we choose the future Ragusnik bride.'

'Then choose a substitute Ragusnik now, by lot,' said Lamorak.

The Chief Councillor said, '*No! Impossible!* How can you suggest that? If we select a baby, that baby is brought up to the life; it knows no other. At this point, it would be necessary to choose an adult and subject him to Ragusnik-hood. No, Dr. Lamorak, we are neither monsters nor abandoned brutes.'

No use, thought Lamorak helplessly. *No use, unless* –

He couldn't bring himself to face that *unless* just yet.

That night, Lamorak slept scarcely at all. Ragusnik asked for only the basic elements of humanity. But opposing that were thirty thousand Elseverians who faced death.

The welfare of thirty thousand on one side; the just demands of one family on the other. Could one say that thirty thousand

who would support such injustice deserved to die? Injustice by
what standards? Earth's? Elsevere's? And who was Lamorak
that he should judge?

And Ragusnik? He was willing to let thirty thousand die,
including men and women who merely accepted a situation
they had been taught to accept and could not change if they
wished to. And children who had nothing at all to do with it.

Thirty thousand on one side; a single family on the other.

Lamorak made his decision in something that was almost
despair; in the morning he called the Chief Councillor.

He said, 'Sir, if you can find a substitute, Ragusnik will see
that he has lost all chance to force a decision in his favor and
will return to work.'

'There can be no substitute,' sighed the Chief Councillor; 'I
have explained that.'

'No substitute among the Elseverians, but I am not an Elseverian; it doesn't matter to me. *I* will substitute.'

They were excited, much more excited than Lamorak himself. A dozen times they asked him if he was serious.

Lamorak had not shaved, and he felt sick, 'Certainly, I'm
serious. And any time Ragusnik acts like this, you can always
import a substitute. No other world has the taboo and there
will always be plenty of temporary substitutes available if you
pay enough.'

(He was betraying a brutally exploited man, and he knew it.
But he told himself desperately: *Except for ostracism, he's very
well treated. Very well.*)

They gave him the handbooks and he spent six hours, reading and re-reading. There was no use asking questions. None of
the Elseverians knew anything about the job, except for what
was in the handbook; and all seemed uncomfortable if the details were as much as mentioned.

'Maintain zero reading of galvanometer A-2 at all times during red signal of the Lunge-howler,' read Lamorak. 'Now what's
a Lunge-howler?'

'There will be a sign,' muttered Blei, and the Elseverians
looked at each other hang-dog and bent their heads to stare at
their finger-ends.

They left him long before he reached the small rooms that

were the central headquarters of generations of working Ragusniks, serving their world. He had specific instructions concerning which turnings to take and what level to reach, but they
hung back and let him proceed alone.

He went through the rooms painstakingly, identifying their in-
struments and controls, following the schematic diagrams in the
handbook.

There's a Lunge-howler, he though, with gloomy satisfaction. The sign did indeed say so. It had a semicircular face bitten
into holes that were obviously designed to glow in separate
colors. Why a 'howler' then?

He didn't know.

Somewhere, thought Lamorak, *somewhere wastes are accu-
mulating, pushing against gears and exits, pipelines and stills,
waiting to be handled in half a hundred ways. Now they just
accumulate.*

Not without a tremor, he pulled the first switch as indicated
by the handbook in its directions for 'Initiation'. A gentle murmur of life made itself felt through the floors and walls. He
turned a knob and lights went on.

At each step, he consulted the handbook, though he knew it
by heart; and with each step, the rooms brightened and the dial-
indicators sprang into motion and a humming grew louder.

Somewhere deep in the factories, the accumulated wastes were
being drawn into the proper channels.

A high-pitched signal sounded and startled Lamorak out of
his painful concentration. It was the communications signal and
Lamorak fumbled his receiver into action.

Ragusnik's head showed, startled; then slowly, the incredulity
and outright shock faded from his eyes. '*That's* how it is, then.'

'I'm not an Elseverian, Ragusnik; I don't mind doing this.'

'But what business is it of yours? Why do you interfere?'

'I'm on your side, Ragusnik, but I must do this.'

'Why, if you're on my side? Do they treat people on your
world as they treat me here?'

'Not any longer. But even if you are right, there are thirty
thousand people on Elsevere to be considered.'

'They would have given in; you've ruined my only chance.'

'They would *not* have given in. And in a way, you've won;
they know now that you're dissatisfied. Until now, they never

dreamed a Ragusnik could be unhappy, that he could make trouble.'

'What if they know? Now all they need do is hire an Outworlder anytime.'

Lamorak shook his head violently. He had thought this through in these last bitter hours. 'The fact that they know means that the Elseverians will begin to think about you; some will begin to wonder if it's right to treat a human so. And if Outworlders are hired, they'll spread the word that this goes on upon Elsevere and Galactic public opinion will be in your favor.'

'And?'

'Things will improve. In your son's time, things will be much better.'

'In my son's time,' said Ragusnik, his cheeks sagging. 'I might have had it now. Well, I lose. I'll go back to the job.'

Lamorak felt an overwhelming relief. 'If you'll come here now, sir, you may have your job and I'll consider it an honor to shake your hand.'

Ragusnik's head snapped up and filled with a gloomy pride. 'You call me "sir" and offer to shake my hand. Go about your business, Earthman, and leave me to my work, for I would not shake yours.'

Lamorak returned the way he had come, relieved that the crisis was over, and profoundly depressed, too.

He stopped in surprise when he found a section of corridor cordoned off, so he could not pass. He looked about for alternate routes, then started at a magnified voice above his head. 'Dr Lamorak, do you hear me? This is Councillor Blei.'

Lamorak looked up. The voice came over some sort of public address system, but he saw no sign of an outlet.

He called out, 'Is anything wrong? Can you hear me?'

'I hear you.'

Instinctively, Lamorak was shouting. 'Is anything wrong? There seems to be a block here. Are there complications with Ragusnik?'

'Ragusnik has gone to work,' came Blei's voice. 'The crisis is over, and you must make ready to leave.'

'Leave?'

'Leave Elsevere; a ship is being made ready for you now.'

'But wait a bit.' Lamorak was confused by this sudden leap of events. 'I haven't completed my gathering of data.'

Blei's voice said, 'This cannot be helped. You will be directed to the ship and your belongings will be sent after you by servomechanisms. We trust – we trust –'

Something was becoming clear to Lamorak. 'You trust *what*?'

'We trust you will make no attempt to see or speak directly to any Elseverian. And of course we hope you will avoid embarrassment by not attempting to return to Elsevere at any time in the future. A colleague of yours would be welcome if further data concerning us is needed.'

'I understand,' said Lamorak, tonelessly. Obviously, he had himself become a Ragusnik. He had handled the controls that in turn had handled the wastes; he was ostracized. He was a corpse-handler, a swineherd, an inside man at the skonk works.

He said, 'Good-bye.'

Blei's voice said, 'Before we direct you, Dr. Lamorak –. On behalf of the Council of Elsevere, I thank you for your help in this crisis.'

'You're welcome,' said Lamorak, bitterly.

In some ways, this story has the strangest background of any I ever wrote. It is also the shortest story I ever wrote – only 350 words. The two go together.

It came about this way. On August 21, 1957, I took part in a panel discussion on means of communicating science on WGBH, Boston's educational TV station. With me were John Hansen, a technical writer of directions for using machinery, and David O. Woodbury, the well-known science writer.

We all bemoaned the inadequacy of most science writing and technical writing and there was some comment on my prolificity. With my usual modesty, I attributed my success entirely to an incredible fluency of ideas and a delightful facility in writing. I stated incautiously that I could write a story anywhere, any time, under any conditions within reason. I was instantly challenged to write one right then and there with the television cameras on me.

I accepted the challenge and began to write, taking for my theme the subject of discussion. The other two did not try to make life easier for me, either. They deliberately kept interrupting in order to drag me into their discussion and interrupt my line of thought, and I was just vain enough to try to answer sensibly while I continued scribbling.

Before that half-hour program was over I had finished and read the story (which is why it is so short, by the way) and it was the one you see here as 'Insert Knob A in Hole B.' In his own introduction to the story, when it appeared in F &SF, Mr. Boucher said he was printing it just as it was (I had sent him the handwritten script, after typing a copy for myself) 'even to the retention of its one grammatical error.' I have kept that error here, too. It's yours for the finding.

I cheated, though. (Would I lie to you?) The three of us were talking before the program started and somehow I got the idea they might ask me to write a story on the program. So, just in case they did, I spent a few minutes before its start blocking out something.

Consequently, when they asked me, I had it roughly in mind. All I had to do was work out the details, write it down, and then read it. After all, I had twenty minutes.

First appearance – The Magazine of Fantasy and Science Fiction, December 1957. ©, 1957, by Fantasy House, Inc.

INSERT KNOB A IN HOLE B

Dave Woodbury and John Hansen, grotesque in their spacesuits, supervised anxiously as the large crate swung slowly out and away from the freight-ship and into the airlock. With nearly a year of their hitch on Space Station A5 behind them, they were understandably weary of filtration units that clanked, hydroponic tubs that leaked, air generators that hummed constantly and stopped occasionally.

'Nothing works,' Woodbury would say mournfully, 'because everything is hand-assembled by ourselves.'

'Following directions', Hansen would add, 'composed by an idiot.'

There were undoubtedly grounds for complaint there. The most expensive thing about a spaceship was the room allowed for freight so all equipment had to be sent across space disassembled and nested. All equipment had to be assembled at the Station itself with clumsy hands, inadequate tools and with blurred and ambiguous direction sheets for guidance.

Painstakingly Woodbury had written complaints to which Hansen had added appropriate adjectives, and formal requests for relief of the situation had made its way back to Earth.

And Earth had responded. A special robot had been designed, with a positronic brain crammed with the knowledge of how to assemble properly any disassembled machine in existence.

That robot was in the crate being unloaded now and Woodbury was trembling as the airlock closed behind it.

'First,' he said, 'it overhauls the Food-Assembler and adjusts the steak-attachment knob so we can get it rare instead of burnt.'

They entered the station and attacked the crate with dainty touches of the demoleculizer rods in order to make sure that not a precious metal atom of their special assembly-robot was damaged.

The crate fell open!

And there within it were five hundred separate pieces – and one blurred and ambiguous direction sheet for assemblage.

I have frequently (rather to my own uneasy surprise) been accused of writing humorously. Oh, I try, I try, but only very cautiously, and for a long time I thought nobody noticed.

You see, there is no margin for error in humor. You can try to write suspense and not quite hit the mark, and have a story that is only moderately suspenseful. In analogous manner, you can have a story be only moderately romantic, moderately exciting, moderately eerie, even moderately science-fictiony.

But what happens when you miss the mark in humor? Is the result moderately humorous? Of course not! The not-quite-humorous remark, the not-quite-witty rejoinder, the not-quite-farcical episode are, respectively, dreary, stupid, and ridiculous.

Well, with a target that is all bull's-eye and no larger than a bull's-eye at that, am I going to blaze away carelessly? Certainly not! I'm fantastically courageous, but I'm not stupid.

So I have tried being funny only occasionally, and usually only gently and unobtrusively (as in 'Nobody Here But – ') On the few occasions in which I tried to write a purely funny story, I wasn't completely satisfied.

Mostly, therefore, I kept my stories grave and sober (as you can tell).

Yet, I never quite gave up, either. One day, at the prodding of Mr. Boucher, I tried my hand at a Gilbert and Sullivan parody and finally (in my own eyes, at any rate) I clicked without reservation. I read the story over and laughed heartily.

That was it. I had found my métier in humor. All I had to do was to assume a very slightly exaggerated pseudo-Victorian style and I found I had no trouble at all in being funny.

Did I enter a full-fledged career as science fiction humorist at once? Not at all. I kept the humor at the previous level and remained, for the most part, grave and sober. That's still what I do best.

However, in the middle 1960s, I took to writing a series of articles for TV Guide which are nothing but this kind of humor, and I love them. (I am sometimes taken to task, by the way, for saying, in my artless way, that I like my own material, but why shouldn't I? Is it conceivable that I would spend seventy hours a week on writing and related reading if I didn't like what I wrote? Come on!)

By the way, a final word about 'The Up-to-Date Sorcerer' – It is not essential to read Gilbert and Sullivan's The Sorcerer

*first, but it would make my story funnier if you did (I think),
and I would like to give it every break.*

First appearance – The Magazine of Fantasy and Science
Fiction, *July 1958*. ©, *1958, by Mercury Press, Inc.*

THE UP-TO-DATE SORCERER

*It always puzzled me that Nicholas Nitely, although a Justice
of the Peace, was a bachelor. The atmosphere of his profession,
so to speak, seemed so conducive to matrimony that surely he
could scarcely avoid the gentle bond of wedlock.*

*When I said as much over a gin and tonic at the Club re-
cently, he said, 'Ah, but I had a narrow escape some time ago,'
and he sighed.*

'Oh, really?'

*'A fair young girl, sweet, intelligent, pure yet desperately ar-
dent, and withal most alluring to the physical sense of even such
an old fogy as myself.'*

I said, 'How did you come to let her go?'

*'I had no choice.' He smiled gently at me and his smooth,
ruddy complexion, his smooth gray hair, his smooth blue eyes,
all combined to give him an expression of near-saintliness. He
said, 'You see, it was really the fault of her fiancé –'*

'Ah, she was engaged to someone else.'

*'– and of Professor Wellington Johns, who was, although an
endocrinologist, by way of being an up-to-date sorcerer. In fact,
it was just that –' He sighed, sipped at his drink, and turned
on me the bland and cheerful face of one who is about to change
the subject.*

*I said firmly, 'Now, then, Nitely, old man, you cannot leave
it so. I want to know about your beautiful girl – the flesh that
got away.'*

He winced at the pun (one, I must admit, of my more abom-

inable efforts) and settled down by ordering his glass refilled. 'You understand,' he said, 'I learned some of the details later on.'

Professor Wellington Johns had a large and prominent nose, two sincere eyes and a distinct talent for making clothes appear too large for him. He said, 'My dear children, love is a matter of chemistry.'

His dear children, who were really students of his, and not his children at all, were named Alexander Dexter and Alice Sanger. They looked perfectly full of chemicals as they sat there holding hands. Together, their age amounted to perhaps 45, evenly split between them, and Alexander said, fairly inevitably, *'Vive la chémie!'*

Professor Johns smiled reprovingly. 'Or rather endocrinology. Hormones, after all, affect our emotions and it is not surprising that one should, specifically, stimulate that feeling we call love.'

'But that's so unromantic,' murmured Alice. 'I'm sure I don't need any.' She looked up at Alexander with a yearning glance.

'My dear,' said the professor, 'your blood stream was crawling with it at that moment you, as the saying is, fell in love. Its secretion had been stimulated by' – for a moment he considered his words carefully, being a highly moral man – 'by some environmental factor involving your young man, and once the hormonal action had taken place, inertia carried you on. I could duplicate the effect easily.'

'Why, Professor,' said Alice, with gentle affection. 'It would be delightful to have you try,' and she squeezed Alexander's hand shyly.

'I do not mean,' said the professor, coughing to hide his embarrassment, 'that I would personally attempt to reproduce – or, rather, to duplicate – the conditions that created the natural secretion of the hormone. I mean, instead, that I could inject the hormone itself by hypodermic or even by oral ingestion, since it is a steroid hormone. I have, you see,' and here he removed his glasses and polished them proudly, 'isolated and purified the hormone.'

Alexander sat erect. 'Professor! And you have said nothing?'

'I must know more about it first.'

'Do you mean to say,' said Alice, her lovely brown eyes shimmering with delight, 'that you can make people feel the wonderful delight and heaven-surpassing tenderness of true love by means of a . . . a pill?'

The professor said, 'I can indeed duplicate the emotion to which you refer in those rather cloying terms.'

'Then why don't you?'

Alexander raised a protesting hand. 'Now, darling, your ardor leads you astray. Our own happiness and forthcoming nuptials make you forget certain facts of life. If a married person were, by mistake, to accept this hormone –'

Professor John said, with a trace of hauteur, 'Let me explain right now that my hormone, or my amatogenic principle, as I call it –' (for he, in common with many practical scientists, enjoyed a proper scorn for the rarefied niceties of classical philology).

'Call it a love-philtre, Professor,' said Alice, with a melting sigh.

'My amatogenic cortical principle,' said Professor Johns, sternly, 'has no effect on married individuals. The hormone cannot work if inhibited by other factors, and being married is certainly a factor that inhibits love.'

'Why, so I have heard,' said Alexander, gravely, 'but I intend to disprove that callous belief in the case of my own Alice.'

'Alexander,' said Alice. 'My love.'

The professor said, 'I mean that marriage inhibits extramarital love.'

Alexander said, 'Why, it has come to my ears that sometimes it does not.'

Alice said, shocked, 'Alexander!'

'Only in rare instances, my dear, among those who have not gone to college.'

The professor said, 'Marriage may not inhibit a certain paltry sexual attraction, or tendencies toward minor trifling, but true love, as Miss Sanger expressed the emotion, is something which cannot blossom when the memory of a stern wife and various unattractive children hobbles the subconscious.'

'Do you mean to say,' said Alexander, 'that if you were to feel your love-philtre – beg pardon, your amatogenic principle – to a number of people indiscriminately, only the *unmarried* individuals would be affected?'

'That is right. I have experimented on certain animals which, though not going through the conscious marriage rite, do form monogamous attachments. Those with the attachments already formed are not affected.'

'Then, Professor, I have a perfectly splendid idea. Tomorrow night is the night of the Senior Dance here at college. There will be at least fifty couples present, mostly unmarried. Put your philtre in the punch.'

'What? Are you mad?'

But Alice had caught fire. 'Why, it's a heavenly idea, Professor. To think that all my friends will feel as I feel! Professor, you would be an angel from heaven. – But oh, Alexander, do you suppose the feelings might be a trifle uncontrolled? Some of our college chums are a little wild and if, in the heat of the discovery of love, they should, well, kiss –'

Professor Johns said, indignantly, 'My dear Miss Sanger. You must not allow your imagination to become overheated. My hormone induces only those feelings which lead to marriage and not to the expression of anything that might be considered indecorous.'

'I'm sorry,' murmured Alice, in confusion. 'I should remember, Professor, that you are the most highly moral man I know – excepting always dear Alexander – and that no scientific discovery of yours could possibly lead to immorality.'

She looked so woebegone that the professor forgave her at once.

'Then you'll do it, Professor?' urged Alexander. 'After all, assuming there will be a sudden urge for mass marriage afterwards, I can take care of that by having Nicholas Nitely, an old and valued friend of the family, present on some pretext. He is a Justice of the Peace and can easily arrange for such things as licenses and so on.'

'I could scarcely agree', said the professor, obviously weakening, 'to perform an experiment without the consent of those experimented upon. It would be unethical.'

'But you would be bringing only joy to them. You would be contributing to the moral atmosphere of the college. For surely, in the absence of overwhelming pressure toward marriage, it sometimes happens even in college that the pressure of continuous propinquity breeds a certain danger of – of –'

'Yes, there is that,' said the professor. 'Well, I shall try a dilute solution. After all, the results may advance scientific knowledge tremendously and, as you say, it will also advance morality.'

Alexander said, 'And, of course, Alice and I will drink the punch, too.'

Alice said, 'Oh, Alexander, surely such love as ours needs no artificial aid.'

'But it would not be artificial, my soul's own. According to the professor, your love began as a result of just such a hormonal effect, induced, I admit, by more customary methods.'

Alice blushed rosily. 'But then, my only love, why the need for the repetition?'

'To place us beyond all vicissitudes of Fate, my cherished one.'

'Surely, my adored, you don't doubt my love.'

'No, my heart's charmer, but –'

'*But?* Is it that you do not trust me, Alexander?'

'Of course I trust you, Alice, but –'

'*But?* Again but!' Alice rose, furious. 'If you cannot trust me, sir, perhaps I had better leave –' And she did leave indeed, while the two men stared after her, stunned.

Professor Johns said, 'I am afraid my hormone has, quite indirectly, been the occasion of spoiling a marriage rather than of causing one.'

Alexander swallowed miserably, but his pride upheld him. 'She will come back,' he said, hollowly. 'A love such as ours is not so easily broken.'

The Senior Dance was, of course, the event of the year. The young men shone and the young ladies glittered. The music lilted and the dancing feet touched the ground only at intervals. Joy was unrestrained.

Or, rather, it was unrestrained in most cases. Alexander Dexter stood in one corner, eyes hard, expression icily bleak. Straight and handsome he might be, but no young woman approached him. He was known to belong to Alice Sanger, and under such circumstances, no college girl would dream of poaching. Yet where was Alice?

She had not come with Alexander and Alexander's pride prevented him from searching for her. From under grim eyelids, he could only watch the circulating couples cautiously.

Professor Johns, in formal clothes that did not fit although made to measure, approached him. He said, 'I will add my hormone to the punch shortly before the midnight toast. Is Mr. Nitely still here?'

'I saw him a moment ago. In his capacity as chaperon he was busily engaged in making certain that the proper distance between dancing couples was maintained. Four fingers, I believe, at the point of closest approach. Mr. Nitely was most diligently making the necessary measurements.'

'Very good. Oh, I had neglected to ask: Is the punch alcoholic? Alcohol would affect the workings of the amatogenic principle adversely.'

Alexander, despite his sore heart, found spirit to deny the unintended slur upon his class. 'Alcholic, Professor? This punch is made along those principles firmly adhered to by all young college students. It contains only the purest of fruit juices, refined sugar, and a certain quantity of lemon peel – enough to stimulate but not inebriate.'

'Good,' said the professor. 'Now I have added to the hormone a sedative designed to put our experimental subjects to sleep for a short time while the hormone works. Once they awaken, the first individual each sees – that is, of course, of the opposite sex – will inspire that individual with a pure and noble ardor that can end only in marriage.'

Then, since it was nearly midnight, he made his way through the happy couples, all dancing at four-fingers distance, to the punch bowl.

Alexander, depressed nearly to tears, stepped out to the balcony. In doing so, he just missed Alice, who entered the ballroom from the balcony by another door.

'Midnight,' called out a happy voice. 'Toast! Toast! Toast to the life ahead of us.'

They crowded about the punch bowl; the little glasses were passed round.

'To the life ahead of us,' they cried out and, with all the enthusiasm of young college students, downed the fiery mixture of pure fruit juices, sugar, and lemon peel, with – of course – the professor's sedated amatogenic principle.

As the fumes rose to their brains, they slowly crumpled to the floor.

Alice stood there alone, still holding her drink, eyes wet with unshed tears. 'Oh, Alexander, Alexander, though you doubt, yet

are you my only love. You wish me to drink and I shall drink.'
Then she, too, sank gracefully downward.

Nicholas Nitely had gone in search of Alexander, for whom
his warm heart was concerned. He had seen him arrive without
Alice and he could only assume that a lovers' quarrel had taken
place. Nor did he feel any dismay at leaving the party to its own
devices. These were not wild youngsters, but college boys and
girls of good family and gentle upbringing. They could be
trusted to the full to observe the four-finger limit, as he well
knew.

He found Alexander on the balcony, staring moodily out at
a star-riddled sky.

'Alexander, my boy.' He put his hand on the young man's
shoulder. 'This is not like you. To give way so to depression,
Chut, my young friend, chut.'

Alexander's head bowed at the sound of the good old man's
voice. 'It is unmanly, I know, but I yearn for Alice. I have been
cruel to her and I am justly treated now. And yet, Mr. Nitely, if
you could but know –' He placed his clenched fist on his chest,
next his heart. He could say no more.

Nitely said, sorrowfully, 'Do you think because I am unmarried that I am unacquainted with the softer emotions? Be
undeceived. Time was when I, too, knew love and heartbreak.
But do not do as I did once and allow pride to prevent your reunion. Seek her out, my boy, seek her out and apologize. Do not
allow yourself to become a solitary old bachelor such as I, myself. – But, tush, I am puling.'

Alexander's back had straightened. 'I will be guided by you,
Mr. Nitely. I will seek her out.'

'Then go on in. For shortly before I came out, I believe I saw
her there.'

Alexander's heart leaped. 'Perhaps she searches for me even
now. I will go – But, no. Go you first, Mr. Nitely, while I stay
behind to recover myself. I would not have her see me a prey to
womanish tears.'

'Of course, my boy.'

Nitely stopped at the door into the ballroom in astonishment.
Had a universal catastrophe struck all low? Fifty couples were
lying on the floor, some heaped together most indecorously.

But before he could make up his mind to see if the nearest were dead, to sound the fire alarm, to call the police, to anything, they were rousing and struggling to their feet.

Only one still remained. A lonely girl in white, one arm outstretched gracefully beneath her fair head. It was Alice Sanger and Nitely hastened to her, oblivious to the rising clamor about him.

He sank to his knees. 'Miss Sanger. My dear Miss Sanger. Are you hurt?'

She opened her beautiful eyes slowly, and said, 'Mr. Nitely! I never realized you were such a vision of loveliness.'

'I?' Nitely started back with horror, but she had now risen to her feet and there was a light in her eyes such as Nitely had not seen in a maiden's eyes for thirty years – and then only weakly.

She said, 'Mr. Nitely, surely you will not leave me?'

'No, no,' said Nitely, confused. 'If you need me, I shall stay.'

'I need you. I need you with all my heart and soul. I need you as a thirsty flower needs the morning dew. I need you as Thisbe of old needed Pyramus.'

Nitely, still backing away, looked about hastily, to see if anyone could be hearing this unusual declaration, but no one seemed to be paying any attention. As nearly as he could make out, the air was filled with other declarations of similar sort, some being even more forceful and direct.

His back was up against a wall, and Alice approached him so closely as to break the four-finger rule to smithereens. She broke, in fact, the no-finger rule, and at the resulting mutual pressure, a certain indefinable something seemed to thud away within Nitely.

'Miss Sanger. Please.'

'Miss Sanger? Am I Miss Sanger to you?' exclaimed Alice, passionately. 'Mr. Nitely! Nicholas! Make me your Alice, your own. Marry me. Marry me!'

All around there was the cry of 'Marry me. Marry me!' and young men and women crowded around Nitely, for they knew well that he was a Justice of the Peace. They cried out, 'Marry us, Mr. Nitely. Marry us!'

He could only cry in return, 'I must get you all licenses.'

They parted to let him leave on that errand of mercy. Only Alice followed him.

Nitely met Alexander at the door of the balcony and turned

him back toward the open and fresh air. Professor Johns came at that moment to join them all.

Nitely said, 'Alexander. Professor Johns. The most extraordinary thing has occurred –'

'Yes,' said the professor, his mild face beaming with joy. 'The experiment has been a success. The principle is far more effective on the human being, in fact, than on any of my experimental animals.' Noting Nitely's confusion, he explained what had occurred in brief sentences.

Nitely listened and muttered, 'Strange, strange. There is a certain elusive familiarity about this.' He pressed his forehead with the knuckles of both hands, but it did not help.

Alexander approached Alice gently, yearning to clasp her to his strong bosom, yet knowing that no gently nurtured girl could consent to such an expression of emotion from one who had not yet been forgiven.

He said, 'Alice, my lost love, if in your heart you could find –'

But she shrank from him, avoiding his arms though they were outstretched only in supplication. She said, 'Alexander, I drank the punch. It was your wish.'

'You needn't have. I was wrong, wrong.'

'But I did, and oh, Alexander, I can never be yours.'

'Never be mine? But what does this mean?'

And Alice, seizing Nitely's arm, clutched it avidly. 'My soul is intertwined indissolubly with that of Mr. Nitely, of Nicholas, I mean. My passion for him – that is, my passion for marriage with him – cannot be withstood. It racks my being.'

'You are false?' cried Alexander, unbelieving.

'You are cruel to say "false",' said Alice, sobbing. 'I cannot help it.'

'No, indeed,' said Professor Johns, who had been listening to this in the greatest consternation, after having made his explanation to Nitely. 'She could scarcely help it. It is simply an endocrinological manifestation.'

'Indeed that is so,' said Nitely, who was struggling with endocrinological manifestations of his own. 'There, there, my – my dear.' He patted Alice's head in a most fatherly way and when she held her enticing face up toward his, swooningly, he considered whether it might not be a fatherly thing – nay, even a neighborly thing – to press those lips with his own, in pure fashion.

But Alexander, out of his heart's despair, cried, 'You are false, false – false as Cressid,' and rushed from the room.

And Nitely would have gone after him, but that Alice had seized him about the neck and bestowed upon his slowly melting lips a kiss that was not daughterly in the least.

It was not even neighborly.

They arrived at Nitely's small bachelor cottage with its chaste sign of JUSTICE OF THE PEACE in Old English letters, its air of melancholy peace, its neat serenity, its small stove on which the small kettle was quickly placed by Nitely's left hand (his right arm being firmly in the clutch of Alice, who, with a shrewdness beyond her years, chose that as one sure method of rendering impossible a sudden bolt through the door on his part).

Nitely's study could be seen through the open door of the dining room, its walls lined with gentle books of scholarship and joy.

Again Nitely's hand (his left hand) went to his brow. 'My dear,' he said to Alice, 'it is amazing the way – if you would release your hold the merest trifle, my child, so that circulation might be restored – the way in which I persist in imagining that all this has taken place before.'

'Surely never before, my dear Nicholas,' said Alice, bending her fair head upon his shoulder, and smiling at him with a shy tenderness that made her beauty as bewitching as moonlight upon still waters, 'could there have been so wonderful a modern-day magician as our wise Professor Johns, so up-to-date a sorcerer.'

'So up-to-date a –' Nitely had started so voilently as to life the fair Alice a full inch from the floor. 'Why, surely that must be it. Dickens take me, if that's not it.' (For on rare occasions, and under the stress of overpowering emotions, Nitely used strong language.)

'Nicholas. What is it? You frighten me, my cherubic one.'

But Nitely walked rapidly into his study, and she was forced to run with him. His face was white, his lips firm, as he reached for a volume from the shelves and reverently blew the dust from it.

'Ah,' he said with contrition, 'how I have neglected the innocent joys of my younger days. My child, in view of this continuing incapacity of my right arm, would you be so kind as to turn the pages until I tell you to stop?'

Together they managed, in such a tableau of preconnubial bliss as is rarely seen, he holding the book with his left hand, she turning the pages slowly with her right.

'I am right!' Nitely said with sudden force. 'Professor Johns, my dear fellow, do come here. This is the most amazing coincidence – a frightening example of the mysterious unfelt power that must sport with us on occasion for some hidden purpose.'

Professor Johns, who had prepared his own tea and was sipping it patiently, as befitted a discreet gentleman of intellectual habit in the presence of two ardent lovers who had suddenly retired to the next room, called out, 'Surely you do not wish my presence?'

'But I do, sir. I would fain consult one of your scientific attainments.'

'But you are in a position –'

Alice screamed, faintly, 'Professor!'

'A thousand pardons, my dear,' said Professor Johns, entering. 'My cobwebby old mind is filled with ridiculous fancies. It is long since I –' and he pulled mightily at his tea (which he had made strong) and was himself again at once.

'Professor,' said Nitely. 'This dear child referred to you as an up-to-date sorcerer and that turned my mind instantly to Gilbert and Sullivan's *The Sorcerer*.'

'What,' asked Professor Johns, mildly, 'are Gilbert and Sullivan?'

Nitely cast a devout glance upward, as though with the intention of gauging the direction of the inevitable thunderbolt and dodging. He said in a hoarse whisper, 'Sir William Schwenck Gilbert and Sir Arthur Sullivan wrote, respectively, the words and music of the greatest musical comedies the world has ever seen. One of these is entitled *The Sorcerer*. In it, too, a philtre was used: a highly moral one which did not affect married people, but which did manage to deflect the young heroine away from her handsome young lover and into the arms of an elderly man.'

'And,' asked Professor Johns, 'were matters allowed to remain so?'

'Well, no. – Really, my dear, the movements of your fingers

in the region of the nape of my neck, while giving rise to undeniably pleasurable sensations, *do* rather distract me. – There is a reunion of the young lovers, Professor.'

'Ah,' said Professor Johns. 'Then in view of the close resemblance of the fictional plot to real life, perhaps the solution in the play will help point the way to the reunion of Alice and Alexander. At least, I presume you do not wish to go through life with one arm permanently useless.'

Alice said, 'I have no wish to be reunited. I want only my own Nicholas.'

'There is something', said Nitely, 'to be said for that refreshing point of view, but tush – youth must be served. There *is* a solution in the play, Professor Johns, and it is for that reason that I most particularly wanted to talk to you.' He smiled with a gentle benevolence. 'In the play, the effects of the potion were completely neutralized by the actions of the gentleman who administered the potion in the first place: the gentleman, in other words, analogous to yourself.'

'And those actions were?'

'Suicide! Simply that! In some manner unexplained by the authors, the effect of this suicide was to break the sp –'

But by now Professor Johns had recovered his equilibrium and said in the most sepulchrally forceful tone that could be imagined, 'My dear sir, may I state instantly that, despite my affection for the young persons involved in this sad dilemma, I cannot under any circumstances consent to self-immolation. Such a procedure might be extremely efficacious in connection with love potions of ordinary vintage, but my amatongenic principle, I assure you, would be completely unaffected by my death.'

Nitely sighed. 'I feared that. As a matter of fact, between ourselves, it was a very poor ending for the play, perhaps the poorest in the canon,' and he looked up briefly in mute apology to the spirit of William S. Gilbert. 'It was pulled out of a hat. It had not been properly foreshadowed earlier in the play. It punished an individual who did not deserve the punishment. In short, it was, alas, completely unworthy of Gilbert's powerful genius.'

Professor Johns said, 'Perhaps it was not Gilbert. Perhaps some bungler had interfered and botched the job.'

'There is no record of that.'

But Professor Johns, his scientific mind keenly aroused by an unsolved puzzle, said at once, 'We can test this. Let us study the mind of this – this Gilbert. He wrote other plays, did he?'

'Fourteen, in collaboration with Sullivan.'

'Were there endings that resolved analogous situations in ways which were more appropriate?'

Nitely nodded, 'One, certainly. There was *Ruddigore*.'

'Who was he?'

'Ruddigore is a place. The main character is revealed as the true bad baronet of Ruddigore and is, of course, under a curse.'

'To be sure,' muttered Professor Johns, who realized that such an eventuality frequently befell bad baronets and was even inclined to think it served them right.

Nitely said, 'The curse compelled him to commit one crime or more each day. Were one day to pass without a crime, he would inevitably die in agonizing torture.'

'How horrible,' murmured the soft-hearted Alice.

'Naturally,' said Nitely, 'no one can think up a crime each day, so our hero was forced to use his ingenuity to circumvent the curse.'

'How?'

'He reasoned thus: If he delibertately refused to commit a crime, he was courting death by his own act. In other words, he was attempting suicide, and attempting suicide is, of course a crime – and so he fulfills the conditions of the curse.'

'I see. I see,' said Professor Johns. 'Gilbert obviously believes in solving matters by carrying them forward to their logical conclusions.' He closed his eyes, and his noble brow clearly bulged with the numerous intense thought waves it contained.

He opened them. 'Nitely, old chap, when was *The Sorcerer* first produced?'

'In eighteen hundred and seventy-seven.'

'Then that is it, my dear fellow. In eighteen seventy-seven, we were faced with the Victorian age. The institution of marriage was not to be made sport of on the stage. It could not be made a comic matter for the sake of the plot. Marriage was holy, spiritual, a sacrament –'

'Enough', said Nitely, 'of this apostrophe. What is in your mind?'

'Marriage. Marry the girl, Nitely. Have all your couples marry, and that at once. I'm sure that was Gilbert's original intention.'

'But that', said Nitely, who was strangely attracted by the notion, 'is precisely what we are trying to avoid.'

'I am not,' said Alice, stoutly (though she was not stout, but, on the contrary, enchantingly lithe and slender).

Professor Johns said, 'Don't you see? Once each couple is married, the amatogenic principle – which does not affect married people – loses its power over them. Those who would have been in love without the aid of the principle remain in love; those who would not are no longer in love – and consequently apply for an annulment.'

'Good heavens,' said Nitely. 'How admirably simple. Of course! Gilbert must have intended that until a shocked producer or theater manager – a bungler, as you say – forced the change.'

'And did it work?' I asked. 'After all, you said quite distinctly that the professor had said its effect on married couples was only to inhibit extra-marital re –'

'It worked,' said Nitely, ignoring my comment. A tear trembled on his eyelid, but whether it was induced by memories or by the fact that he was on his fourth gin and tonic, I could not tell.

'It worked,' he said. 'Alice and I were married, and our marriage was almost instantly annulled by mutual consent on the grounds of the use of undue pressure. And yet, because of the incessant chaperoning to which we were subjected, the incidence of undue pressure between ourselves was, unfortunately, virtually nil.' He sighed again. 'At any rate, Alice and Alexander were married soon after and she is now, I understand, as a result of various concomitant events, expecting a child.'

He withdrew his eyes from the deep recesses of what was left of his drink and gasped with sudden alarm. 'Dear me! She again.'

I looked up, startled. A vision in pastel blue was in the doorway. Imagine, if you will, a charming face made for kissing; a lovely body made for loving.

She called, 'Nicholas! Wait!'

'Is that Alice?' I asked.

'No, no. This is someone else entirely: a completely different story. – But I must not remain here.'

He rose and, with an agility remarkable in one so advanced in years and weight, made his way through a window. The fe-

minine vision of desirability, with an agility only slightly less remarkable, followed.

I shook my head in pity and sympathy. Obviously, the poor man was continually plagued by these wondrous things of beauty who, for one reason or another, were enamored of him. At the thought of this horrible fate, I downed my own drink at a gulp and considered the odd fact that no such difficulties had ever troubled me.

And at that thought, strange to tell, I ordered another drink savagely, and a scatological exclamation rose, unbidden, to my lips.

*Not long after the appearance of 'The Up-to-Date Sorcerer,'
Mr. Boucher retired as editor of F & SF, and was succeeded in
the post by Robert P. Mills.*

*Mr. Mills proceeded to do me the largest single favor of my
writing life since Mr. Campbell had started the discussion that
had led to 'Nightfall'. Mr. Mills asked me to write a monthly
column on science for F & SF and I complied at once. Since the
November 1958 issue, in which my first column appeared, I have
kept right on going, month after month, and, as I write this, I
am about to celebrate my tenth anniversary as monthly column-
ist for the magazine.*

*Of all the writing I do, fiction, non-fiction, adult, or juvenile,
these F & SF articles are by far the most fun, and in them, during Mr. Mills' tenure I never referred to him as other than
the 'Kindly Editor'.*

*Anyway, over lunch one day, Mr. Mills said he had seen the
name Lefkowitz on several different and unrelated occasions
that day, which struck him as a curious coincidence. Could I
make a story out of it? In my usual offhand manner, I said,
'Sure!' and gave it a little thought.*

*The result was a story that served as a tribute to Mr. Boucher,
too. He was, you see, a devout Catholic. (I must say 'was', for
he died in April 1968 to the heartfelt grief of all who knew him.
He was so kind a man that he was loved by the very authors
he rejected, even while he was rejecting them, and there simply
isn't any harsher test of true love than that.) And because Mr.
Boucher was a sincere Catholic, there was very often a faintly
Catholic air about F & SF under his leadership; always a pleasant and liberal one, though, for that was the kind of man he
was.*

*So I thought that as my tribute to Mr. Boucher's editorship, I
would try my hand at that kind of flavor myself. I couldn't
handle it Catholic-fashion, of course, for I am not Catholic. I
did it the only way I could manage, and wrote a Jewish story –
the only Jewish story it ever occurred to me to write, I think.*

*And I made Mr. Mills' remark about Lefkowitz become 'Unto
the Fourth Generation.'*

First appearance – The Magazine of Fantasy and Science
Fiction, *April 1959. ©, 1959 by Mercury Press, Inc.*

UNTO THE FOURTH GENERATION

At ten of noon, Sam Marten hitched his way out of the taxi-cab, trying as usual to open the door with one hand, hold his briefcase in another and reach for his wallet with a third. Having only two hands, he found it a difficult job and, again as usual, he thudded his knee against the cab-door and found himself still groping uselessly for his wallet when his feet touched pavement.

The traffic of Madison Avenue inched past. A red truck slowed its crawl reluctantly, then moved on with a rasp as the light changed. White script on its side informed an unresponsive world that its ownership was that of *F. Lewkowitz and Sons, Wholesale Clothiers.*

Levkowich, thought Marten with brief inconsequence, and finally fished out his wallet. He cast an eye on the meter as he clamped his briefcase under his arm. Dollar sixty-five, make that twenty cents more as a tip, two singles gone would leave him only one for emergencies, better break a fiver.

'Okay,' he said, 'take out one-eighty-five, bud.'

'Thanks,' said the cabbie with mechanical insincerity and made the change.

Marten crammed three singles into his wallet, put it away, lifted his briefcase and breasted the human currents on the sidewalk to reach the glass doors of the building.

Levkovich? he thought sharply, and stopped. A passerby glanced off his elbow.

'Sorry,' muttered Marten, and made for the door again.

Levkovich? That wasn't what the sign on the truck had said. The name had read Lewkowitz, Loo-koh-itz. Why did he *think* Levkovich? Even with his college German in the near past changing the w's to v's, where did he get the '–ich' from?

Levkovich? He shrugged the whole matter away roughly. Give it a chance and it would haunt him like a Hit Parade tinkle.

Concentrate on business. He was here for a luncheon appointment with this man, Naylor. He was here to turn a contract into an account and begin, at twenty-three, the smooth business rise which, as he planned it, would marry him to Elizabeth in two years and make him a paterfamilias in the suburbs in ten.

He entered the lobby with grim firmness and headed for the banks of elevators, his eye catching at the white-lettered directory as he passed.

It was a silly habit of his to want to catch suite numbers as he passed, without slowing, or (heaven forbid) coming to a full halt. With no break in his progress, he told himself, he could maintain the impression of belonging, of knowing his way around, and that was important to a man whose job involved dealing with other human beings.

Kulin-etts was what he wanted, and the word amused him. A firm specializing in the production of minor kitchen gadgets, striving manfully for a name that was significant, feminine, and coy, all at once –

His eyes snagged at the M's and moved upward as he walked. Mandel, Lusk, Lippert Publishing Company (two full floors), Lafkowitz, Kulin-etts. There it was – 1024. Tenth floor. OK.

And then, after all, he came to a dead halt, turned in reluctant fascination, returned to the directory, and stared at it as though he were an out-of-towner.

Lafkowitz?

What kind of spelling was that?

It was clear enough. Lafkowitz, Henry J., 701. With an A. That was no good. That was useless.

Useless? Why useless? He gave his head one violent shake as though to clear it of mist. Damn it, what did he care how it was spelled? He turned away, frowning and angry, and hastened to an elevator door, which closed just before he reached it, leaving him flustered.

Another door opened and he stepped in briskly. He tucked his briefcase under his arm and tried to look bright alive – junior executive in its finest sense. He had to make an impression on Alex Naylor, with whom so far he had communicated only by telephone. If he was going to brood about Lewkowitzes and Lafkowitzes –

The elevator slid noiselessly to a halt at seven. A youth in shirtsleeves stepped off, balancing what looked like a desk-drawer in which were three containers of coffee and three sandwiches.

Then, just as the doors began closing, frosted glass with black lettering loomed before Marten's eyes. It read: 701 – HENRY J. LEFKOWITZ – IMPORTER and was pinched off by the inexorable coming together of the elevator doors.

Marten leaned forward in excitement. It was his impulse to say: Take me back down to 7.

But there were others in the car. And after all, he had no reason.

Yet there was a tingle of excitement within him. The Directory *had* been wrong. It wasn't A, it was E. Some fool of a nonspelling menial with a packet of small letters to go on the board and only one hind foot to do it with.

Lefkowitz. Still not right, though.

Again, he shook his head. Twice. Not right for what?

The elevator stopped at ten and Marten got off.

Alex Naylor of Kulin-etts turned out to be a bluff, middle-aged man with a shock of white hair, a ruddy complexion, and a broad smile. His palms were dry and rough, and he shook hands with a considerable pressure, putting his left hand on Marten's shoulder in an earnest display of friendliness.

He said, 'Be with you in two minutes. How about eating right here in the building? Excellent restaurant, and they've got a boy who makes a good martini. That sound all right?'

'Fine. Fine.' Marten pumped up enthusiasm from a some-how-clogged reservoir.

It was nearer ten minutes than two, and Marten waited with the usual uneasiness of a man in a strange office. He stared at the upholstery on the chairs and at the little cubby-hole within which a young and bored switchboard operator sat. He gazed at the pictures on the wall and even made a half-hearted attempt to glance through a trade journal on the table next to him.

What he did not do was think of Lev —

He did *not* think of it.

The restaurant was good, or it would have been good if Marten had been perfectly at ease. Fortunately, he was freed of the necessity of carrying the burden of the conversation. Naylor talked rapidly and loudly, glanced over the menu with a practiced eye, recommended the Eggs Benedict, and commented on the weather and the miserable traffic situation.

On occasion, Marten tried to snap out of it, to lose that edge of fuzzed absence of mind. But each time the restlessness would return. Something was wrong. The name was wrong. It stood in the way of what he had to do.

With main force, he tried to break through the madness. In

sudden verbal clatter, he led the conversation into the subject of wiring. It was reckless of him. There was no proper foundation; the transition was too abrupt.

But the lunch had been a good one; the dessert was on its way; and Naylor responded nicely.

He admitted dissatisfaction with existing arrangements. Yes, he had been looking into Marten's firm and, actually, it seemed to him that, yes, there was a chance, a good chance, he thought, that –

A hand came down on Naylor's shoulder as a man passed behind his chair. 'How's the boy, Alex?'

Naylor looked up, grin ready-made and flashing. 'Hey, Lefk, how's business?'

'Can't complain. See you at the –' He faded into the distance.

Marten wasn't listening. He felt his knees trembling, as he half-rose. 'Who was that man?' he asked, intensely. It sounded more peremptory than he intended.

'Who? Lefk? Jerry Lefkovitz. You know him?' Naylor stared with cool surprise at his lunch companion.

'No. How do you spell his name?'

'L-E-F-K-O-V-I-T-Z, I think. Why?'

'With a V?'

'An F. . . . Oh, there's a V in it, too.' Most of the good nature had left Naylor's face.

Marten drove on. 'There's a Lefkowitz in the building. With a W. You know, Lef-COW-itz.'

'Oh?'

'Room 701. This is not the same one?'

'Jerry doesn't work in this building. He's got a place across the street. I don't know this other one. This is a big building, you know. I don't keep tabs on every one in it. What is all this, anyway?'

Marten shook his head and sat back. He didn't know what all this was, anyway. Or at least, if he did, it was nothing he dared explain. Could he say: I'm being haunted by all manner of Lefkowitzes today.

He said, 'We were talking about wiring.'

Naylor said, 'Yes. Well, as I said, I've been considering your company. I've got to talk it over with the production boys, you understand. I'll let you know.'

'Sure,' said Marten, infinitely depressed. Naylor wouldn't let him know. The whole thing was shot.

And yet, through and beyond his depression, there was still that restlessness.

The hell with Naylor. All Marten wanted was to break this up and get on with it. (*Get on with what?* But the question was only a whisper. Whatever did the questioning inside him was ebbing away, dying down . . .)

The lunch frayed to an ending. If they had greeted each other like long-separated friends at last reunited, they parted like strangers.

Marten felt only relief.

He left with pulses thudding, threading through the tables, out of the haunted building, onto the haunted street.

Haunted? Madison Avenue at 1.20 p.m. in an early fall afternoon with the sun shining brightly and ten thousand men and women be-hiving its long straight stretch.

But Marten felt the haunting. He tucked his briefcase under his arm and headed desperately northward. A last sigh of the normal within him warned him he had a three o'clock appointment on 36th Street. Never mind. He headed uptown. Northward.

At 54th Street, he crossed Madison and walked west, came abruptly to a halt and looked upward.

There was a sign on the window, three stories up. He could make it out clearly: A. S. LEFKOWICH, CERTIFIED ACCOUNTANT.

It had an F and an EW, but it was the first '-ich' ending he had seen. The first one. He was getting closer. He turned north again on Fifth Avenue, hurrying through the unreal streets of an unreal city, panting with the chase of something, while the crowds about him began to fade.

A sign in a ground floor window, M. R. LEFKOWICH, M.D.

A small gold-leaf semi-circle of letters in a candy-store window: JACOB LEVKOW.

(Half a name, he thought savagely. Why is he disturbing me with half a name?)

The streets were empty now except for the varying clan of Lefkowitz, Levkowitz, Lefkowicz to stand out in the vacuum.

He was dimly aware of the park ahead, standing out in painted motionless green. He turned west. A piece of newspaper fluttered at the corner of his eyes, the only movement in a dead world. He veered, stooped, and picked it up, without slackening his pace.

It was in Yiddish, a torn half-page.

He couldn't read it. He couldn't make out the blurred Hebrew letters, and could not have read it if they were clear. But one word was clear. It stood out in dark letters in the center of the page, each letter clear in its every serif. And it said Lefkovitsch, he knew, and as he said it to himself, he placed its accent on the second syllable: Lef-KUH-vich.

He let the paper flutter away and entered the empty park.

The trees were still and the leaves hung in odd, suspended attitudes. The sunlight was a dead weight upon him and gave no warmth.

He was running, but his feet kicked up no dust and a tuft of grass on which he placed his weight did not bend.

And there on a bench was an old man; the only man in the desolate park. He wore a dark felt cap, with a visor shading his eyes. From underneath it, tufts of gray hair protruded. His grizzled beard reached the uppermost button of his rough jacket. His old trousers were patched, and a strip of burlap was wrapped about each worn and shapeless shoe .

Marten stopped. It was difficult to breathe. He could only say one word and he used it to ask his question: 'Levkovich?'

He stood there, while the old man rose slowly to his feet; brown old eyes peering close.

'Marten,' he sighed. 'Samuel Marten. You have come.' The words sounded with an effect of double exposure, for under the English, Marten heard the faint sigh of a foreign tongue Under the 'Samuel' was the unheard shadow of a 'Schmu-el'.

The old man's rough, veined hands reached out, then withdrew as though he were afraid to touch. 'I have been looking but there are so many people in this wilderness of a city-that-is-to-come. So many Martins and Martines and Mortons and Mertons. I stopped at last when I found greenery, but for a moment only – I would not commit the sin of losing faith. And then you came.'

'It is I,' said Marten, and knew it was. 'And you are Phinehas Levkovich. Why are we here?'

'I am Phinehas ben Jehudah, assigned the name Levkovich

by the ukase of the Tsar that ordered family names for all. And we are here,' the old man said, softly, 'because I prayed. When I was already old, Leah, my only daughter, the child of my old age, left for America with her husband, left the knouts of the old for the hope of the new. And my sons died, and Sarah, the wife of my bosom, was long dead and I was alone. And the time came when I, too, must die. But I had not seen Leah since her leaving for the far country and word had come but rarely. My soul yearned that I might see sons born unto her; sons of my seed; sons in whom my soul might yet live and not die.'

His voice was steady and the soundless shadow of sound beneath his words was the stately roll of an ancient language.

'And I was answered and two hours were given me that I might see the first son of my line to be born in a new land and in a new time. My daughter's daughter's daughter's son, have I found you, then, amidst the splendor of this city?'

'But why the search? Why not have brought us together at once?'

'Because there is pleasure in the hope of the seeking, my son,' said the old man, radiantly, 'and in the delight of the finding. I was given two hours in which I might seek, two hours in which I might find ... and behold, thou art here, and I have found that which I had not looked to see in life.' His voice was old, caressing. 'Is it well with thee, my son?'

'It is well, my father, now that I have found thee,' said Marten, and dropped to his knees. 'Give me thy blessing, my father, that it may be well with me all the days of my life, and with the maid whom I am to take to wife and the little ones yet to be born of my seed and thine.'

He felt the old hand resting lightly on his head and there was only the soundless whisper.

Marten rose.

The old man's eyes gazed into his yearningly. Were they losing focus?

'I go to my fathers now in peace, my son,' said the old man, and Marten was alone in the empty park.

There was an instant of renewing motion, of the Sun taking up its interrupted task, of the wind reviving, and even with that first instant of sensation, all slipped back –

At ten of noon, Sam Marten hitched his way out of the taxi-cab, and found himself groping uselessly for his wallet while traffic inched on.

A red truck slowed, then moved on. A white script on its side announced: *F. Lewkowitz and Sons, Wholesale Clothiers.* ...

Marten didn't see it. Yet somehow he knew that all would be well with him. Somehow, as never before, he knew. ...

This one is complicated. It goes back to 1938–39 when, for some half a dozen issues or so, a magazine I won't name tried to make a go of what I can only call 'spicy science fiction stories.' Considering the sexual freedom allowed the writers of today, those old spicy s.f. stories read like 'The Bobbsey Twins in Outer Space' now, but they were sizzlers to the magazine's few readers then.

The stories dealt very heavily with the hot passion of alien monsters for Earth-women. Clothes were always getting ripped off and breasts were described in a variety of elliptical phrases. (Yes, I know that's a pun.) The magazine died a deserved death, not so much for its sex and sadism, as for the deadly sameness of its stories and the abysmal quality of its 'writing.'

The curtain falls, and rises again in 1960. The magazine Playboy decided to have a little fun with science fiction. They published an article entitled 'Girls for the Slime God' in which they pretended (good-naturedly) that all science fiction was sex and sadism. They could find very little real stuff to satirize, however, for until 1960 there was no branch of literature anywhere (except perhaps for the children's stories in Sunday school bulletins) as puritanical as science fiction. Since 1960, to be sure, sexual libertarianism has penterated even science fiction.

Playboy therefore had to illustrate its article with the funny-sexy covers of fictitious magazines and had to draw all its quotations from only one source – that 1938–39 magazine I mentioned above.

Cele Goldsmith, the editor of Amazing Stories, *read the article and called me at once. She suggested I write a story entitled 'Playboy and the Slime God' satirizing the satire. I was strongly tempted to do so for several reasons:*

1) Miss Goldsmith had to be seen to be believed. She was the only science fiction editor I've ever seen who looked like a show girl, and I happen to be aesthetically affected (or something) by show-girl types.

2) I take science fiction seriously and I was annoyed that that 1938–39 magazine should have given Playboy a handle for satire. I wanted to satire back at them.

3) I quickly thought up exactly what I wanted to say.

So I wrote 'Playboy and the Slime God' using some of the same quotes that Playboy had used and trying to show what an encounter between sex-interested aliens and an Earth-woman might really be like. (I might say that Miss Goldsmith wrote the final three paragraphs of the story. I had a quite pretentious ending and Miss Goldsmith's was much better. So I let it stand, not only in the magazine, but here.)

The title was a problem, though. It's disgusting. When the late (alas!) Groff Conklin, who was one of the most indefatigable anthologizers in the business, was considering the story for one of his collections, he asked rather piteously if I had an alternate title. 'You bet!' I said. 'How about "What Is This Thing Called Love?"'

Mr. Conklin was delighted and so was I, and that is the title that he used, and the one that I am now using.

First appearance – Amazing Stories, March 1961, under the title 'Playboy and the Slime God.' Copyright © 1961, by Ziff-Davis Publishing Company.

WHAT IS THIS THING CALLED LOVE?

'But these are two species,' said Captain Garm, peering closely at the creatures that had been brought up from the planet below. His optic organs adjusted focus to maximum sharpness, bulging outwards as they did so. The color patch above them gleamed in quick flashes.

Botax felt warmly comfortable to be following color-changes once again, after months in a spy cell on the planet, trying to make sense out of the modulated sound waves emitted by the natives. Communication by flash was almost like being home in the far-off Perseus arm of the Galaxy. 'Not two species,' he said, 'but two forms of one species.'

'Nonsense, they look quite different. Vaguely Perse-like, thank the Entity, and not as disgusting in appearance as so many outforms are. Reasonable shape, recognizable limbs. But no colorpatch. Can they speak?'

'Yes, Captain Garm,' Botax indulged in a discreetly disapproving prismatic interlude. 'The details are in my report. These creatures form sound waves by way of throat and mouth, something like complicated coughing. I have learned to do it myself.' He was quietly proud. 'It is very difficult.'

'It must be stomach-turning. Well, that accounts for their flat, unextensible eyes. Not to speak by color makes eyes largely useless. Meanwhile, how can you insist these are a single species? The one on the left is smaller and has longer tendrils, or whatever it is, and seems differently proportioned. It bulges where this other does not. Are they alive?'

'Alive but not at the moment conscious, Captain. They have been psycho-treated to repress fright in order that they might be studied easily.'

'But are they worth study? We are behind our schedule and have at least five worlds of greater moment than this one to check and explore. Maintaining a Time-stasis unit is expensive and I would like to return them and go on –'

But Botax's moist spindly body was fairly vibrating with anxiety. His tubular tongue flicked out and curved up and over his flat nose, while his eyes sucked inward. His splayed three-fingered hand made a gesture of negation as his speech went almost entirely into the deep red.

'Entity save us, Captain, for no world is of greater moment to us than this one. We may be facing a supreme crisis. These creatures could be the most dangerous life-forms in the Galaxy, Captain, just *because* there are two forms.'

'I don't follow you.'

'Captain, it has been my job to study this planet, and it has been most difficult, for it is unique. It is so unique that I can scarcely comprehend its facets. For instance, almost all life on the planet consists of species in two forms. There are no words to describe it, no concepts even. I can only speak of them as first form and second form. If I may use their sounds, the little one is called "female", and the big one, here, "male", so the creatures themselves are aware of the difference.'

Garm winced, 'What a disgusting means of communication.'

'And, Captain, in order to bring forth young, the two forms must cooperate.'

The Captain, who had bent forward to examine the specimens closely with an expression compounded of interest and revulsion, straightened at once. 'Cooperate? What nonsense is this? There is no more fundamental attribute of life than that each living creature bring forth its young in innermost communication with itself. What else makes life worth living?'

'The one form does bring forth life but the other form must cooperate.'

'How?'

'That has been difficult to determine. It is something very private and in my search through the available forms of literature I could find no exact and explicit description. But I have been able to make reasonable deductions.'

Garm shook his head. 'Ridiculous. Budding is the holiest, most private function in the world. On tens of thousands of worlds it is the same. As the great photo-bard, Levuline, said, "In budding-time, in budding time, in sweet, delightful budding time; when –" '

'Captain, you don't understand. This cooperation between forms brings about somehow (and I am not certain exactly how) a mixture and recombination of genes. It is a device by which in every generation, new combinations of characteristics are brought into existence. Variations are multiplied; mutated genes hastened into expression almost at once where under the usual budding system, millennia might pass first.'

'Are you trying to tell me that the genes from one individual can be combined with those of another? Do you know how completely ridiculous that is in the light of all the principles of cellular physiology?'

'It must be so,' said Botax nervously under the other's pop-eyed glare. 'Evolution is hastened. This planet is a riot of species. There are supposed to be a million and a quarter different species of creatures.'

'A dozen and a quarter more likely. Don't accept too completely what you read in the native literature.'

'I've seen dozens of radically different species myself in just a small area. I tell you, Captain, give these creatures a short space of time and they will mutate into intellects powerful enough to overtake us and rule the Galaxy.'

'Prove that this cooperation you speak of exists, Investigator, and I shall consider your contentions. If you cannot, I shall dismiss all your fancies as ridiculous and we will move on.'

'I can prove it.' Botax's color-flashes turned intensely yellow-green. 'The creatures of this world are unique in another way. They foresee advances they have not yet made, probably as a consequence of their belief in rapid change which, after all, they constantly witness. They therefore indulge in a type of literature involving the space-travel they have never developed. I have translated their term for the literature as "science-fiction". Now I have dealt in my readings almost exclusively with science-fiction, for there I thought, in their dreams and fancies, they would expose themselves and their danger to us. And it was from that science-fiction that I deduced the method of their inter-form cooperation.'

'How did you do that?'

'There is a periodical on this world which sometimes publishes science-fiction which is, however, devoted almost entirely to the various aspects of the cooperation. It does not speak entirely freely, which is annoying, but persists in merely hinting. Its name is nearly as I can put into flashes is "Recreationlad". The creature in charge, I deduce, is interested in nothing but inter-form cooperation and searches for it everywhere with a systematic and scientific intensity that has roused my awe. He has found instances of cooperation described in science-fiction and I let material in his periodical guide me. From the stories he instanced I have learned how to bring it about.

'And Captain, I beg of you, when the cooperation is accomplished and the young are brought forth before your eyes, give orders not to leave an atom of this world in existence.'

'Well,' said Captain Garm, wearily, 'bring them into full consciousness and do what you must do quickly.'

Marge Skidmore was suddenly completely aware of her surroundings. She remembered very clearly the elevated station at the beginning of twilight. It had been almost empty, one man standing near her, another at the other end of the platform. The approaching train had just made itself known as a faint rumble in the distance.

There had then come the flash, a sense of turning inside out, the half-seen vision of a spindly creature, dripping mucus, a rushing upward, and now –

'Oh, God,' she said, shuddering. 'It's still here. And there's another one, too.'

She felt a sick revulsion, but no fear. She was almost proud of herself for feeling no fear. The man next to her, standing quietly as she herself was, but still wearing a battered fedora, was the one that had been near her on the platform.

'They got you too?' she asked. 'Who else?'

Charlie Grimwold, feeling flabby and paunchy, tried to lift his hand to remove his hat and smooth the thin hair that broke up but did not entirely cover the skin of his scalp and found that it moved only with difficulty against a rubbery but hardening resistance. He let his hand drop and looked morosely at the thin-faced woman facing him. She was in her middle thirties, he decided, and her hair was nice and her dress fit well, but at the moment, he just wanted to be somewhere else and it did him no good at all that he had company; even female company.

He said, 'I don't know, lady. I was just standing on the station platform.'

'Me, too.'

'And then I see a flash. Didn't hear nothing. Now here I am. Must be little men from Mars or Venus or one of them places.'

Marge nodded vigorously, 'That's what I figure. A flying saucer? You scared?'

'No. That's funny, you know. I think maybe I'm going nuts or I *would* be scared.'

'Funny thing. I ain't scared, either. Oh, God, here comes one of them now. If he touches me, I'm going to scream. Look at those wiggly hands. And that wrinkled skin, all slimy; makes me nauseous.'

Botax approached gingerly and said, in a voice at once rasping and screechy, this being the closest he could come to imitating the native timbre, 'Creatures! We will not hurt you. But we must ask you if you would do us the favor of cooperating.'

'Hey, it talks!' said Charlie. 'What do you mean, cooperate?'

'Both of you. With each other,' said Botax.

'Oh?' He looked at Marge. 'You know what he means, lady?'

'Ain't got no idea whatsoever,' she answered loftily.

Botax said, 'What I mean –' and he used the short term he had once heard employed as a synonym for the process.

Marge turned red and said, 'What!' in the loudest scream she could manage. Both Botax and Captain Garm put their hands over their mid-regions to cover the auditory patches that trembled painfully with the decibels.

Marge went on rapidly, and nearly incoherently. 'Of all things. I'm a married woman, you. If my Ed was here, you'd hear from *him*. And you, wise guy,' she twisted toward Charlie against rubbery resistance, 'whoever you are, if you think –'

'Lady, lady,' said Charlie in uncomfortable desperation. 'It ain't my idea. I mean, far be it from me, you know, to turn down some lady, you know; but me, I'm married, too. I got three kids. Listen –'

Captain Garm said, 'What's happening, Investigator Botax? These cacophonous sounds are awful.'

'Well,' Botax flashed a short purple patch of embarrassment. 'This forms a complicated ritual. They are supposed to be reluctant at first. It heightens the subsequent result. After that initial stage, the skins must be removed.'

'They have to be *skinned*?'

'Not really skinned. Those are artificial skins that can be removed painlessly, and must be. Particularly in the smaller form.'

'All right, then. Tell it to remove the skins. Really, Botax, I don't find this pleasant.'

'I don't think I had better tell the smaller form to remove the skins. I think we had better follow the ritual closely. I have here sections of those space-travel tales which the man from the "Recreationlad" periodical spoke highly of. In those tales the skins are removed forcibly. Here is a description of an accident, for instance "which played havoc with the girl's dress, ripping it nearly off her slim body. For a second, he felt the warm firmness of her half-bared bosom against his cheek –" It goes on that way. You see, the ripping, the forcible removal, acts as a stimulus.'

'Bosom?' said the Captain. 'I don't recognize the flash.'

'I invented that to cover the meaning. It refers to the bulges on the upper dorsal region of the smaller form.'

'I see. Well, tell the larger one to rip the skins off the smaller one. What a dismal thing this is.'

Botax turned to Charlie. 'Sir,' he said, 'rip the girl's dress nearly off her slim body, will you? I will release you for the purpose.'

Marge's eyes widened and she twisted toward Charlie in instant outrage. 'Don't you dare do that, you. Don't you *dast touch* me, you sex maniac.'

'Me?' said Charlie plaintively. 'It ain't my idea. You think I go around ripping dresses? Listen,' he turned to Botax, 'I got a wife and three kids. She finds out I go around ripping dresses, I get clobbered. You know what my wife does when I just look at some dame? *Listen* –'

'Is he still reluctant?' said the Captain impatiently.

'Apparently,' said Botax. 'The strange surroundings, you know, may be extending that stage of the cooperation. Since I know this is unpleasant for you, I will perform this stage of the ritual myself. It is frequently written in the space-travel tales that an outer-world species performs the task. For instance, here,' and he riffled through his notes finding the one he wanted, 'they describe a very awful such species. The creatures on the planet have foolish notions you understand. It never occurs to them to imagine handsome individuals such as ourselves, with a fine mucous cover.'

'Go on! Go on! Don't take all day,' said the Captain.

'Yes, Captain. It says here that the extraterrestrial "came forward to where the girl stood. Shrieking hysterically, she was cradled in the monster's embrace. Talons ripped blindly at her body, tearing the kirtle away in rags." You see, the native creature is shrieking with stimulation as her skins are removed.'

'Then go ahead, Botax, remove it. But please, allow no shrieking. I'm trembling all over with the sound waves.'

Botax said politely to Marge, 'If you don't mind –'

One spatulate finger made as though to hook on to the neck of the dress.

Marge wiggled desperately. 'Don't touch. Don't touch! You'll get slime on it. Listen, this dress cost $24.95 at Ohrbach's. Stay away, you monster. Look at those eyes on him.' She was panting in her desperate efforts to dodge the groping, extraterrestrial hand. 'A slimy, bug-eyed monster, that's what he is. Listen, I'll take it off myself. Just don't touch it with slime, for God's sake.'

She fumbled at the zipper, and said in a hot aside to Charlie, 'Don't you dast look.'

Charlie closed his eyes and shrugged in resignation.

She stepped out of the dress. 'All right? You satisfied?'

Captain Garm's fingers twitched with unhappiness. 'Is that the bosom? Why does the other creature keep its head turned away?'

'Reluctance. Reluctance,' said Botax. 'Besides, the bosom is still covered. Other skins must be removed. When bared, the bosom is a very strong stimulus. It is constantly described as ivory globes, or white spheres, or otherwise after that fashion. I have here drawings, visual picturizations, that come from the outer covers of the space-travel magazines. If you will inspect them, you will see that upon every one of them, a creature is present with a bosom more or less exposed.'

The Captain looked thoughtfully from the illustrations to Marge and back. 'What is ivory?'

'That is another made-up flash of my own. It represents the tusky material of one of the large sub-intelligent creatures on the planet.'

'Ah,' and Captain Garm went into a pastel green of satisfaction. 'That explains it. This small creature is one of a warrior sect and those are tusks with which to smash the enemy.'

'No, no. They are quite soft, I understand.' Botax's small brown hand flicked outward in the general direction of the objects under discussion and Marge screamed and shrank away.

'Then what other purpose do they have?'

'I think,' said Botax with considerable hesitation, 'that they are used to feed the young.'

'The young eat them?' asked the Captain with every evidence of deep distress.

'Not exactly. The objects produce a fluid which the young consume.'

'Consume a fluid from a living body? Yech-h-h.' The Captain covered his head with all three of his arms, calling the central supernumerary into use for the purpose, slipping it out of its sheath so rapidly as almost to knock Botax over.

'A three-armed, slimy, bug-eyed monster,' said Marge.

'Yeah,' said Charlie.

'All right you, just watch those eyes. Keep them to yourself.'

'Listen, lady. I'm trying not to look.'

Botax approached again. 'Madam, would you remove the rest?'

Marge drew herself up as well as she could against the pinioning field. 'Never!'

'I'll remove it, if you wish.'

'Don't touch! For God's sake, don't touch. Look at the slime on him, will you? All right, I'll take it off.' She was muttering under her breath and looking hotly in Charlie's direction as she did so.

'Nothing is happening,' said the Captain, in deep dissatisfaction, 'and this seems an imperfect specimen.'

Botax felt the slur on his own efficiency. 'I brought you two perfect specimens. What's wrong with the creature?'

'The bosom does not consist of globes or spheres. I know what globes or spheres are and in these pictures you have shown me, they are so depicted. Those are large globes. On this creature, though, what we have are nothing but small flaps of dry tissue. And they're discolored, too, partly.'

'Nonsense,' said Botax. 'You must allow room for natural variation. I will put it to the creature herself.'

He turned to Marge, 'Madam, is your bosom imperfect?'

Marge's eyes opened wide and she struggled vainly for moments without doing anything more than gasp loudly. '*Really!*' she finally managed. 'Maybe I'm no Gina Lollobrigida or Anita Ekberg, but I'm perfectly all right, thank you. Oh boy, if my Ed were only here.' She turned to Charlie. 'Listen, you, you tell this bug-eyed slimy thing here, there ain't nothing wrong with my development.'

'Lady,' said Charlie, softly. 'I ain't looking, remember?'

'Oh, sure, you ain't looking. You been peeking enough, so you might as well just open your crummy eyes and stick up for a lady, if you're the least bit of a gentleman, which you probably ain't.'

'Well,' said Charlie, looking sideways at Marge, who seized the opportunity to inhale and throw her shoulders back, 'I don't like to get mixed up in a kind of delicate matter like this, but you're all right – I guess.'

'You *guess?* You blind or something? I was once runner-up for Miss Brooklyn, in case you don't happen to know, and where I missed out was on waist-line, *not* on –'

Charlie said, 'All right, all right. They're fine. Honest.' He nodded vigorously in Botax's direction. 'They're okay. I ain't that much of an expert, you understand, but they're okay by me.'

Marge relaxed.

Botax felt relieved. He turned to Garm. 'The bigger form expresses interest, Captain. The stimulus is working. Now for the final step.'

'And what is that?'

'There is no flash for it, Captain. Essentially, it consists of placing the speaking-and-eating apparatus of one against the equivalent apparatus of the other. I have made up a flash for the process, thus: kiss.'

'Will nausea never cease?' groaned the Captain.

'It is the climax. In all the tales, after the skins are removed by force, they clasp each other with limbs and indulge madly in burning kisses, to translate as nearly as possible the phrase most frequently used. Here is one example, just one, taken at random: "He held the girl, his mouth avid on her lips." '

'Maybe one creature was devouring the other,' said the Captain.

'Not at all,' said Botax impatiently. 'Those were burning kisses.'

'How do you mean, burning? Combustion takes place?'

'I don't think literally so. I imagine it is a way of expressing the fact that the temperature goes up. The higher the temperature, I suppose, the more successful the production of young. Now that the big form is properly stimulated, he need only place his mouth against hers to produce young. The young will not be produced without that step. It is the cooperation I have been speaking of.'

'That's all? Just this –' The Captain's hands made motions of coming together, but he could not bear to put the thought into flash form.

'That's all,' said Botax. 'In none of the tales; not even in "Re-creationlad", have I found a description of any further physical activity in connection with young-bearing. Sometimes after the kissing, they write a line of symbols like little stars, but I suppose that merely means more kissing; one kiss for each star, when they wish to produce a multitude of young.'

'Just one, please, right now.'

'Certainly, Captain.'

Botax said with distinctiveness, 'Sir, would you kiss the lady?'
Charlie said, 'Listen, I can't move.'

'I will free you, of course.'

'The lady might not like it.'

Marge glowered. 'You bet your damn boots, I won't like it.
You just stay away.'

'I would like to, lady, but what do they do if I don't? Look,
I don't want to get them mad. We can just – you know – make
like a little peck.'

She hesitated, seeing the justice of the caution. 'All right. No
funny stuff, though. I ain't in the habit of standing around like
this in front of every Tom, Dick and Harry, you know.'

'I know that, lady. It was none of my doing. You got to admit
that.'

Marge muttered angrily, 'Regular slimy monsters. Must
think they're some kind of gods or something, the way they
order people around. Slime gods is what they are!'

Charlie approached her. 'If it's okay now, lady.' He made a
vague motion as though to tip his hat. Then he put his hands
awkwardly on her bare shoulders and leaned over in a gingerly
pucker.

Marge's head stiffened so that lines appeared in her neck.
Their lips met.

Captain Garm flashed fretfully. 'I sense no rise in temperature.' His heat-detecting tendril had risen to full extension at
the top of his head and remained quivering there.

'I don't either,' said Botax, rather at a loss, 'but we're doing it
just as the space travel stories tell us to. I think his limbs should
be more extended – Ah, like that. See, it's working.'

Almost absently, Charlie's arm had slid around Marge's soft,
nude torso. For a moment, Marge seemed to yield against him
and then she suddenly writhed hard against the pinioning field
that still held her with fair firmness.

'Let go.' The words were muffled against the pressure of Charlie's lips. She bit suddenly, and Charlie leaped away with a
wild cry, holding his lower lip, then looking at his fingers for
blood.

'What's the idea, lady?' he demanded plaintively.

She said, 'We agreed just a peck, is all. What were you starting

there? You some kind of playboy or something? What am I surrounded with here? Playboy and the slime gods?'

Captain Garm flashed rapid alternations of blue and yellow.
'Is it done? How long do we wait now?'

'It seems to me it must happen at once. Throughout all the
universe, when you have to bud, you bud, you know. There's no
waiting.'

'Yes? After thinking of the foul habits you have been describ-
ing, I don't think I'll ever bud again. Please get this over with.'

'Just a moment, Captain.'

But the moments passed and the Captain's flashes turned
slowly to a brooding orange, while Botax's nearly dimmed out
altogether.

Botax finally asked hesitantly, 'Pardon me, madam, but when
will you bud?'

'When will I *what*?'

'Bear young?'

'I've got a kid.'

'I mean bear young now.'

'I should say not. I ain't ready for another kid yet.'

'What? What?' demanded the Captain. 'What's she saying?'

'It seems,' said Botax, weakly, 'she does not intend to have
young at the moment.'

The Captain's color patch blazed brightly. 'Do you know what
I think, Investigator? I think you have a sick, perverted mind.
Nothing's happening to these creatures. There is no cooperation
between them, and no young to be borne. I think they're two
different species and that you're playing some kind of foolish
game with me.'

'But, Captain –' said Botax.

'Don't but Captain me,' said Garm. 'I've had enough. You've
upset me, turned my stomach, nauseated me, disgusted me with
the whole notion of budding and wasted my time. You're just
looking for headlines and personal glory and I'll see to it that
you don't get them. Get rid of these creatures now. Give that
one its skins back and put them back where you found them.
I ought to take the expense of maintaining Time-stasis all this
time out of your salary.'

'But, Captain –'

'Back, I say. Put them back in the same place and at the same instant of time. I want this planet untouched, and I'll see to it that it stays untouched.' He cast one more furious glance at Botax. 'One species, two forms, bosoms, kisses, cooperation, BAH – You are a fool, Investigator, a dolt as well, and most of all a sick, sick, sick creature.'

There was no arguing. Botax, limbs trembling, set about returning the creatures.

They stood there at the elevated station, looking around wildly. It was twilight over them, and the approaching train was just making itself known as a faint rumble in the distance.

Marge said, hesitantly, 'Mister, did it really happen?'

Charlie nodded. 'I remember it.'

Marge said, 'We can't tell anybody.'

'Sure not. They'd say we was nuts. Know what I mean?'

'Uh-huh. Well,' she edged away.

Charlie said, 'Listen. I'm sorry you was embarrassed. It was none of my doing.'

'That's all right. I know.' Marge's eyes considered the wooden platform at her feet. The sound of the train was louder.

'I mean, you know, lady, you wasn't really bad. In fact, you looked good, but I was kind of embarrassed to say that.'

Suddenly, she smiled. 'It's all right.'

'You want maybe to have a cup of coffee with me just to relax you? My wife, she's not really expecting me for a while.'

'Oh? Well, Ed's out of town for the weekend so I got only an empty apartment to go home to. My little boy is visiting at my mother's,' she explained.

'Come on, then. We been kind of introduced.'

'I'll say.' She laughed.

The train pulled in, but they turned away, walking down the narrow stairway to the street.

They had a couple of cocktails actually, and then Charlie couldn't let her go home in the dark alone, so he saw her to her door. Marge was bound to invite him in for a few moments, naturally.

Meanwhile, back in the space-ship, the crushed Botax was making a final effort to prove his case. While Garm prepared the ship for departure Botax hastily set up the tight-beam viviscreen for a last look at his specimens. He focused in on Charlie and

Marge in her apartment. His tendril stiffened and he began flashing in a coruscating rainbow of colors.

'Captain Garm! Captain! Look what they're doing now!'

But at that very instant the ship winked out of Time-stasis.

Toward the end of the 1950s some rather unexpected changes took place in my life. My writing career had been constantly expanding. I had been driven on by my own compulsion and by editorial cooperation to undertake more and more tasks in greater and greater variety and by 1958 I found that I could no longer do the writing I wanted to do and maintain a full academic schedule.

The Medical School and I came to an amicable understanding, therefore. I kept my title (Associate Professor of Biochemistry, if you're curious) and continued to do odd jobs, like giving several lectures a year, sitting on committees, and so on. In the main, however, I became a full-time writer and relieved them of the trouble of paying me a salary.

For a while, it seemed to me that with virtually no academic duties and an infinite amount of time each and every day, I could finally do all the writing I had to do with plenty of time left over for fun and games.

It didn't work out. One of Parkinson's laws is: 'Work expands to fill the time available.' It did in my case. In no time at all, I found I was typing as assiduously full-time as I had previously been typing half-time and I quickly discovered the Asimov corollary to Parkinson's law: 'In ten hours a day you have time to fall twice as far behind your commitments as in five hours a day.'

The worst of it was that just about the time I was arranging to make myself a full-time writer, the Soviet Union sent up Sputnik I and the United States went into a kind of tizzy, and so did I.

I was overcome by the ardent desire to write popular science for an America that might be in great danger through its neglect of science, and a number of publishers got an equally ardent desire to publish popular science for the same reason. As a result of combining the two ardencies I found myself plunging into a shoreless sea in which I am still immersed.

The trouble is – it's all non-fiction. In the last ten years, I've done a couple of novels, some collections, a dozen or so stories, but that's nothing.

From the aggrieved letters I get, one would think I was doing this on purpose. I'm not. I try desperately not to lose touch with science fiction altogether. It's my life in a way that nothing else *can quite be. There's my monthly article in* F & SF, *of course, but that's not quite the same thing.*

And so it happens that each short individual piece of fiction I manage to get the typewriter to put out for me is dearer to me in the nowadays of my dimness, than in the old times when I did two dozen or more long ones a year.

'The Machine That Won the War' is one of those that serves as my periodic proof to the world of fandom that I am, too, alive.

First appearance – The Magazine of Fantasy and Science Fiction, *October 1961.* ©, *1961, by Mercury Press Inc.*

THE MACHINE THAT WON THE WAR

The celebration had a long way to go and even in the silent depths of Multivac's underground chambers, it hung in the air.

If nothing else, there was the mere fact of isolation and silence. For the first time in a decade, technicians were not scurrying about the vitals of the giant computer, the soft lights did not wink out their erratic patterns, the flow of information in and out had halted.

It would not be halted long, of course, for the needs of peace would be pressing. Yet now, for a day, perhaps for a week, even Multivac might celebrate the great time, and rest.

Lamar Swift took off the military cap he was wearing and looked down the long and empty main corridor of the enormous computer. He sat down rather wearily in one of the technician's swing-stools, and his uniform, in which he had never been comfortable, took on a heavy and wrinkled appearance.

He said, 'I'll miss it all after a grisly fashion. It's hard to remember when we weren't at war with Deneb, and it seems against nature now to be at peace and to look at the stars without anxiety.'

The two men with the Executive Director of the Solar Federation were both younger than Swift. Neither was as gray. Neither looked quite as tired.

John Henderson, thin-lipped and finding it hard to control the relief he felt in the midst of triumph, said, 'They're destroyed! They're destroyed! It's what I keep saying to myself over and over and I still can't believe it. We all talked so much, over so many years, about the menace hanging over Earth and all its worlds, over every human being, and all the time it was true, every word of it. And now we're alive and it's the Denebians who are shattered and destroyed. They'll be no menace now, ever again.'

'Thanks to Multivac,' said Swift, with a quiet glance at the imperturbable Jablonsky, who through all the war had been Chief Interpreter of science's oracle. 'Right, Max?'

Jablonsky shrugged. Automatically, he reached for a cigarette and decided against it. He alone, of all the thousands who had lived in the tunnels within Multivac, had been allowed to smoke, but toward the end he had made definite efforts to avoid making use of the privilege.

He said. 'Well, that's what *they* say.' His broad thumb moved in the direction of his right shoulder, aiming upward.

'Jealous, Max?'

'Because they're shouting for Multivac? Because Multivac is the big hero of mankind in this war?' Jablonsky's craggy face took on an air of suitable contempt. 'What's that to me? Let Multivac be the machine that won the war, if it pleases them.'

Henderson looked at the other two out of the corners of his eyes. In this short interlude that the three had instinctively sought out in the one peaceful corner of a metropolis gone mad; in this entr'acte between the dangers of war and the difficulties of peace; when, for one moment, they might all find surcease; he was conscious only of his weight of guilt.

Suddenly, it was as though that weight were too great to be borne longer. It had to be thrown off, along with the war; now!

Henderson said, 'Multivac had nothing to do with victory. It's just a machine.'

'A big one,' said Swift.

'Then just a big machine. No better than the data fed it.' For a moment, he stopped, suddenly unnerved at what he was saying.

Jablonsky looked at him, his thick fingers once again fumbling for a cigarette and once again drawing back. 'You should know. You supplied the data. Or is it just that you're taking the credit?'

'*No*,' said Henderson, angrily. 'There is no credit. What do you know of the data Multivac had to use; predigested from a hundred subsidiary computers here on Earth, on the Moon, on Mars, even on Titan. With Titan always delayed and always that feeling that its figures would introduce an unexpected bias.'

'It would drive anyone mad,' said Swift, with gentle sympathy.

Henderson shook his head. 'It wasn't just that. I admit that eight years ago when I replaced Lepont as Chief Programmer, I was nervous. But there was an exhilaration about things in those days. The war was still long-range; an adventure without real danger. We hadn't reached the point where manned vessels had had to take over and where interstellar warps could swallow up a planet clean, if aimed correctly. But then, when the real difficulties began –'

Angrily – he could finally permit anger – he said, 'You know nothing about it.'

'Well,' said Swift. 'Tell us. The war is over. We've won.'

'Yes.' Henderson nodded his head. He had to remember that. Earth had won so all had been for the best. 'Well, the data became meaningless.'

'Meaningless? You mean that literally?' said Jablonsky.

'Literally. What would you expect? The trouble with you two was that you weren't out in the thick of it. You never left Multivac, Max, and you, Mr. Director, never left the Mansion except on state visits where you saw exactly what they wanted you to see.'

'I was not as unaware of that', said Swift, 'as you may have thought.'

'Do you know', said Henderson, 'to what extent data concerning our production capacity, our resource potential, our trained man-power – everything of importance to the war effort, in fact – had become unreliable and untrustworthy during the last half of the war? Group leaders, both civilian and military, were intent on projecting their own improved image, so to speak, so they obscured the bad and magnified the good. Whatever the machines might do, the men who programmed them and interpreted the results had their own skins to think of and competitors to stab. There was no way of stopping that. I tried, and failed.'

'Of course,' said Swift, in quiet consolation. 'I can see that you would.'

This time Jablonsky decided to light his cigarette. 'Yet I presume you provided Multivac with data in your programming. You said nothing to us about unreliability.'

'How could I tell you? And if I did, how could you afford to believe me?' demanded Henderson, savagely. 'Our entire war effort was geared to Multivac. It was the one great weapon on our side, for the Denebians had nothing like it. What else kept up morale in the face of doom but the assurance that Multivac would always predict and circumvent any Denebian move, and would always direct and prevent the circumvention of our moves? Great Space, after our Spy-warp was blasted out of hyperspace we lacked any reliable Denebian data to feed Multivac and we didn't dare make *that* public.'

'True enough,' said Swift.

'Well, then,' said Henderson, 'if I'd told you the data was unreliable, what could you have done but replace me and refuse to believe me? I couldn't allow that.'

'What did you do?' said Jablonsky.

'Since the war is won, I'll tell you what I did. I corrected the data.'

'How?' asked Swift.

'Intuition, I presume. I juggled them till they looked right. At first, I hardly dared. I changed a bit here and there to correct what were obvious impossibilities. When the sky didn't collapse about us, I got braver. Toward the end, I scarcely cared. I just wrote out the necessary data as it was needed. I even had the Multivac Annex prepare data for me according to a private programming pattern I had devised for the purpose.'

'Random figures?' said Jablonsky.

'Not at all. I introduced a number of necessary biases.'

Jablonsky smiled, quite unexpectedly, his dark eyes sparkling behind the crinkling of the lower lids. 'Three times a report was brought me about unauthorized uses of the Annex, and I let it go each time. If it had mattered, I would have followed it up and spotted you, John, and found out what you were doing.

But, of course, nothing about Multivac mattered in those days, so you got away with it.'

'What do you mean, nothing mattered?' asked Henderson, suspiciously.

'Nothing did. I suppose if I had told you this at the time, it would have spared you your agony, but then if you had told me what you were doing, it would have spared me mine. What made you think Multivac was in working order, whatever the data you supplied it?'

'Not in working order?' said Swift.

'Not really. Not reliably. After all, where were my technicians in the last years of the war? I'll tell you, they were feeding computers on a thousand different space devices. They were gone! I had to make do with kids I couldn't trust and veterans who were out-of-date. Besides, do you think I could trust the solid-state components coming out of Cryogenics in the last years? Cryogenics wasn't any better placed as far as personnel was concerned than I was. To me, it didn't matter whether the data being supplied Multivac were reliable or not. The *results* weren't reliable. That much I knew.'

'What did you do?' asked Henderson.

'I did what you did, John. I introduced the bugger factor. I adjusted matters in accordance with intuition – and that's how the machine won the war.'

Swift leaned back in the chair and stretched his legs out before him. 'Such revelations. It turns out then that the material handed me to guide me in my decision-making capacity was a man-made interpretation of man-made data. Isn't that right?'

'It looks so,' said Jablonsky.

'Then I perceive I was correct in not placing too much reliance upon it,' said Swift.

'You didn't?' Jablonsky, despite what he had just said, managed to look professionally insulted.

'I'm afraid I didn't. Multivac might seem to say, Strike here, not there; do this, not that; wait, don't act. But I could never be certain that what Multivac seemed to say, it really did say; or what it really said, it really meant. I could never be certain.'

'But the final report was always plain enough, sir,' said Jablonsky.

'To those who did not have to make the decision, perhaps. Not to me. The horror of the responsibility of such decisions was unbearable and not even Multivac was sufficient to remove the weight. But the point is I was justified in doubting and there is tremendous relief in that.'

Caught up in the conspiracy of mutual confession, Jablonsky put titles aside, 'What was it you did then, Lamar? After all, you did make decisions. How?'

'Well, it's time to be getting back perhaps but – I'll tell you first. Why not? I did make use of a computer, Max, but an older one than Multivac, much older.'

He groped in his own pocket for cigarettes, and brought out a package along with a scattering of small change; old-fashioned coins dating to the first years before the metal shortage had brought into being a credit system tied to a computer-complex.

Swift smiled rather sheepishly. 'I still need these to make money seem substantial to me. An old man finds it hard to abandon the habits of youth.' He put a cigarette between his lips and dropped the coins one by one back into his pocket.

He held the last coin between his fingers, staring absently at it. 'Multivac is not the first computer, friends, nor the best-known, nor the one that can most efficiently lift the load of decision from the shoulders of the executive. A machine *did* win the war, John; at least a very simple computing device did; one that I used every time I had a particularly hard decision to make.'

With a faint smile of reminiscence, he flipped the coin he held. It glinted in the air as it spun and came down in Swift's outstretched palm. His hand closed over it and brought it down on the back of his left hand. His right hand remained in place, hiding the coin.

'Heads or tails, gentlemen?' said Swift.

One of the side effects of the growing respectability of science fiction was that it began to appear in markets where, a few short years earlier, the Sanitation Department would have been called in to remove any such manuscripts that had inadvertently found their way into the editorial office.

I'll never forget the shock that rumbled through the entire world of science fiction fandom when, after World War II, our own Robert A. Heinlein broke the 'slicks' barrier by having an undiluted science fiction story of his published in The Saturday Evening Post.

Nowadays, it is routine to find science fiction writers and their science fiction in such wide-circulation markets as Playboy. Indeed, the competition of the mass markets is such that the small speciality science fiction magazines find it hard to hold on to the more experienced writers and they do not benefit, as they ought, from the field's new-won respectability. It is unjust!

But the strangest market for science fiction, in my opinion, was the advertising columns of that excellent and, for me, indispensable) periodical, Scientific American. It seems that a company called Hoffman Electronics Corporation got the idea of running a series of advertisements that would include a two-page (minus one column) illustrated science fiction story – real science fiction stories by the acknowledged masters. The final column would then be used to promote their product in a dignified manner. There was no direct tie-in between story and advertising and the writer was to have carte blanche, except that it would be nice to have the story involve communications in one form or another (since communications technology was what Hoffman was selling).

The challenge was interesting and artistic integrity was preserved, so when I was asked to do a story for the program, I accepted and wrote 'My Son, the Physicist.' As you see, it deals with communications but is in no way a 'commercial' for such things. Hoffman accepted the story without changing a word or a comma and it ran not only in the ad columns of Scientific American but in Fortune as well.

It was an experience, you may be sure, because it is not likely that my by-line would ever have appeared in either magazine otherwise. Not under a piece of science fiction, anyway.

I am a little uneasy, though, as to how well the idea worked out. There were only six such advertisements altogether, as far *as I know, and then they stopped. Well, maybe they just had difficulty getting appropriate stories. I don't know.*

First appearance – Scientific American, *February 1962.* ©, *1962, Hoffman Electronics Corporation.*

MY SON, THE PHYSICIST

Her hair was a light apple-green in color, very subdued, very old-fashioned. You could see she had a delicate hand with the dye, the way they did thirty years ago, before the streaks and stipples came into fashion.

She had a sweet smile on her face, too, and a calm look that made something serene out of elderliness.

And, by comparison, it made something shrieking out of the confusion that enfolded her in the huge government building.

A girl passed her at a half-run, stopped and turned toward her with a blank stare of astonishment. 'How did you get in?'

The woman smiled. 'I'm looking for my son, the physicist.'

'Your son, the –'

'He's a communications engineer, really. Senior Physicist Gerard Cremona.'

'Dr. Cremona. Well, he's – Where's your pass?'

'Here it is. I'm his mother.'

'Well, Mrs. Cremona, I don't know. I've got to – His office is down there. You just ask someone.' She passed on, running.

Mrs. Cremona shook her head slowly. Something had happened, she supposed. She hoped Gerard was all right.

She heard voices much farther down the corridor and smiled happily. She could tell Gerard's.

She walked into the room and said, 'Hello, Gerard.'

Gerard was a big man, with a lot of hair still and the gray just beginning to show because he didn't use dye. He said he was too busy. She was very proud of him and the way he looked.

Right now, he was talking volubly to a man in army uniform. She couldn't tell the rank, but she knew Gerard could handle him.

Gerard looked up and said, 'What do you — Mother! What are you doing here?'

'I was coming to visit you today.'

'Is today Thursday? Oh Lord, I forgot. Sit down, Mother, I can't talk now. Any seat. Any seat. Look, General.'

General Reiner looked over his shoulder and one hand slapped against the other in the region of the small of his back. 'Your mother?'

'Yes.'

'Should she be here?'

'Right now, no, but I'll vouch for her. She can't even read a thermometer so nothing of this will mean anything to her. Now look, General. They're on Pluto. You see? They are. The radio signals can't be of natural origin so they must originate from human beings, from our men. You'll have to accept that. Of all the expeditions we've sent out beyond the planetoid belt, one turns out to have made it. And they've reached Pluto.'

'Yes, I understand what you're saying, but isn't it impossible just the same? The men who are on Pluto now were launched four years ago with equipment that could not have kept them alive more than a year. That is my understanding. They were aimed at Ganymede and seem to have gone eight times the proper distance.'

'Exactly. And we've got to know how and why. They may — just — have — had — help.'

'What kind? How?'

Cremona clenched his jaws for a moment as though praying inwardly. 'General,' he said, 'I'm putting myself out on a limb but it is just barely possible non-humans are involved. Extra-terrestrials. We've got to find out. We don't know how long contact can be maintained.'

'You mean' (the General's grave face twitched into an almost-smile) 'they may have escaped from custody and they may be recaptured again at any time.'

'Maybe. Maybe. The whole future of the human race may depend on our knowing exactly what we're up against. Knowing it *now*.'

'All right. What is it you want?'

'We're going to need Army's Multivac computer at once. Rip out every problem it's working on and start programing our general semantic problem. Every communications engineer you have must be pulled off anything he's on and placed into co-ordination with our own.'

'But why? I fail to see the connection.'

A gentle voice interrupted. 'General, would you like a piece of fruit? I brought some oranges?'

Cremona said, 'Mother! Please! Later! General, the point is a simple one. At the present moment Pluto is just under four billion miles away. It takes six hours for radio waves, traveling at the speed of light, to reach from here to there. If we say something, we must wait twelve hours for an answer. If they say something and we miss it and say "what" and they repeat – bang goes a day.'

'There's no way to speed it up?' said the General.

'Of course not. It's the fundamental law of communications. No information can be transmitted at more than the speed of light. It will take months to carry on the same conversation with Pluto that would take hours between the two of us right now.'

'Yes, I see that. And you really think extra-terrestrials are involved?'

'I do. To be honest, not everyone here agrees with me. Still, we're straining every nerve, every fiber, to devise some method of concentrating communication. We must get in as many bits per second as possible and pray we get what we need before we lose contact. And there's where I need Multivac and your men. There must be some communications strategy we can use that will reduce the number of signals we need send out. Even an increase of ten per cent in efficiency can mean perhaps a week of time saved.'

The gentle voice interrupted again. 'Good grief, Gerard, are you trying to get some talking done?'

'Mother.' There was a hysterical edge to Cremona's voice.

'Well, all right, but if you're going to say something and then wait twelve hours for an answer, you're silly. You shouldn't.'

The General snorted. 'Dr. Cremona, shall we consult –'

'Just one moment, General,' said Cremona. 'What are you getting at, Mother?'

'While you're waiting for an answer,' said Mrs. Cremona, earnestly, 'just keep on transmitting and tell them to do the same. You talk all the time and they talk all the time. You have someone listening all the time and they do, too. If either one of you says anything that needs an answer, you can slip one in at your end, but chances are, you'll get all you need without asking.'

Both men stared at her.

Cremona whispered, 'Of course. Continuous conversation. Just twelve hours out of phase, that's all. God, we've got to get going.'

He strode out of the room, virtually dragging the General with him, then strode back in.

'Mother,' he said, 'if you'll excuse me, this will take a few hours, I think. I'll send in some girls to talk to you. Or take a nap, if you'd rather.'

'I'll be all right, Gerard,' said Mrs. Cremona.

'Only, how did you think of this, Mother? What made you suggest this?'

'But, Gerard, all women know it. Any two women – on the video-phone, or on the stratowire, or just face to face – know that the whole secret to spreading the news is, no matter what, to Just Keep Talking.'

Cremona tried to smile. Then, his lower lip trembling, he turned and left.

Mrs. Cremona looked fondly after him. Such a fine man, her son, the physicist. Big as he was and important as he was, he still knew that a boy should always listen to his mother.

I have a rule which I state loudly on every possible occasion. The rule is that I never write anything unless I am asked to do so. That sounds awfully haughty and austere, but it's a fake. As a matter of fact, I take it for granted that the various science fiction magazines and certain of my book publishers have standing requests for material, so I write for them freely. It's just the scattering of others that have to ask.

In 1946, I was finally asked by Playboy to write a story for them. They sent me a dim photograph of a clay head, without ears, and with the other features labeled in block letters, and asked me to write a story based on that photo. Two other writers were also asked to write a story based on that same photo and all three stories were to be published together.

It was an interesting challenge and I was tempted. I wrote 'Eyes Do More Than See'.

In case I have given the impression in the previous introductions in this volume that my writing career has been one long succession of triumphs ever since 'Nightfall'; that with me, to write is to sell; that I wouldn't recognize a rejection slip if some fellow writer showed me one – rest easy, it is not so.

'Eyes Do More Than See' was rejected with muscular vigor. The manuscript came flying through my window all the way from Chicago, bounced off the wall and lay there quivering. (At least that's how it seemed.) The other two stories were accepted by Playboy, and a third story, by someone hastily called in to backstop me, was also accepted.

Fortunately, I am a professional of enviable imperturbability and these things do not bother me. I doubt whether anyone could have guessed that I was disturbed except for the short screaming fit of rage I indulged myself with.

I checked with Playboy and made sure the story was mine to do with as I pleased, despite the fact it was based on their photo. It was!

My next step was to send the story to F & SF explaining to them (as is my wont in such cases) that it was a reject and giving them the exact circumstances. They took it, anyway.

Fortunately, F & SF works reasonably quickly and Playboy works abominably slowly. Consequently 'Eyes Do More Than See' appeared in F & SF a year and a half before the story-triad appeared in Playboy. I spent an appreciable length of time hoping Playboy would get indignant letters complaining that the

*situations in the triad had been stolen from an Asimov story. I
was even tempted to write such a letter myself under a false name
(but I didn't).*

I contented myself, instead, with the thought that by the time
Playboy *had published its triad, my little story had not only
been published elsewhere but had been reprinted twice and was
slated to appear in still a third anthology. (And this collection
represents a fourth, and how do you like that, Mr. Hefner?)*

First appearance – The Magazine of Fantasy and Science
Fiction, *April 1965.* ©, *1965, by Mercury Press, Inc.*

EYES DO MORE THAN SEE

After hundreds of billions of years, he suddenly thought of himself as Ames. Not the wavelength combination which, through
all the universe was now the equivalent of Ames – but the sound
itself. A faint memory came back of the sound waves he no longer heard and no longer could hear.

The new project was sharpening his memory for so many
more of the old, old, eons-old things. He flattened the energy
vortex that made up the total of his individuality and its lines
of force stretched beyond the stars.

Brock's answering signal came.

Surely, Ames thought, he could tell Brock. Surely he could
tell somebody.

Brock's shifting energy pattern communed, 'Aren't you coming, Ames?'

'Of course.'

'Will you take part in the contest?'

'Yes!' Ames' lines of force pulsed eratically. 'Most certainly. I have thought of a whole new art-form. Something really
unusual.'

'What a waste of effort! How can you think a new variation

can be thought of after two hundred billion years. There can be nothing new.'

For a moment Brock shifted out of phase and out of communion, so that Ames had to hurry to adjust his lines of force. He caught the drift of other-thoughts as he did so, the view of the powdered galaxies against the velvet of nothingness, and the lines of force pulsing in endless multitudes of energy-life, lying between the galaxies.

Ames said, 'Please absorb my thoughts, Brock. Don't close out. I've thought of manipulating Matter. Imagine! A symphony of Matter. Why bother with Energy. Of course, there's nothing new in Energy; how can there be? Doesn't that show we must deal with Matter?'

'Matter!'

Ames interpreted Brock's energy-vibrations as those of disgust.

He said, 'Why not? We were once Matter ourselves back – back – Oh, a trillion years ago anyway! Why not build up objects in a Matter medium, or abstract forms or – listen, Brock – why not build up an imitation of ourselves in Matter, ourselves as we used to be?'

Brock said, 'I don't remember how that was. No one does.'

'I do,' said Ames with energy, 'I've been thinking of nothing else and I am beginning to remember. Brock, let me show you. Tell me if I'm right. Tell me.'

'No. This is silly. It's – repulsive.'

'Let me try, Brock. We've been friends; we've pulsed energy together from the beginning – from the moment we became what we are. Brock, please!'

'Then, quickly.'

Ames had not felt such a tremor along his own lines of force in – well, in how long? If he tried it now for Brock and it worked he could dare manipulate Matter before the assembled Energy-beings who had so drearily waited over the eons for something new.

The Matter was thin out there between the galaxies, but Ames gathered it, scraping it together over the cubic light-years, choosing the atoms, achieving a clayey consistency and forcing matter into an ovoid form that spread out below.

'Don't you remember, Brock?' he asked softly. 'Wasn't it something like this?'

Brock's vortex trembled in phase. 'Don't make me remember, I don't remember.'

'That was the head. They called it the head. I remember it so clearly, I want to say it. I mean with sound.' He waited, then said, 'Look, do you remember that?'

On the upper front of the ovoid appeared HEAD.

'What is that?' asked Brock.

'That's the word for head. The symbols that meant the word in sound. Tell me you remember, Brock!'

'There was something,' said Brock hesitantly, 'something in the middle.' A vertical bulge formed.

Ames said, 'Yes! Nose, that's it!' And NOSE appeared upon it. 'And those are eyes on either side,' LEFT EYE – RIGHT EYE.

Ames regarded what he had formed, his lines of force pulsing slowly. Was he sure he liked this?

'Mouth,' he said, in small quiverings, 'and chin and Adam's apple, and the collarbones. How the words come back to me.' They appeared on the form.

Brock said, 'I haven't thought of them for hundreds of billions of years. Why have you reminded me? Why?'

Ames was momentarily lost in his thoughts, 'Something else. Organs to hear with; something for the sound waves. Ears! Where do they go? I don't remember where to put them.'

Brock cried out, 'Leave it alone! Ears and all else! Don't remember!'

Ames said, uncertainly, 'What is wrong with remembering?'

'Because the outside wasn't rough and cold like that but smooth and warm. Because the eyes were tender and alive and the lips of the mouth trembled and were soft on mine.' Brock's lines of force beat and wavered, beat and wavered.

Ames said, 'I'm sorry! I'm sorry!'

'You're reminding me that once I was a woman and knew love; that eyes do more than see and I have none to do it for me.'

With violence, she added matter to the rough-hewn head and said, 'Then let *them* do it' and turned and fled.

And Ames saw and remembered, too, that once he had been a man. The force of his vortex split the head in two and he fled back across the galaxies on the energy-track of Brock – back to the endless doom of life.

And the eyes of the shattered head of Matter still glistened with the moisture that Brock had placed there to represent tears. The head of Matter did that which the energy-beings could do no longer and it wept for all humanity, and for the fragile beauty of the bodies they had once given up, a trillion years ago.

In the spring of 1967, I received an interesting request.

It seems there is a periodical called Abbotempo, *supported by Abbott Laboratories, a respected pharmaceutical firm. It is a slick-paper, impressively designed job, with excellent articles on various medical and near-medical subjects. It is printed in the Netherlands and is distributed free of charge to physicians in Great Britain and on the Continent. It is not distributed in the United States.*

The editor of Abbottempo *wrote to ask me to write a 2000 -word science fiction story on a subject of medical interest that physicians would find at once interesting, amusing, and thought-provoking.*

I was just as swamped with work at that moment as I am at all other moments, so I sighed and put a piece of letter paper in the typewriter, intending to write out a polite refusal.

Unfortunately, or fortunately, it takes time to pick up letter paper and a yellow second sheet, put a piece of carbon paper in the typewriter. It takes additional time to center the paper properly, type the date, address, and salutation.

What with all that time, I happened to think up a story I couldn't resist, so when I actually got past 'Dear Sir,' I found myself typing a polite acceptance.

I wrote 'Segregationist' in April 1967, on a theme that was completely and entirely science-fictional. It appeared in December 1967, just in time to be slightly behind the headlines in some respects.

The nicest result of the publication of the story, by the way, was that Abbottempo *published it in each of their eight editions. They sent me a boxed collection of the set in 1) English, 2) French, 3) Spanish, 4) German, 5) Italian, 6) Japanese, 7) Greek, and 8) Turkish, and the set remains one of the more interesting oddities of my personal library of Asimoviana.*

First appearance – Abbottempo, Book 4, 1967. Copyright, 1968, by Isaac Asimov.

The surgeon looked up without expression. 'Is he ready?'

'Ready is a relative term,' said the med-eng. '*We*'re ready. He's restless.'

'They always are. . . . Well, it's a serious operation.'

'Serious or not, he should be thankful. He's been chosen for it over an enormous number of possibles and frankly, I don't think . . .'

'Don't say it,' said the surgeon. 'The decision is not ours to make.'

'We accept it. But do we have to agree?'

'Yes,' said the surgeon, crisply. 'We agree. Completely and wholeheartedly. The operation is entirely too intricate to approach with mental reservations. This man has proven his worth in a number of ways and his profile is suitable for the Board of Mortality.'

'All right,' said the med-eng, unmollified.

The surgeon said, 'I'll see him right in here, I think. It is small enough and personal enough to be comforting.'

'It won't help. He's nervous, and he's made up his mind.'

'Has he indeed?'

'Yes. He wants metal; they always do.'

The surgeon's face did not change expression. He stared at his hands. 'Sometimes one can talk them out of it.'

'Why bother?' said the med-eng, indifferently. 'If he wants metal, let it be metal.'

'You don't care?'

'Why should I?' The med-eng said it almost brutally. 'Either way it's a medical engineering problem and I'm a medical engineer. Either way, I can handle it. Why should I go beyond that?'

The surgeon said stolidly, 'To me, it is a matter of the fitness of things.'

'Fitness! You can't use that as an argument. What does the patient care about the fitness of things?'

'I care.'

'You care in a minority. The trend is against you. You have no chance.'

'I have to try.' The surgeon waved the med-eng into silence

with a quick wave of his hand – no impatience to it, merely quickness. He had already informed the nurse and he had already been signaled concerning her approach. He pressed a small button and the double-door pulled swiftly apart. The patient moved inward in his motor-chair, the nurse stepping briskly along beside him.

'You may go, nurse,' said the surgeon, 'but wait outside. I will be calling you.' He nodded to the med-eng, who left with the nurse, and the door closed behind them.

The man in the chair looked over his shoulder and watched them go. His neck was scrawny and there were fine wrinkles about his eyes. He was freshly shaven and the fingers of his hands, as they gripped the arms of the chair tightly, showed manicured nails. He was a high-priority patient and he was being taken care of. . . . But there was a look of settled peevishness on his face.

He said, 'Will we be starting today?'

The surgeon nodded. 'This afternoon, Senator.'

'I understand it will take weeks.'

'Not for the operation itself, Senator. But there are a number of subsidiary points to be taken care of. There are some circulatory renovations that must be carried through, and hormonal adjustments. These are tricky things.'

'Are they dangerous?' Then, as though feeling the need for establishing a friendly relationship, but patently against his will, he added, '. . . doctor?'

The surgeon paid no attention to the nuances of expression. He said, flatly, 'Everything is dangerous. We take our time in order that it be less dangerous. It is the time required, the skill of many individuals united, the equipment, that makes such operations available to so few . . .'

'I know that,' said the patient, restlessly. 'I refuse to feel guilty about that. Or are you implying improper pressure?'

'Not at all, Senator. The decisions of the Board have never been questioned. I mention the difficulty and intricacy of the operation merely to explain my desire to have it conducted in the best fashion possible.'

'Well, do so, then. That is my desire, also.'

'Then I must ask you to make a decision. It is possible to supply you with either of two types of cyber-hearts, metal or . . .'

'Plastic!' said the patient, irritably. 'Isn't that the alternative you were going to offer, doctor? Cheap plastic. I don't want that. I've made my choice. I want the metal.'

'But . . .'

'See here. I've been told the choice rests with me. Isn't that so?'

The surgeon nodded. 'Where two alternate procedures are of equal value from a medical standpoint, the choice rests with the patient. In actual practice, the choice rests with the patient even when the alternate procedures are *not* of equal value, as in this case.'

The patient's eyes narrowed. 'Are you trying to tell me the plastic heart is superior?'

'It depends on the patient. In my opinion, in your individual case, it is. And we prefer not to use the term, plastic. It is a fibrous cyber-heart.'

'It's plastic as far as I am concerned.'

'Senator,' said the surgeon, infinitely patient, 'that material is not plastic in the ordinary sense of the word. It is a polymeric material true, but one that is far more complex than ordinary plastic. It is a complex protein-like fibre designed to imitate, as closely as possible, the natural structure of the human heart you now have within your chest.'

'Exactly, and the human heart I now have within my chest is worn out although I am not yet sixty years old. I don't want another one like it, thank you. I want something better.'

'We all want something better for you, Senator. The fibrous cyber-heart will be better. It has a potential life of centuries. It is absolutely non-allergic . . .'

'Isn't that so for the metallic heart, too?'

'Yes, it is,' said the surgeon. 'The metallic cyber is of titanium alloy that . . .'

'And it doesn't wear out? And it is stronger than plastic? Or fibre or whatever you want to call it?'

'The metal is physically stronger, yes, but mechanical strength is not a point at issue. Its mechanical strength does you no particular good since the heart is well protected. Anything capable of reaching the heart will kill you for other reasons even if the heart stands up under manhandling.'

The patient shrugged. 'If I ever break a rib, I'll have that replaced by titanium, also. Replacing bones is easy. Anyone can have that done anytime. I'll be as metallic as I want to be, doctor.'

'That is your right, if you so choose. However, it is only fair to tell you that although no metallic cyber-heart has ever broken down mechanically, a number have broken down electronically.'

'What does that mean?'

'It means that every cyber-heart contains a pacemaker as part of its structure. In the case of the metallic variety, this is an electronic device that keeps the cyber in rhythm. It means an entire battery of miniaturized equipment must be included to alter the heart's rhythm to suit an individual's emotional and physical state. Occasionally something goes wrong there and people have died before that wrong could be corrected.'

'I never heard of such a thing.'

'I assure you it happens.'

'Are you telling me it happens often?'

'Not at all. It happens very rarely.'

'Well, then, I'll take my chance. What about the plastic heart? Doesn't that contain a pacemaker?'

'Of course it does, Senator. But the chemical structure of a fibrous cyber-heart is quite close to that of human tissue. It can respond to the ironic and hormonal controls of the body itself. The total complex that need be inserted is far simpler than in the case of the metal cyber.'

'But doesn't the plastic heart ever pop out of hormonal control?'

'None has ever yet done so.'

'Because you haven't been working with them long enough. Isn't that so?'

The surgeon hesitated. 'It is true that the fibrous cybers have not been used nearly as long as the metallic.'

'There you are. What is it anyway, doctor? Are you afraid I'm making myself into a robot . . . into a Metallo, as they call them since citizenship went through?'

'There is nothing wrong with a Metallo as a Metallo. As you say, they are citizens. But you're *not* a Metallo. You're a human being. Why not stay a human being?'

'Because I want the best and that's a metallic heart. You see to that.'

The surgeon nodded. 'Very well. You will be asked to sign the necessary permissions and you will then be fitted with a metal heart.'

'And you'll be the surgeon in charge? They tell me you're the best.'

'I will do what I can to make the changeover an easy one.'

The door opened and the chair moved the patient out to the waiting nurse.

The med-eng came in, looking over his shoulder at the receding patient until the doors had closed again.

He turned to the surgeon. 'Well, I can't tell what happened just by looking at you. What was his decision?'

The surgeon bent over his desk, punching out the final items for his records. 'What you predicted. He insists on the metallic cyber-heart.'

'After all, they are better.'

'Not significantly. They've been around longer; no more than that. It's this mania that's been plaguing humanity ever since Metallos have become citizens. Men have this odd desire to make Metallos out of themselves. They yearn for the physical strength and endurance one associates with them.'

'It isn't one-sided, doc. You don't work with Metallos but I do; so I know. The last two who came in for repairs have asked for fibrous elements.'

'Did they get them?'

'In one case, it was just a matter of supplying tendons; it didn't make much difference there, metal or fibre. The other wanted a blood system or its equivalent. I told him I couldn't; not without a complete rebuilding of the structure of his body in fibrous material. . . . I suppose it will come to that some day. Metallos that aren't really Metallos at all, but a kind of flesh and blood.'

'You don't mind that thought?'

'Why not? And metallized human beings, too. We have two varieties of intelligence on Earth now and why bother with two. Let them approach each other and eventually we won't be able to tell the difference. Why should we want to? We'd have the best of both worlds; the advantages of man combined with those of robot.'

'You'd get a hybrid,' said the surgeon, with something that approached fierceness. 'You'd get something that is not both, but neither. Isn't it logical to suppose an individual would be too proud of his structure and identity to want to dilute it with something alien? Would he *want* mongrelization?'

'That's segregationist talk.'

'Then let it be that.' The surgeon said with calm emphasis, 'I believe in being what one is. I wouldn't change a bit of my own structure for any reason. If some of it absolutely required replacement, I would have that replacement as close to the original in nature as could possibly be managed. I am *myself*; well pleased to be myself; and would not be anything else.'

He had finished now and had to prepare for the operation. He placed his strong hands into the heating oven and let them reach the dull red-hot glow that would sterilize them completely. For all his impassioned words, his voice had never risen, and on his burnished metal face there was (as always) no sign of expression.